Thank you support!

Enjoy

J Messina

TRUMP

JOE MESSINA

Order this book online at www.trafford.com
or email orders@trafford.com

Most Trafford titles are also available at major online book retailers.

© Copyright 2013 Joe Messina.
Cover Illustration Copyright © 2013 by Yanik Mayer

All rights reserved. No part of this publication may be reproduced, stored in a retrieval system, or transmitted, in any form or by any means, electronic, mechanical, photocopying, recording, or otherwise, without the written prior permission of the author.

This is a work of fiction. Names, characters, businesses, places, events and incidents are either the products of the author's imagination or used in a fictitious manner. Any resemblance to actual persons, living or dead, or actual events is purely coincidental.

Printed in the United States of America.

ISBN: 978-1-4907-1439-4 (sc)
ISBN: 978-1-4907-1438-7 (hc)
ISBN: 978-1-4907-1440-0 (e)

Library of Congress Control Number: 2013916877

Trafford rev. 10/03/2013

 www.trafford.com

North America & international
toll-free: 1 888 232 4444 (USA & Canada)
fax: 812 355 4082

To my wife Rose, for her patience and encouragement.
And also to my daughter, Sarah, and my stepson, Kevin.

Prologue

IT WAS RAINING STEADY. The wind was gentle, and the leaves on the trees were blowing softly. The moon was covered in thick clouds. No one could be seen walking the streets at such a late hour, except for a lone, dark figure who purposely walked in one direction. Preferring these types of nights when it was raining and dark, most people wouldn't even think about leaving their homes unless they had to. On these nights, the dark figure could go slow and not worry if anyone saw. Oh yes! He could enjoy himself and that would have put a smile on his lips, if he had any.

A few minutes later, he approached the house that he intended to visit. He slid into the shadows behind the huge oak tree so as not to be seen. There he waited for the occupant of the house to come out—just as he did every night around this time. He would get in his car, be gone about twenty minutes, and then return with a woman—probably his girlfriend. It made him mad. People like that always have girls swarming over them. Any time they wanted.

The dark figure remembers years ago when in high school, the pretty girls would never go out with him, let alone talk to him. It always made him mad.

He remembers telling his own mother that all the girls hate him. His mother would only laugh at him and say he was imagining it, putting too much into it. He would find someone eventually. Not to rush it. But she was laughing at him.

What mother laughs at her own son? His dad would never laugh at him. His dad would understand.

But why did he leave him? He was only seven years old when he left them. It must have been his mother's fault. It had to be.

Mother was always saying things that were not nice. She would put his father down. Maybe that's why he left them. Maybe he just left his mother, and not the boy. But that doesn't make sense. Does it?

Shortly after that, Mother would punish the boy for no reason. Being punished every day!

For no reason! But now he's had enough!

Mother would be sorry she's ever treated him that way! He'll get revenge!

Later that night, he snuck into the kitchen to steal the butcher knife. He waited until Mother was sound asleep and crept into her room and loomed over her. He stabbed her in the back again and again and again, only stopping when he couldn't raise his arm anymore.

He went into the garage to look for the gasoline that he knew was there. He picked it up and carried it into the house, up the stairs, and into his mother's room.

He looked at his mother one last time with hate in his eyes.

Trump

You will never laugh at me again, Mother.

With that thought, he uncapped the gasoline and poured it all over his mother, soaking the curtains hanging on the window and the floor leading to the door. He spread some gas in the hallway outside the door leading down stairwell. As he got to the bottom of the stairs, he finally ran out of gas and threw the container aside. Taking a deep breath he walked toward the kitchen to go get some matches. Coming back to the bottom of the staircase, he lit the matches and tossed them on the drenched staircase. He took a step back and covered his face he watched the fire trail going up the stairs toward his mother's room. Satisfied, he left the house and raced down the street. He never looked back until he heard the explosion.

Only then he finally stopped and watched.

Never again, Mother!

Movement in the house caught the dark figure's attention and snapped him out of his daze. Stepping farther into the shadows, the occupant pushed the drapes aside and peered out. It lasted less than a minute before the drapes were back in their normal position.

Tony Reid checked his watch and saw it was still half an hour before midnight. He still had time before he went to get Nancy Trusk, his girlfriend, who worked as a waitress at Trent's Restaurant. Her shift usually finished at midnight unless they were extremely busy. She would call Tony so he wouldn't have to go get her. She would call Joe's Cab. But tonight was not that night. He only had a couple of blocks to go so he wouldn't have to leave until five minutes to the hour. Suddenly he thought he heard a noise outside. What could it be this time of night? Nobody in their right mind would be out in this rain. Could it have been raccoons? He moved the drapes aside and peered out for a bit. He didn't see anything out of the ordinary. In this small town of Havenburg, nothing was ever out of the ordinary. What a boring place. Often he talked about leaving this town, but where would he go? His roots were here. He had no family, few friends, and a beautiful girlfriend whom he loved very much. He thought about the orphanage he grew up in. It had caught fire ten years ago, and no one was ever charged. It was said some kids from the orphanage started the fire, but it couldn't be proved. So he stayed here in Havenburg and grew into a handsome young man. Thirty years old, blond hair, blue eyes, five feet and eleven inches tall, and a smile that drove the ladies mad. Finishing the last of his coffee, it was time to go. He grabbed his jacket out of the closet, shut the lights, and went out the door.

As he turned to lock the door, he turned and felt a sharp pain in the back. His last thoughts before he died were of Nancy. Beautiful Nancy.

Never see my beautiful Nancy ever again. Please forgive me, sweetheart.

XXXXX

Once the lights were shut off and the door opened, the dark figure took out a butcher knife and left the shadow of the oak tree. Just as Tony turned to lock door, the dark figure sprang with the knife held high and plunged it into his back.

The dark figure then took out the ace of spades.

1

It was thunder and lightning steady all night, but the boy was determined to keep running. He was at it for quite some time, but the shape kept getting closer and closer. He wanted to slow down and rest for a minute, but he knew the figure could close the distance in a heartbeat. He cut through some yards, hoping to put some distance, but he was too tired. Still, he leaned against a fence he came across to catch his breath when a sheet of lightning lit up the sky.

At that precise moment, a black cat jumped over the fence, and he woke up screaming to the sound of the telephone ringing. It took him a minute or two to catch his bearings before he flipped the lid from his cell growling "Ya, what is it?"

"And a good morning to you too, grouchy. Same dream again?"

"Ya, for the past three months. It's three thirty in the morning. Don't you ever sleep, Claire"

"Yes, Luke, I sleep very well actually, thank you very much, except when there's been another murder last night."

"What, another one? That's the third one in the last two months. When will we clobber this maniac? We gotta get him, Claire. I want this bastard."

"Then get up, shower, and get dressed. I'm pulling into your driveway as we speak."

Twenty minutes later, detectives Luke Myers and Claire Davis were pulling up to the murder site where the coroner and paramedics were just finishing with the body. As they were approaching, Claire noticed a woman with a blanket draped around her. She nudged Luke and started toward her. Luke continued toward the coroner.

"Morning, Phil, whataya got?"

Phil Blake was the coroner for the small town of Havenburg for the past twenty years. All emergency, medical, and law enforcement came to respect and like him. He just turned fifty-one, and he felt every one of them this morning. He was five feet ten inches tall with curly, black hair, brown eyes, and thin lips, weighing about two hundred and forty pounds.

"Well, stab wounds in the back, which is the cause of death . . . left his calling card."

Luke winced at that. The killer went to the trouble of leaving the ace of spades on the forehead of all his victims, as though he wouldn't get credit for his killings if he didn't leave them. All of the victims were men, around thirty years of age, all in great physical shape.

"Phil, who discovered the body?"

"The girlfriend over there with your partner. She came here to his apartment looking for him when he didn't pick her up after her shift. He didn't answer his phone, and she got worried."

Luke Myers, twenty-seven, estimated to be six feet tall, weighing two hundred and ten pounds, had dark shoulder-length hair and green eyes. He lived in an old house with white siding, left to him when both his parents were killed in an automobile accident three years before. He became a detective five years ago.

Claire Davis, twenty-five, was five feet three inches, short blond hair, hazel eyes, and weighing 110 pounds and soaking wet. She lived in the heart of downtown Havenburg. She had made detective two years ago and was Myers's partner. They were inseparable.

Luke noticed two cigarettes of the same variety half-smoked and squished by the body. He put on a pair of surgical gloves from his pocket and picked the butts up and put them in a plastic bag. He handed them to Blake to have them analyzed, then went to join Claire.

He waited until she was finished in her interview. He steered her by the elbow until they were at her three-year-old Dodge Neon. When they were seated inside the car, she looked at him with concern.

"What's with you?" she said. "You look like the cat that swallowed the canary. Did you find something out while I was interviewing the girlfriend?"

"Maybe, it's definitely our guy. He left his calling card, no pun intended, the ace of spades on the victim's forehead. I also found two half-smoked cigarettes of the same brand. Could be our killer's. I had Phil bring them in to the lab to get examined. We should hear something in a couple days or so. What about you? Did you find anything out, or is that your new bridge partner?"

"Ho ho ha ha—real funny! Did you think that up all by yourself, or did your friend Phil help you? Anyway, no nothing useful, her name is Nancy Trusk. She's a waitress at Trent's Restaurant, and her shift finished at midnight. When he didn't show to pick her up, she called his cell. When he didn't answer, she began to worry, thinking maybe he fell asleep. So she walked over to his place two blocks away. When she arrived, she found him in the exact same spot we saw him."

"Did you at least get the victim's name?

"Yup, his name was Tony Reid. He was a mechanic at Wayne's Garage at the other end of town."

"Well, later on we're going to have to talk to his boss. In the meantime, let's go back to my place and fix some breakfast."

Ten minutes later, they pulled up in his driveway. Claire put the car in park, shut the engine, and pulled out the keys. As she put them in her purse, Luke opened his door, stepped out, and waited for her by her door. Entering the house through the back door, he threw his jacket on a nearby chair, while Claire threw her jacket and purse on an opposite chair.

"Now let's see, I remember somebody mentioned something about fixing breakfast, or was I dreaming?" mused Claire.

"No, you weren't dreaming, and I'll be sitting in the living room watching the news. Don't forget I like my eggs sunny-side up and my toast a little burnt."

"What? You male chauvinist pig, this is your place. You should be doing the cooking."

"My house, my rules. If you don't like it, move in."

At that moment, Claire's face dropped, and for once she had nothing to say.

Later that afternoon, they were seated in Captain Bruce Willard's office, going over the evidence of the last three killings. Captain Willard was a big man weighing two hundred and sixty-three pounds. He was five feet eleven inches tall with thin, gray hair and a wavy mustache. He was a no-nonsense boss, expected the most from his detectives but was a fair man. That fairness had earned him the respect of the small Havenburg Police Department, with ten police officers, including four detectives.

"You mean to tell me all you have is two cigarette butts to go on? That's all you got? Listen, guys. I don't need to remind you that the chief is on my butt to get this psycho off the streets."

Luke stood up and started to pace. "Don't forget, Cap, I should get an answer later today, tomorrow at the latest. Hopefully we'll know whose butts those are, and we can interview him. Maybe he knows something we don't."

"Okay, do that and keep me posted."

Two days later, Luke pulled into his parking spot in his green, nine-year-old Toyota Tercel. Luke and Claire were climbing the front stairs when they heard their names being called from behind. They turned to see the lab tech jogging up the stairs to catch up with them.

Eyeing the coffee, Luke replied, "Where's mine?"

"Sorry, Luke, but I hoped to make it to the lab before you. The results are in, but there's nothing major, I'm afraid."

"What do you mean?" Luke asked as they entered the building and headed to the elevators.

"The fingerprints we found belong to the dead man, and his were the only ones on it. I'm sorry, but it looks like a dead end."

Luke and Claire were visibly upset at the discovery. Back to the drawing board and they hadn't even started yet.

They stopped by the captain's office just as he was getting off the phone. Seeing his detectives, he waved them in to sit down.

"That was the chief down my back to see if my detectives came up with any leads yet. Well, did you?"

"Sorry, Cap, but we came to a dead end with the lab. The fingerprints on those butts belonged to the victim, and his were the only ones on it. We're headed to the garage where Reid worked to interview some of his coworkers."

Captain Willard got up to open the door, practically tripping over Claire's chair as he did so, yelling "What are you still doing here? Don't you have somewhere to be?"

As they were getting into the car, Claire started giggling.

"What's so funny, Claire?"

"Didn't you see how fast Cap got up from his chair?" asked Claire. "He practically tripped over my chair to get rid of us. I've never seen him move so fast."

Luke chimed in, "The last time I saw him move that fast was when—okay, I never seen him move that fast either."

At that they both started laughing and pulled out of the parking lot. Fifteen minutes later, they arrived at Wayne's Garage. They approached a mechanic working underneath a car. It took a minute before the worker dragged himself out and stood up. "Can I help you with something?" he asked.

Luke and Claire showed him their badges and asked to see who was in charge. They thanked the man and went to find the manager. As they entered the garage, Claire spotted a door at the far end and pointed. "There it is."

They knocked on the door, and a gruff voice yelled, "It's open."

"Are you the manager?" asked Luke.

"Yes," replied the manager. "Who are you?"

"I'm Detective Myers, and this is my partner Detective Davis." They showed him their badges. "What is your name, sir?"

"My name is Bob Gerald. I manage eight, I mean seven people now." Bob Gerald was a short, hefty man, balding in the middle, and gray on the sides. He weighed about two hundred and fifty pounds and was sweating profusely.

"We're investigating the murder of Tony Reid. We believe he was your employee." It was a statement.

"Well yes. He worked for me for a long time."

"What was his relationship like with his coworkers?"

"Everybody gets along here. We all respect one another."

"In your opinion, would you say there was anybody working here who would want to hurt him—maybe kill him?"

"Absolutely not. I resent you even suggesting it. Every Friday night all the mechanics go out to Dan's Cooler to unwind."

"Dan's Cooler?"

"Yes, Dan's Cooler. The bar two blocks over."

"Oh right, the bar. Well, what about anyone else? People pretending to look busy but maybe watching the place? Maybe a certain car parked down the road that looked out of place?"

"No, nothing. I didn't notice anything. Lots of people come and go or walk by. Just like lots of cars drive up and down this street."

"All right then. That's all the questions for now. I'm sorry for taking up your time. I'll leave you my card in case you think of anything. Thank you!"

Fifteen minutes later, they were sitting in Captain Willard's office with coffee in front of them. Captain Willard was leafing through the report that Luke had given him. "It says here that Tony Reid often visited Dan's Cooler after his shift was done."

"Yes, Cap. Tomorrow night Claire and I are going to see if we can interview some of the regulars."

"What's wrong with tonight?"

"Too tired and it's been a long day already. I need to go home and get some sleep!"

"All right, tomorrow then but don't forget and keep me posted!"

"Don't I always?"

After a good-night's sleep and a big breakfast, Luke took Claire's hands and drew her to him. He put his arms around her and gave her a kiss on the lips. When he released her, she stepped back and looked at him. "What in devil's name was that all about?"

"Just trying to convince you to move in with me."

"You were serious about that?"

"I sure was. Otherwise, I wouldn't have mentioned it. Look, you're here all the time, and you sleep in my bed more than you sleep in yours. It would just make more sense."

"Is that what you really want? It's a really big step, you know."

"Yes, I know it is, but that is what I really want."

"I don't know. I'll have to give it some thought."

"Yes, please do and don't rush. Take your time. In the meantime, we should go over our case before we head to Dan's Cooler tonight."

But in the pit of Luke's stomach, he had a bad feeling about this.

A very bad feeling.

2

IF ONE WAS TO drive through the little town of Havenburg, they would come to the conclusion that it is a peaceful place. They would even surmise that it has beautiful scenery, and the wind blowing softly. They would even be impressed with the woods on the edge of town as they were leaving. They would not notice the little dirt road that leads farther into the woods; the little dirt road that was covered by thick branches, leaves, and other odds and ends blowing in the wind. Even some of the townsfolk that lived there didn't seem to notice it. It appeared that the little dirt road never got used much—maybe it didn't get used at all. No cars or trucks were ever seen using it. For that matter, no one seemed to notice people even walking on that path. On this day, however, a dark figure entered that dirt road, walked briskly, and never looked back. Not hesitating, knowing the way. Farther into the woods until a small clearing opens up.

Nobody knows of this spot, for the tiny cabin has not been run down, and everything is just as it was left. With all the leaves and trees surrounding the cabin, not even Mother Nature could destroy it. When the dark figure arrived at the door, a light kick was all that was needed to open it because of the rotting wood. When the door flew open and hit the wall, a couple of small strides was all it took to step inside.

Home!

XXXXX

Luke and Claire arrived at Dan's Cooler around ten o'clock that evening. They hoped by coming out at this late hour, a good number of the regulars would be there by then. Luke parked his car around the side of the building as there was no room in the front. As they stepped out of the car, they could hear laughter coming from the front. As they approached the front door, Luke hesitated and took a deep breath. Claire nudged him as to ask what's up, but he shook his head and continued in.

Entering the room, they saw the bar took up the whole wall on the right with a flap near the end for the waitresses to come and go. At the back of the room was a doorway for the bar staff to leave when their shifts were done or just beginning. To the left, about ten tables with six chairs around each were placed, and about seven tables were filled at the moment. In the middle of the room, not much room was left, was for dancing whenever they played music. Tonight was not that night. Toward the back of the room were two big picture windows with hunter-green drapes hanging from them. Around the corner in the back were two bathrooms. All the floors were hardwood except the bathrooms and the bar, which were tiled. After years of wear and tear it, wouldn't hurt to have them changed.

Luke and Claire made their way toward the bar, keeping their eyes open. Sitting at the bar, the bartender stopped cleaning glasses and walked over to them. "What can I get you guys?"

"I'll just have a large Coke," Luke replied.

"That's it?"

"Yes, sir, if that's all right?"

"Sure if that's what you want." He gazed toward Claire. "And what would the lady like?"

"I'll have the same, please," Claire answered.

"Of course you will," He turned the way he came to go get the glasses.

"So, boss, what's our next move?" Claire teased.

"First, we chat with our friend the bartender and see what he has to say. After that, we play it by ear."

"Sounds good, but the bartender doesn't sound very friendly."

Just then the bartender brought two Cokes and placed them in front of them. As he turned to leave, Luke raised his finger to get his attention. "Excuse me, sir, but I'm wondering if you could help us out?"

"Help you out," he answered, "with what?"

Luke and Claire produced their badges and introduced themselves. "We'd like to ask you a few questions if you don't mind."

"Questions?" he asked. "About what?"

"First, what is your name sir?"

"Fred," he said. "Fred Dwyer."

"We're investigating the murder of Tony Reid. We understand that he was a regular here every Friday evening." Luke pulled out a photo of the victim and placed it on the bar in front of them so that Fred could take a look. "He was a mechanic at Wayne's Garage for several years. I wonder if you can tell us anything about him."

"Well yes, I do recognize him. He did come in here every Friday night. He always came in with his buddies from work. There were always eight of them. I remember because we always put two tables together so that they could all sit together. Anyways, they always had a good time. Not troublemakers like some of the other customers. Kept to themselves."

"Did any of the troublemakers ever give them a hard time? Maybe wanting to start a fight?"

"No, not that I was aware of. They'd be here a couple of hours or so and then leave."

"Did they always leave together?"

"Most of the time they would, but sometimes he would leave first. He had a girlfriend that he talked about all the time. He couldn't wait to get back home to her."

"Do you know the girlfriend's name?"

"No, I don't. I'm usually busy Friday nights, so I'm at all the tables bringing drinks."

"What about when he would leave? Did you notice anybody leaving shortly after he did?"

"You mean somebody who might want to hurt him?"

"Hurt him—or worse."

"You mean kill him? Heavens no! I mean, I never noticed anything like that. Like I said, I was always busy serving drinks."

"Okay, Fred, that's enough questions for now. Thank you very much for your time. If I think of any more questions, we'll be back. If you think of anything you might have forgotten to mention, here's my card. Call anytime, day or night."

The following morning, Luke and Claire met with Captain Willard at Mary's Coffee and Doughnut Shop. They were sitting in the far corner overlooking the street. Luke was sipping his coffee when Willard asked, "What's our next move? From what you told me about your visit to Dan's Cooler's last night, we're back to square one. We still don't know anything about this killer or when he might strike next."

Luke answered back, "At the rate that he's going, it will probably be in about two weeks—maybe three tops—before he strikes again unless we can find him and stop him!"

Claire added, "I think we need to talk to Nancy Trusk, the girlfriend, again. She might know something even if she doesn't think it's important. We need to ask her more detailed questions than we did before. It will open new wounds, but we have no choice. Like you said, Luke, we have to find him and stop him!"

At one o'clock that afternoon, Luke and Claire knocked softly on Nancy Trusk's front door. When there was no answer, they knocked again, more insistently. When there was still no answer, Luke peeked into the front window. Satisfied that there was nothing out of place, he stepped away. Defeated, the two detectives started back toward the car.

"Now what's our next move going to be?" asked Claire. "I really believed that she might have been able to help us."

Luke noticed how upset his partner was getting; he never saw her like that. "We go visit Trent's Restaurant. Maybe she's at work. That's what our next move is going to be."

When they entered the restaurant, they looked around and saw that is was mostly empty. Two occupants took up one table at the far end of the room. There were no waitresses anywhere to be seen, so Luke took a walk around the counter and went toward the kitchen. Almost at the door, a waitress pushed through the door toward him. Startled, she almost dropped the plate of food all over Luke.

Apologizing, Luke identified himself and asked if he could speak with Nancy Trusk.

"She took an extended leave of absence to go visit her mother and sister. She took her boyfriend's death pretty hard. She said she needed to get out of this place before she went crazy," the waitress replied.

"That's understandable, and I feel like a heel, but my partner and I need to talk to her about that. We're hoping she can help us in our investigation. Do you know how we can reach her?"

"No, I'm sorry. All she said was her family lived up north, but she didn't say where."

"That's okay. Thanks for your time."

Leaving the restaurant, Luke told Claire about the conversation he had with the waitress.

Claire was deep in thought and then replied, "We're going to have to figure out a different angle. It could take months before she comes back—months that we don't have."

Luke seemed to be deep in his own thoughts when he said, "I think we have to go over the reports of all three murders. There's something that I'm sure we overlooked. Something that will bring us closer to this psycho!"

Back at Willard's office, the three of them were leafing through all the reports in front of them. Luke broke the silence, asking, "Why does he attack all his victims from behind? There has to be a reason for that, but what?"

Willard looked up from the report that he was looking at and said, "That's a good point, Luke. I was wondering the same thing, but damned if I could figure it out!"

"They all went to *Havenburg High*!"

Both Luke and Willard answered, "What did you say?"

Claire looked at both men. "I said, all three victims went to the same high school—Havenburg High at around the same time. We need to get over to the high school and take a look at some yearbooks."

Luke and Willard gazed at Claire. "That's it. That's what we were looking for. Maybe someone at the school can help us out." Luke was getting excited. Finally a break, but they had to work quickly. Time was of the essence.

As Luke and Claire mounted the stairs, the last bell rang, and kids were dashing out the door and darting down the stairs, almost knocking them down. Once all the kids cleared out, they entered the building and stopped. What a beautiful school it was. The hallway was long, with four classrooms on the right side of the building. Two-thirds of the way down was a stairway leading to a second floor, probably more classrooms. On the left side were five classrooms to complete the hallway. At the back wall on the right side were two bathrooms. Beside that was an office with a sign that read Office—just what they were looking for.

When they entered, they saw a small waiting room with three chairs off to one side. As they closed the door, the receptionist greeted them warmly. Luke and Claire showed their credentials and were asked to have a seat. The receptionist buzzed an inner office to announce them. A couple of minutes later, the receptionist gestured for them to go through the door behind her.

Upon entering the office, a woman stood up and extended her hand. "I'm Principal Kim Lacy. My secretary tells me you're detectives? How may I help you?"

"Yes, that's correct," Luke replied. They both showed the principal their badges. "We're investigating a rash of murders, and we believe that you may be able to help."

"I'll be able to help? In what way?"

"We believe that the three victims may have been students here around the same time, about ten, maybe twelve, years ago."

"I've been principal here for eight years ago. Anything before that I wouldn't know much about."

Claire was looking out the window when she asked, "May we see the photo books dating back that far?"

Principal Lacy retorted, "That would be against our policy. Confidentiality for all our students, you understand."

Luke chimed in, "Yes, we do understand, but you need to understand that there is something going on in this town, and there may be information you can provide to help us figure out why these murders are happening. If we have to go to a judge to get a warrant, then that's what we'll do."

"There's no need for that, I was just pointing out our policy. If you leave me your card, I'll have my secretary dig them out, but it's going to take a couple of days or so. Will that be all right?"

"Yes, that will be fine. We'll be waiting for your call. Have a nice day."

XXXXX

The dark figure finished sharpening the knives and picked up the hunting knife to feel how sharp the blade was. Satisfied, the dark figure tucked the blade into a jacket pocket. Stepping outside, there was a trail that led behind the cabin and into the woods. After walking for nearly ten minutes, the dark figure was soon lost in all the foliage, but that was okay. The woods were home, they were friends, and nobody could trespass here. They weren't allowed. The woods wouldn't let them. The woods were protection. Soon the dark figure arrived at a boulder, sat, and waited.

Forty-five minutes later, two tiny creatures emerged from the brush that concealed them from the scorching sun. They were eating the grass and the leaves that were hanging low from the trees. Three more creatures emerged from under the same brush and started eating the grass. After a while, they would stop and sniff at the air as though they were expecting something to happen.

Slowly, very slowly, the dark figure took out the hunting knife and held it by the handle. Still as a statue, the knife held overhead—and struck!

The creature that had been sniffing the air died instantly when the knife went through its neck and protruded from the other side. The rest of the creatures went back into hiding, leaving the slaughtered creature unprotected.

The dark figure picked up the knife from where it stuck into the ground, and with it the creature that was claimed. Famished, the dark figure slid against the boulder and looked at the knife. Saliva slowly trickling down the face, onto the blade, onto the creature, driving the dark figure into a frenzy! With mutilating speed, he tore at the rabbit and feasted!

3

In the following days when no leads came up, Luke and Claire were overjoyed when Principal Lacy called. "I have what you asked for, sorry it took longer than I thought."

"That's okay," replied Luke. "We were busy ourselves, looking on other leads. We'll be there shortly!"

When the two detectives arrived at the high school, they went directly to the principal's office.

Lacy was pointing in the corner where the seven or eight boxes were with the photos. "Those are all the photos in the last twelve years. If you can't find what you're looking for in there, then I won't be able to help you."

"You've helped us enough already. We appreciate it. Would it be all right if we brought these down to the station?"

Later that afternoon, they were in Willard's office going over the photos. "Any luck?" the captain asked.

"Not really. We have pictures of the three victims, two in the same class, the other a year younger, but I don't understand it. I mean, they all look athletic even in the photos. How can somebody kill them?" Claire asked. "I mean, there didn't seem to be any struggle at all. These victims are huge, and they didn't even fight back!"

"Claire's right, Cap," Luke added. "I've been thinking the same thing. What kind of person can do that to athletic men?"

Willard was scratching his chin, lost in thought. "I don't know but the kind of person that could do that is probably in those books somewhere. So keep looking!"

"Cap, are you saying that the psycho went to that school too?" asked Luke.

"I don't know what I'm saying. But anything is possible, especially when you have no other leads!"

On that note, the two detectives looked at all the photos again but still couldn't see anything. "I don't know about you, but I'm bushed, and I can't see anything," Luke muttered. "What do you say we pack it up and finish looking tomorrow?"

"I'm with you," Claire agreed. "I'm starved!"

The next morning, Luke and Claire were in the main office studying the photos again. There were eight desks, two rows of four facing each other. The walls were shaded light gray, with floor tiles that looked like they would need an overhaul soon. There was a door at either end of the room, one of which they had just entered. At the other end of the room was Captain Willard's office.

They were seated at the two desks closest to Willard's office, drinking coffee. Luke was studying one page closely when he said, "Now that we've established a connection among the victims, being that they all went to the same school together, we need to look at the pictures of the men that are alive."

Claire looked up from her photo book and said, "Do you know how many that is? There's a ton of men that are alive!"

"I know. But not nearly enough of the ones that are in great shape. Those are the ones that we look for. If the psycho is one of these guys, then we have to work fast. We have to figure out who the next victim is, if we're not too late already!"

Toward the end of the day, Luke and Claire came up with six names they thought could be the next possible victims. They studied the photos a little longer when Willard stepped out of his office to join them.

"Any luck?" he asked.

Luke handed him the sheet of names, saying, "Maybe. We think one of these men could possibly be the next victim."

Willard studied the names. "You're sure?"

"Not exactly sure but it's a start. They have the same physical shape. It appeals to the psycho."

"Okay. You take the top two names. Claire, you take the middle two names, and I'll take the bottom two names. It's four thirty now. I know you guys are tired, but we need to work fast. Maybe one of these guys can actually help us nail this creep."

Forty minutes later, Luke pulled into a driveway and parked his Toyota behind a black pickup. He knocked on the door twice and rang the bell when finally a thirtyish-looking woman opened the door. "Yes, may I help you?" she asked.

Luke pulled out his badge, introduced himself, and asked, "I'm sorry to interrupt, but would Larry Haswell be home?"

"My husband?" she asked. "What's wrong?!"

"Nothing to worry about, ma'am, I would just like to ask your husband a few questions."

Before Mrs. Haswell could say anything, a voice cut in, "You're a detective?" Larry Haswell walked up to the door from the yard.

"Yes, sir, I am, and I need to ask you a couple of questions. It's important."

"Well then, ask away."

"My partner and I are investigating a few murders that happened recently."

"What does that have to do with me?"

"Well, sir, all three victims went to the same high school. Two were in the same grade, the other a year behind. They all went Havenburg High. I believe you went there also?"

"Ya, so what?"

"The killer is targeting men from twenty-five to thirty-five years old. The victims all had a good build, were in excellent shape. You fit that pattern. You could be in danger."

"Are you saying that because I went to the same high school and I'm thirty-three years old that I could become a victim? I'm sorry but I don't buy that."

"I'm sorry too, sir, but that doesn't change the fact that you will be targeted. My job is to see that doesn't happen."

"Well, it probably won't happen, so I won't be needing your help."

"Sir, listen to me. You don't understand. This psycho is never seen; it's like fighting a ghost. You have to let us help you."

"Now you listen to me, Detective, I don't have to let you do anything where I'm concerned. Now I suggest you leave before I lose my temper."

Luke just stood there and looked at Haswell. He couldn't believe how stubborn this person was. If Haswell didn't want help, he couldn't force him. His hands were tied for now, but he would find a way. He had to, or else Haswell would die.

"I'm leaving now, but I'm leaving my card with your wife in case you do change your mind. Mr. Haswell, I really hope you change your mind. For your sake and for your wife's sake."

XXXXX

As Luke left the Haswell house, the dark figure watched. The dark figure had been watching the Haswell house for some time. After a few moments, all was quiet again. Except for Mother's voice. *Be patient. Soon it will be time to kill again. The time will be right. Then they will fear you, and nobody will be able to stop you. Hahahahaha!*

Then her voice and laughter disappeared as though it had never there. The dark figure disappeared.

XXXXX

After leaving the Haswell residence, Luke met with Claire at Mary's Coffee and Doughnut Shop. Claire hadn't fared much better. Shortly after seven, getting up from their chairs, Luke mentioned he would have time to go see the last person on the list. Just then Luke's cell phone buzzed. Willard's voice almost sounded distorted but managed to say, "Meet me at the station. One of my names is going to look at the photos."

Fifteen minutes later, Luke handed Jim Parent a coffee while he was studying the photos. "See anything out of the ordinary?" Luke asked.

"Not yet. It's hard to believe that one of these guys is a killer!"

"I know, but we're pretty sure that it's true. Just try to see something that doesn't fit. We'll do the rest!"

So it went on for two more hours; for all the good it did, they were back to square one.

"All right," Luke said. "Enough for tonight. Thank you, Jim. You were helpful. If you come up with anything, anything at all, please let us know!"

After Jim left, Luke started looking through the photos again. "Who the hell could kill these people? Look how big they are. Who's doing it?"

That night Luke was tossing and turning in his sleep. His face was drenched as though he was doing a one-hundred-yard sprint. He awoke to shouting. Claire was right beside him.

"Same dream, sweetheart?" asked Claire.

"Exactly the same, dear. Always at the same time—when the sheet of lightning appears, and the black cat jumps over the fence, is when I scream and wake up!"

"I'm going to say this for your own good, darling. You need to seek professional help about your dreams and get to the bottom of this."

"I don't need help; it's just a dream. They don't mean anything!"

"Are you sure about that? Don't you want to know who this man is that's chasing you is? Don't you want to know anything about the dream just so you can put it to rest? Just so you can sleep at night?"

"I'm sure it's nothing. Besides, I don't dream every night."

"Almost every night!"

At that moment, deep into the woods, at a small clearing, there was a figure, a dark figure, who was in a small cabin just staring out the window, thinking about Mother. What had Mother meant? She said soon the time would be right. What did she mean by that? Nobody told the dark figure what to do! *Not even Mother!*

Slowly turning around, the rocking chair moved!

XXXXX

The following morning, after breakfast, Luke felt much better and apologized to Claire for keeping her up most of the night.

When they got to the office, Willard was waiting for them. "Did you guys interview your list yet?"

Luke took a sip of his coffee before answering. "Cap, not yet. We were going to finish today. It was a late night."

"Make sure you do! We need to catch this maniac before he kills again!"

"We're leaving shortly," Luke answered. "But this time we're bringing the photo book with us."

George Boudreaux's long, narrow driveway led to the back of the house. Trees on both sides of the driveway made it hard to see the house until you were practically on it. There was a small window and a door, but just looking at the layout, you knew the entrance would be the back door.

Claire felt chilled. "Something's wrong!" she said.

Luke turned to look at her. "Wrong?" he replied. "Wrong, how?"

"I don't know, but I feel like we're being watched. Like something's going to happen!"

That made Luke uneasy. Ever since he'd known Claire, whenever she had a woman's intuition, it was usually correct.

Before opening his door, Luke looked around but didn't notice anything out of the ordinary. Satisfied, he got out of the car. Approaching the back stoop, about to knock, the door opened on creaking hinges. Claire gasped and jumped back. "I told you something's wrong!"

Luke stood where he was, then took a step forward. Entering, he shouted, "Hello, is anyone here? Hello? Police, is anyone here!"

Looking at each other, they both silently drew their guns. They entered deeper into the house. The kitchen overlooked an unkempt backyard. Dirty dishes were stacked in the sink, the faucet was dripping, and open food was on the counter.

"Looks like they left in a rush," Claire pointed out.

"Yup," replied Luke, "but why?"

Past the kitchen was a cluttered living room. The television was on at low volume, a couple of hooks from the curtains were off the track, and newspapers scattered the floor.

The hallway had a closet with towels and linen. At the end of the hallway was a bathroom with no shower. It was empty. Two bedrooms and another bathroom were at the end of the hall. Both bedroom doors were closed, so they checked the bathroom first. It proved to be empty. They started for the bedroom door that was closest to where they were standing. Opening the door slowly, Luke pushed it open all the way with his gun drawn. After a full minute, Luke and Claire made their way into the room. Checking both sides of the bed and underneath, they were satisfied that it was empty.

Going toward the last door, Luke opened it slowly again and pushed it wide open with his gun. The stench was incredible. They both took a couple of deep breaths before going in. The first thing they saw was the bed in the middle of the room with a dead man in it.

4

THE HOUSE WAS ALIVE with people. Luke and Claire, Captain Willard, Phil Blake, and a couple of paramedics were present. Outside, the driveway was lined with emergency vehicles.

"That's George Boudreaux all right!" Luke said. "I recognize his photo. Looking in his room, he must have been dead for a while. It smelled so bad I thought I was going to be sick. I wonder if he was married, and if so, where's the wife?"

Blake entered the kitchen; taking off his gloves, he said, "Judging by the way his blood was coagulating, I'd say he was dead for at least forty-eight hours. Sixty tops. With the stabbing in the back and the ace of spades on his forehead, it definitely is our psycho."

Willard motioned to Luke and Claire. "You'll have to talk to the neighbors. Maybe somebody saw something that can help us out."

"I was thinking the same thing. But we'll look around the yard first. Maybe the killer left some clues," Luke replied as he and Claire made their way out the door.

Watching them go, Blake pointed out to Willard, "I don't believe George Boudreaux was married. He had no ring on his finger and no tan line of a ring if he took it off earlier."

Willard looked back at him and said, "That explains why no one else was in the house, and the killer managed to break in."

The police captain and the coroner moved to the door to give the paramedics room to wrap the body up and take it away.

When they were finally alone, Blake excused himself, saying he had some work to catch up with.

Willard went back into the house to look around. Maybe something was missed. But he doubted that, since he had the two best detectives he'd ever known. Putting on some gloves, he started opening drawers, cupboards, fridge, and anything else he could see. Nothing seemed to be missing. Stepping into the living room, he went to the newspapers that were sprawled all over the floor and checked the date. August 9. The date on his watch read August 12. Three days. That sounds about right. Blake said the victim was dead between two and three days. He was about to check the bathroom when the television caught his eye. He went up to it and watched closely. Then he realized what he was watching. Quickly he picked up his cell.

Luke and Claire were in the living room with Willard watching what was playing on the screen. "I can't believe it," Luke was saying. "I can't believe that I missed it earlier. I thought he was just watching the tube when he was killed."

Willard just shrugged and said, "I wouldn't be too hard on yourself. Anybody could have missed it."

While the two men were talking, Claire was watching George Boudreaux, wrists and ankles tied to his bed, being slowly tortured. Claire was visualizing how poor George was suffering. It was disgusting. How could anyone put another person through tragedy like that? Only psychotic people could do that. The killer was truly psychotic, and then some. The video finished with George screaming. That must be when he was killed. Claire closed her eyes momentarily and said a short prayer. When she opened them, both Luke and Willard were watching her.

"Are you okay?" Luke asked her.

"Ya, just peachy. It's always entertaining when you see a victim being tortured. Listen, Cap, we have to get this sicko soon!"

"Well, we're trying, Claire, but we don't have much to go on. Actually, the both of you have to go back and convince Haswell that he is going to be a target. Just don't know when, and, Claire, you still have one more name on your list that needs to be checked. So get going, both of you. We still have a lot of work to do."

XXXXX

When the fawn darted out from behind the brush to follow its mother, the doe turned around and chased it back behind the brush. The doe just stood in front of the fawn for a few seconds. When the doe was satisfied that the fawn would not come out from behind the brush, it darted away. The fawn stayed behind the brush and waited for its mother to return. It waited and waited and still would not move. Soon it was getting dark, and the full moon was high above. The fawn was tired and lay down on the ground beside a big oak. The fawn was startled as she felt something on her back nudging her to see the doe had come back for her.

XXXXX

Early the next morning, Luke and Claire were in Willard's office going over their plan for the day. Luke was saying Haswell was still uncooperative while they were planning on talking to the last name on Claire's list. "Let's hope with this guy, we don't run into a dead end. We need all the help we can get!" Luke exclaimed.

Claire continued, "We still need to try to help Haswell, but he does have that right, if he doesn't think he's in danger."

"We have to convince him—somehow; otherwise he will definitely end up dead."

Willard was listening to all this talk before cutting in, "But you still have two people to go see. I suggest you go soon. It will take up most of your day if you run into any more difficulties. So let's move, people."

XXXXX

Darren Peters was taking his early morning jog as he did every morning. His last mile took him to Gore Buff Road. The path went in and was almost instantly swallowed up by trees and vegetation. He was going at a slow pace enjoying the greenery. As he jumped a log that was knocked down in his path, he heard rustling noises toward his right. He glanced over but couldn't see anything. Farther down, he heard more rustling noises, along with a low growl. This time he stopped to look around, but to no avail. He continued jogging, staying in the path. Out of nowhere a black squirrel scurried past him and over to the other side. He stopped to catch his breath, and then he started to laugh. He was never scared of the woods before, nor was he scared of them now. He must have imagined the low growl. He didn't imagine the hunting knife going straight into his spine. With a twist of the blade, the knife came out easily, and he dropped to the ground hard. Maybe he should have been scared of the woods after all.

XXXXX

Turning the corner, Luke slowed down just a bit so they could see which house they needed. By concentrating their efforts, they failed to see Gore Buff Road as they drove by it. Finally reaching the house, Luke pulled into Darren Peters's driveway. Cutting the engine, Luke and Claire got out of the car and went up to the door. Luke knocked a couple of times before a little girl peeked through the curtains.

"Who, who is it?" she sniffed.

Luke looked at Claire, not knowing what to do.

Claire said, "We're police officers, sweetheart. We just want to talk."

"About what?" the little girl was still sniffling. By then a boy a little older stood beside her.

"We're looking for Darren Peters. We believe he lives here."

Now the little boy cut in. "That's our dad. What do you want with him?"

"We just want to talk to him, son."

"Well, he's not here!"

"Can you tell us where he is?"

"He went jogging like he does every morning."

"Well, can you tell us when he'll be back?"

The little boy and girl looked at each other.

Claire continued, "Please, son, it's important."

The boy said, "We don't know when he'll be back. We're not lying to you. He should have been back two hours ago."

Luke and Claire looked at each other.

"Listen, son," Luke said. "We're going to show you our badges through the window so that you know we really are the police, okay?"

The boy looked at his sister and nodded his head. "Okay," he said.

Luke and Claire showed their badges and noticed that both children looked relieved, like a weight had lifted off their shoulders.

"May we come in?" Claire asked.

After a moment's hesitation, the boy unlocked the door and let them in. When entering the house, Claire said, "You kids are very smart. Your mom and dad must be proud of you both."

"Our mother died a long time ago, and our dad is very proud of us," the girl said.

Upon hearing about their mom, Claire said, "I'm so sorry to hear that. I didn't know she died."

"That's okay," the boy said. "We're fine."

Luke and Claire took out their badges again and let the kids hold them. Their little fingers were feeling the edges. You could tell they had never seen a real badge before.

Luke turned the badge over and showed the two kids the numbers on it. "This is my badge number, so if I ever lost it, and someone found it and brought it to police headquarters, it would be returned to me."

"Wow," the boy said, "ever neat!"

"Yes," Luke replied. "It is neat. Now listen, we need to ask you a few questions. Is that okay?"

The little boy answered, "Sure, I guess."

"Good boy," Luke said. "First, I would like to know your name and age and your sister's name and age."

"My name is Mark, and this is my sister, Vicky," Mark said. "I'm twelve, and my sister is ten."

"Mark, listen, this is very important. You said your father should have been home two hours ago?"

"Yes," Mark answered. "He always comes home in plenty of time before we go to school. But he didn't show up today. I'm scared something happened to him."

"Listen, Mark, we need to know your dad's jogging route. That way we can go find him and bring him home."

"We don't know his route. Honest. He never talks about it. But he does mention sometimes about the nice trees and squirrels and other little animals he sees. But you don't see too many around here, except maybe in the woods."

"The woods?" asked Luke.

"Yes, the woods. There's a path at the end of this road that leads into the woods. Maybe that's where he ran."

"Well, that's a good place for us to start looking," Luke said.

"Mark, Vicky, thank you very much for your help. We'll do our very best to find your dad."

When they were in the car, Luke said, "I don't like where this is going. He should have been home more than two hours ago. The kids are by themselves. He would have been there as soon as possible, without changing his routine. I have a feeling something really is wrong."

Claire looked over at him. "So now you have the feeling. I guess we do make a good team. But you're right; I don't have a good feeling about this!"

5

FINDING THE LITTLE DIRT path named Gore Buff Road, Luke pulled the car over and shut it off. Neither one of them said anything for a few minutes. Then Luke said, "I guess this is where we get out and start looking for Darren Peters.

"Ya," replied Claire. "Let's hope it's good news." Luke cringed at that last remark. "We'll never know until we find him. Let's get going."

They got out of the car and began walking toward the path. "Does it ever look spooky?" Luke declared. "Even in the daytime."

"It sure does," Claire agreed. "Maybe we should go in armed."

They both pulled out their guns and advanced onto the path that led into the woods. Claire took the right side of the path, while Luke took the left. They could hear a lot of animal noises as they got farther down the path.

"Is it ever noisy?" Claire announced. "I'm glad that I don't jog in these woods. Is it ever creepy?"

Luke looked at her and said, "I didn't know you jogged. You never told me."

"Okay, okay, so I don't jog. Sue me. But just the same, I'm glad I don't come here."

Ten minutes later, they came across a fallen log in the pathway. When they reached the log, they stood still.

"Now it's really quiet," Luke observed. "It's like all the creatures of the woods know something is up."

As they started farther down the path, they saw something. About twenty feet down on the edge of the path, they saw an arm and a leg sticking out from behind a tree.

"Oh my God," cried Claire. "Not again!"

As they got closer, they could see the whole body, but they had to walk around the tree to view the face.

"That's Darren Peters all right," Luke said. "I recognize his photo. I'll call Willard."

Forty minutes later, Willard showed up with Phil Blake and two paramedics. Willard was saying, "The body count is five as far as we know. I'm surprised the media haven't gotten their mitts dirty yet!"

Phil responded, "Another stabbing to the back and the ace of spades on the forehead. Definitely our guy."

Luke cut in, "I'm going to have to tell the kids about their dad. They're going to be heartbroken. They already lost their mother a few years ago. I don't know if they have any other relatives they can go to."

"Luke," Willard went up to him. "You don't have to be the one to tell them, you know. We have people who can do that."

"No! I'm going to tell them. I told them that I would find their dad."

Driving back to the Peters' place, Luke and Claire were quiet. Both lost in their own thoughts, Claire finally broke the silence as they were pulling into the driveway. "I know it's going to be hard, especially telling a little boy and little girl their dad is dead. You know I'm going in with you, right?"

Luke looked at her; his eyes were red. When he didn't say anything, she repeated, "Right?"

Luke finally answered, "Ya, I know. Thanks." Claire put her hand on his and gave it a reassuring squeeze.

Knocking on the front door, Mark answered almost immediately. He must have been watching and saw the look in Luke's eyes. "Oh no, something's wrong, isn't it! Something's happened to my dad, hasn't it?"

"Mark," Luke choked. "I'm afraid . . . I'm afraid something bad has happened to your dad." But Luke couldn't finish the rest.

Claire cut in, "Mark, honey, something awful has happened to your dad, and I'm afraid he won't be able to come back home anymore. He—"

"He's dead, isn't he?" Mark interrupted. "Isn't he!"

Claire looked at him, "Yes, Mark, he's dead. I'm very sorry!"

Mark's eyes flooded with tears, running down his face. Vicky had walked into the room by then and heard the important part. Her dad was dead. She was sobbing uncontrollably, and Claire hugged her. They stayed with the kids until their aunt was notified and came to get them.

"Well, that's that," Claire said. "How are you holding out?" she asked Luke.

"I'm okay," he answered, his eyes still moist. "I was more upset for the kids because now they're orphans."

XXXXXX

The dark figure hid behind a big tree, watching the scene unfold. What a bunch of sheep they were.

One lamb falls and they all come running about.

Why should they care if there is one less of them? It made no sense. When you slaughter a deer, a moose, a rabbit, they don't care. They don't mope around. They continue on with their pathetic lives. They go on as though there is nothing amiss. Not people though. They have to make a big show as though they will miss the dead; never heard of anything so stupid. That would be their downfall, because they care too much for one another.

They will all fall at the hands of the dark figure because they were so stupid, just waiting to be killed.

I will oblige every single one of them.

Once everyone left, the dark figure returned to the cabin. Walking toward Mother, the rocking chair started to move.

Soon child, very soon, everything will come to an end. Mother's voice was screeching, so loud, like nails on a chalkboard, until just as suddenly, everything stopped. It was quiet again. The rocking chair stopped moving.

XXXXX

Phil Blake was feeling his age. He was always tired. It was hard for him to move around without feeling some kind of pain. But today was probably the worst. Maybe he was getting tired of his job. Maybe it was because with five murders, they still weren't any closer to catching the killer than they were when it all began. He couldn't understand why they couldn't find a lead, couldn't understand any of it. That's why he was looking at Darren Peters's body again. Perhaps he had missed something. Not likely, he was always thorough with his autopsies, never taking shortcuts. But here he was, going over his work again. Oh well!

Luke was having a fitful sleep that night. Being in a terrible mood all day and all night because of what happened earlier didn't help matters. Claire tried to help, but she couldn't snap him out of it. Later when they went to bed, he started dreaming almost immediately, keeping them both awake. Claire pointed out again that he should go see someone about the dreams.

"No!" he yelled. "I told you before there is nothing wrong. It's just a dream!"

"I don't believe that at all. I think as soon as you know who that man chasing you is, the sooner you'll stop having that dream!"

"Claire, stop it!" Luke growled. "I'm not going to do it."

With that comment, Claire said, "Well, in that case, I'm going to go home tonight! Maybe you'll come to your senses."

"Claire, don't go. I need you. Please," Luke begged.

Claire stopped to look at him. "Right now you don't need me, but you do need help. I'll see you at the office in the morning."

The following morning, Claire was in Willard's office. Willard looked at her and then looked at the empty chair Luke usually sat in.

"Where the hell is your partner?" he asked.

"Home would be a good guess," she replied.

"You guess? You mean you don't know?"

"No. We had an argument last night. I went to my place after that, never heard from him."

"Well, you better hear from him. The two of you have lots of work to do."

Just then the door burst open wide, and Luke came in with three cups of coffee. He put one in front of Willard, one in front of Claire, who kept staring at him, and kept one for himself.

"Did I miss much?" he asked as he sat down.

"Not much," the captain replied. "Only wondering if we were ever going to hear from you again!"

"Sorry about that. I should have called to tell you I'd be late, won't happen again."

"Well, you're here now. That's the main thing. I was just telling Detective Davis there that we still have lots of work to get done. Whatever problems the two of you have, get them fixed. I won't have my detectives at each other's throats. I pay you for results, not insults. You got that!"

"Yes, sir. We sure do, don't we, Claire? Got it, I mean."

"Yes, Luke. We do, crystal clear. I mean, it couldn't be clearer."

"Okay, people, enough already. Just get back to work pronto."

Back at their own desk, Luke broke the awkwardness when he blurted out to Claire, "I was late this morning because I went to see a lady about this dream I keep having. I still don't think it's anything, but it's not worth fighting with you over it."

When he looked up, he saw tears in her eyes. After she composed herself, Claire asked, "What did she say?"

"Nothing," he replied.

"Nothing?" she repeated.

"Nothing because she wasn't there."

"Wasn't there? Well, where the heck is she."

"Apparently, she's still on holidays. She won't be back for the rest of the month."

"But you could go find someone else. There are other people that can help, aren't there?"

"I don't want anyone else. I was told she's the best around. If anyone can help, it would be her."

"All right, Luke, I won't argue. At least you're looking into it. That's all I can ask."

"We're still going to have to check the photo book. I'm sure if the killer went to that school, he's in there. But we need help. We need to find someone who knows those kids. Except for Haswell, we don't have any leads."

Claire pointed at the photo book. "Maybe no leads yet, but there are still more photos that we haven't looked at yet. Maybe one of them will help us."

Luke looked up at her, smiling. "See, I told you I needed you."

For the next three hours, Luke and Claire poured over the photo book but could not make heads or tails. Getting up to get a cup of coffee, Luke said, "We're not getting anything accomplished. Maybe we should go find Haswell and try to convince him of the danger he's in."

Claire got up, agreeing. "All right. I hope we have better luck than before."

As they were pulling into the Haswell's driveway, they could see something was different than the last time they were here. The screen door was closed, but the inside door was open. They could see into the house. A hurricane must have gone through it. Everything was thrown all over the place. As they were about to knock, they heard crying coming from farther into the house. Drawing their guns, Luke opened the door and yelled, "Police, is anyone here?"

"B-b-back here," sobbed a female. "I'm in the bathroom."

Claire went forward to be the one to talk to Mrs. Haswell.

As she entered the bathroom, she asked, "What the heck happened? It's like a tornado came through here."

"It's my husband. I tried to get him to seek help, but he just gets more upset. Today was the last straw. He was like a raving madman, throwing everything in sight. It was like he didn't even know I was here. I was lucky not to get hit. Then just like that, he stops throwing things and leaves."

"What? He just left?"

"He does that when he gets upset."

"He's done this before?"

"Oh yes. He has a little temper, but most of the time, he can control it."

"That temper that he controlled with my partner, the other day when we were here? Has that temper ever hit you?"

"Heavens no! He never hits me. That's why he left. He'll be back when he's over his mood."

"Does he have a lot of outbursts like today?"

"No, not at all, thank goodness for that."

"Do you know where he went? Where we could find him?"

"He always goes to this bar called Dan's Cooler. That's not far from here. About two or three blocks away. That's probably where he is now."

"Well, thank you for your time, Mrs. Haswell."

"Call me Diana. Diana Haswell."

"Well, okay. Again, thank you for your time, Diana. If there is anything else you might remember, please don't hesitate to call. Anytime."

"Of course, thank you again for everything."

When they were in the car, heading toward Dan's Cooler, Claire repeated her conversation with Diana. As she finished her story, she asked Luke, "Do you mind telling me what you were doing all that time?"

"Not too much," he answered. "I was poking through the debris but didn't find anything useful."

Pulling into Dan's Cooler, Luke had a thought. "If Haswell gave us a hard time before, and he just trashed his place, we're going to have our hands full."

"Ya, I know. I was having the same thought myself."

As they entered the bar, they noticed only four men and one woman scattered through the room. At the bar, two men were sitting at opposite ends, nursing a drink. Haswell was one of those patrons, at the far end. Luke and Claire sat about two stools away from Haswell but did not make eye contact. Luke, being closer to

Haswell, said out loud to Claire, "They serve any type of people here."

At the sound of his voice, Haswell turned and sneered at Luke. "Following me in here now? Why don't you leave me alone! It's not enough you come to my home and make accusations, now you follow me here?"

"Accusations?" repeated Luke. "I never accused you of anything. We came here to help you. You're a target, and if you don't take us seriously, you're going to wind up dead."

"I still don't buy all that crap about somebody at my school being the killer. That's ridiculous."

"Really," snickered Luke. "You still think so? Do you remember Darren Peters? Do you? You should. He was in every one of your classes. The two of you chummed around together. You were like Siamese twins. Inseparable. The two of you went everywhere together. Remember that?! Well, he's dead now. He left behind a little girl and a little boy. They're all alone now except for an aunt. Darren Peters is victim number 5. Everyone from your school in the same era is dying. You're going to be in that group also."

Luke was about to order a soda when Haswell grabbed him by the shirt collar and punched him in the jaw. The blow was so hard, so sudden and unexpected, that Luke fell off his stool and onto the floor. As he was gathering himself up, Haswell stood beside his stool, watching Luke. Luke moved toward Haswell and punched him on the left cheekbone. He fell back onto the bar. As Luke pursued Haswell, he grabbed him and flipped him over the bar. Luke leaped over the bar but received a kick to the gut. As he reeled over in pain, Haswell punched him to the side of the head. Haswell got up to his feet to continue the onslaught. Watching

Haswell approach, Luke ran hard and butted him on the side. Both men fell, with Luke ending up on top. He got to his feet, picked up Haswell, and spun him against the bar. He put Haswell's hands behind his back and cuffed him.

"You're under arrest for assault," Luke informed him. "Tonight you're going to cool down in a nice, big cage. Maybe tomorrow you'll decide to play nice, asshole." He glanced over and saw Claire smiling at him.

"What?" His mouth hurt to talk.

"My hero, my knight in shining armour, my dreamboat."

"Does that mean we're okay now?"

"It sure does."

Luke looked at Fred the bartender. "All damages can be billed to Mr. Haswell."

That evening in the emergency room, getting his injuries checked over, Willard looked at his bruised jaw and said, "Look at you. Two inches to the right, and you wouldn't have any front teeth."

Luke looked up at him and replied, "Ya, but look at it this way. To inches to the left, he would have missed me completely."

Willard threw his hands up in surrender and said, "I give up. It's like trying to make friends with a rattlesnake. Just impossible."

When he left, Luke and Claire started laughing. "Seriously, Luke, the captain does have a point. Your face sure took a beating. It must hurt like hell."

"Not much, only when I breathe. But the doc says my face should be as good as new in a couple of weeks. So I'm not complaining."

"Maybe not, but don't go making a habit of it. Otherwise, I might take a round out of you."

"Oooohhh tough talk from a tough lady. I'm starting to get scared of you. I'm shaking in my boots. I promise I won't make a habit of this—much."

6

AFTER A SOUND SLEEP, Luke was somewhat sore, but feeling much better, he was looking forward to the day. This time Claire was doing the driving. When they entered the precinct, Willard waved at them to go in his office.

When they seated themselves, Willard asked Luke, "How's your face this morning?"

"A little sore, hurts to talk a lot, but otherwise just fine."

"Good, because now we have to figure out how to convince Haswell to change his viewpoint. I have a feeling he holds the key."

"I believe you're right, Cap," Luke answered. "But I'm thinking maybe I want to go back to Dan's Cooler and talk to Fred the bartender."

"You do? May I ask why?" Willard was confused.

"I was thinking last night that maybe our psycho friend drinks here and there. Maybe Fred will recognize him."

Willard was pondering this. "Maybe you're onto something there. I like it. When would you go talk to him?"

"Tonight. I'll bring the photo book with me and show him some pictures."

"That's a brilliant idea. Let's hope it works. But in the meantime, we work on Haswell."

When Luke and Claire went to talk to Haswell in the interrogation room, he was sporting a grin so horrific; it'd be enough to crack the face of a tarantula. Seeing that grin, Luke asked him, "What's so funny?"

That made Haswell grin even more. "Your face, that's what's so funny. Any minute now my wife will come here and spring me loose."

"You think so?" Now it was Luke's turn to grin. "I wouldn't count on that. In fact, you'll be lucky if she's still home waiting for you. The way you trashed the place, scaring her like that. But I tell you what I will do. You help us with some photos, and I'll help you with the charges against you. But only if you help; otherwise, I'll ride this through to the end."

Haswell just looked at Luke, not knowing if he was on the level. "How do I know you're telling the truth?" inquired Haswell.

"Well, that's the thing. You don't. Take it or leave it. We'll come back for your answer." With that, Luke and Claire left the room.

While watching Haswell through the two-way mirror next door, Claire said, "Well, that was pretty smooth the way you handled him. I didn't know you had it in you. But how do you know his wife will leave him?"

"I don't. I was just blowing smoke to make him mad. We'll just watch him stew for a while, and then we'll go back in."

"Very impressive, Detective Myers."

"Why, thank you, Detective Davis."

It was almost forty minutes later when they decided to return to Haswell.

"It's damn well time you showed up. You can't treat me this way."

"What way would that be?" challenged Luke.

"Like a criminal! I've never been in jail in all my life, let alone have a police record."

"Well," Luke responded. "You're going to have a record now. So unless you help me, I'll treat you like a criminal and don't tell me otherwise."

Haswell's face turned bright red. He had to take a deep breath to calm down.

"All right, all right, don't get your tie all knotted up. I'll look at the damn photos, but that don't mean I'll see anything that you couldn't see."

While Haswell was leafing through the photo book, Luke and Willard were watching him through the two-way. Willard said, "What do you think?"

"Claire is keeping tabs on him in there. We decided Haswell might work better if I stepped out for a bit. So now we'll see if it works."

"Well, I hope it does. We're running out of time. He needs to find something soon."

Claire was watching Haswell closely as he looked through the photo book. Haswell was turning page after page, but nothing seemed to register. He looked up at Claire and apologized. "I'm sorry, I truly am. But I can't see anything that might help."

Claire sighed and stood up. She shook her head no to the glass where she knew Luke and Willard were watching.

"Keep trying," she told him. "I'll get you a coffee."

She joined Luke and Willard. "How's he holding out," Willard asked.

"Not good so far, but I can tell by watching him he really is trying. I'm going to get him a coffee."

Back in the interrogation room, Haswell was stumped. According to these pictures, only five—maybe six—guys would not be considered a potential victim. They all looked small and weak, with none of the good looks that all the victims had. If the killer was one of those guys, he didn't know how he could manhandle the victims. They were all too small. He must have been right. None of these guys could have killed them. It was somebody who had not gone to this school. Ever. He couldn't have. Could he?

Claire entered the room and put a coffee in front of him.

"Well, did you find anything?" Claire asked hopefully.

Taking a sip of his coffee, Haswell said, "Well, I did, and I didn't."

Claire said, "I don't follow."

Haswell said, "Well, see here?" He turned the book around so she could get a better look. "See all these guys here?"

"Ya, so."

"See how big and strong they look? They would be difficult to kill."

"Go on."

"Now, see these other guys? See how small they look? Even weak? How could they kill those big guys like that? They would have needed help."

"Yes, I noticed that too. That's why we need your help. We can't figure it out. No leads."

Haswell said, "Well, that's all I can do. The faces themselves don't look familiar. Other than what I've already told you, I don't know how else I can help."

"I know you tried, that's all I can ask. You're free to go."

Haswell just stared at her. "I'm free to go? Just like that? No charges?"

"Just like that—no charges. Now go, before I change my mind."

Claire watched Haswell leave. When he was gone, she just sat there looking at some of the photos. Luke and Willard came in from the next room and sat with her.

Luke asked, "You just let him go?"

Without looking at him, Claire said, "Yup."

"Why? You said he wasn't helping."

"But he was helping. You didn't see his eyes. I did. Besides, he just gave us our biggest clue without even knowing."

Luke and Willard looked at each other and then looked back at Claire. Luke said, "He did? What clue would that be?"

Claire turned the book around so that both men could see the pictures clearly.

"If we're right about the killer being one of the classmates, and I think we are, I bet it would have to be one of these six guys right here."

Both Luke and Willard studied the pictures but saw nothing. Willard spoke, "I don't see anything, Claire. Suppose you just tell us."

"All right," she said. Claire pointed to the six photos and remarked, "Not one of these guys would be victim material because they look small, weak, and even ugly. Am I right so far?"

When neither man spoke, she continued. "Having said that, it must be one of these six men that is probably our killer."

"But, Claire," Willard said. "Those men wouldn't be able to kill those big men, at least not as easily. There was no evidence of any resistance from the victims. Not one!"

"Exactly, because they were killed from behind, not the front. Evidence would show he struck from the back, where the stab wounds are. He had to be directly behind them, shoulder to shoulder, not from the side. So that means if he was quiet enough, they may not have heard him. Killing them would not be difficult."

Both Luke and Willard swore silently.

Luke, breaking the silence, said, "Wow, Claire, even if that's true, the stab wounds are so high, just under the neck, and these guys are pretty short, how would they reach, bring a stool?"

Luke and Willard chuckled at that.

"It's not funny, guys. Did you ever think that if he was running behind them, he could jump and then stab?"

Luke said, "If he was running, the victims would have heard the footsteps and turn around to see who it was. Just basic instinct."

Claire had to agree with Luke on that one.

"But that doesn't mean we're wrong. I still think it's one of those guys. Maybe it's two guys teaming up."

Both men were quiet on that last remark. When Luke spoke, he said, "When I go see my friend the bartender tonight, maybe he'll recognize one of them, and we can go from there."

"Sounds good to me," Willard said. "It's better than what we have now."

XXXXX

The dark figure was in a state of panic. Mother was screaming furiously. Not knowing what upset her made it even worse. Why won't Mother just say what's on her mind instead of just screaming like that? To make matters worse, Mother's chair began to move. Now she's really mad. It was thunder and lightning all of a sudden—must be because of Mother. Big trees were waving their big arms back and forth, almost touching the ground. Branches were scraping against the cabin walls and windows. The sound was deafening.

The dark figure was unable to escape the image of what it must be doing to the cabin. When the lightning struck, it felt like the trees would split in half. The cabin shook. The rocking chair was moving faster and faster, from the front tip of the chair to the back tip. It was squeaking louder and louder, seeming to drown out the thunder. The squeaking was so loud; the dark figure screamed and fell on the floor. Flailing like a fish out of water, the dark figure sobbed like a little baby.

Mother's voice was haunting. *Why did you kill that nobody here in the woods! Do you know what you've done? Do you? Now sooner or later, those sheep as you call them will find us! Do you understand that? Do you even comprehend? Get up, boy, get up and look at me when I'm talking! Look at me and see what you've done to me! Take a good long look, for you're going to look at this image for the rest of your miserable life. No wonder you could never get any girls to go out with you! Or even like you! They saw your nothingness—that's why they laughed at you! So get up and feel my fury!*

The dark figure stood up on shaky legs.

Why would you say that, Mother? I did everything you asked me to do. Why would you treat me so mean? I would never do that to you.

Then everything stopped. The rocking chair stopped. The thunder and lightning stopped. The branches and trees stopped moving. The wind stopped. Most importantly, Mother's voice stopped taunting him. Everything stopped as though it had never begun. When the dark figure turned to look at Mother again, the rocking chair was directly in front of him.

XXXXX

Luke and Claire were driving to Luke's place when the storm hit. The wind picked up velocity. Trees were bending, almost reaching the road where Luke was driving. Anything that was not tied down was blowing westward. Branches were hitting the car as they broke off the trees with a snap. A few of the smaller trees uprooted and fell. Some were lying in ditches, while other trees were lying alongside the road. Wind gusts seemed to reach up near ninety kilometers an hour. But where did this storm come from? It was clear and sunny all day with clear, blue skies. So how could this happen? That's what Luke was thinking.

"How the hell could this freak thunder and lightning just happen? Because that's what it is. Freak of nature or maybe freak of hell." He had pulled to the curb to wait it out. Couldn't see two feet in front of you, let alone drive in it.

"Calm yourself down, handsome, or you'll work yourself to a heart attack. Besides, these storms don't usually last long."

To prove her point, the storm stopped suddenly, as though it had never begun. The only evidence it ever happened were the trees that were lying about. Eventually, they made it to his place. Luke looked at her, saying, "How on the ball was that?"

"What do you mean?"

"What do you mean—what do I mean? About the storm not lasting long. It stopped as soon as you said that."

"Well, it's true. Most storms don't last long."

"But it stopped as soon as you said that. What are the chances of that?"

"Slim to none, I suppose. But it happened. Maybe I have a magic power. Yes, that's it. I think I will call myself Weather Woman!" Then she started laughing. "You should have seen the look on your face. So adorable."

"I guess you're right. But it's so uncanny, the way that happened."

"Yes, it was, but let's not worry about that anymore. We have other fish to fry, like going to see our friend Fred the bartender tonight."

7

WHEN THE STORM HIT, Captain Bruce Willard spilled his coffee all over his clean, new shirt. Where the hell did this weather come from all of a sudden? It was warm and sunny just a minute ago. How could it be stormy? It was thunder and lightning to beat the band. What the heck was going on? His office shook and knocked pencils and pens from his desk that were loose. The curtain was trying to do the high jump where the window was open. The trembling felt like a minor earthquake. But that was impossible. We never had earthquakes here in Havenburg since he was around. His whole life here and not once any earthquakes. So what gives? Why now? As suddenly it started, it stopped. Everything went back to normal. Only the mess of his office and the mess of his brand-new shirt would tell you otherwise.

Along with Willard's office, the rest of the police station was hit worse. Two officers were drinking coffee with a shot of rye, while putting their feet up on the desk. The heavy winds blew both officers backward with their drinks all over them. With the curtain blowing, everything that was loose blew over, and the desk tipped on end. The two police officers barely managed avoided being crushed. They got to their feet but couldn't get out of the room, losing their balance. They were on one knee, and when they fought to gain control, the wind was keeping them at a standstill. The buzz that they managed to achieve didn't do them any good.

Once again the two officers fell on the floor and tried to crawl toward the door. The lightning managed to split a few trees along the sidewalk directly leading up to the police station. The thunder was so loud it was unbelievable. People had to shout to be heard, and when everything stopped, all of a sudden, people were yelling, not knowing the storm passed.

When people came out to look around, lots of damage was done. But the most damage was done to the mind. How could a storm like this happen? If it happened this one time, how will we know if it'll happen again? That is the worst damage it could do.

When the storm hit, the animals in the woods were well sheltered. With their sense of smell, they knew the storm was coming quickly. The smell was coming from the west. They stayed away from the west knowing what lay beyond the hills leading west. The cabin. The cabin was very dangerous. Something bad happened when the cabin was involved. All the animals avoid the cabin. They saw death emanating from beyond the walls. They stayed sheltered, and they stayed away from the cabin.

Later that night, nursing their two Cokes at Dan's Cooler, Luke scanned the crowd.

"This is the most people I've seen here, not that I come here lots," Luke was saying. "But it seems it usually wasn't so busy."

Claire took a drink while looking through the crowd and said, "I don't recognize anyone here." When she turned toward Luke, she saw him gazing across the room. She looked also and saw a couple of ladies looking back at him. Taking another drink, she jabbed him in the side, and he winced in pain. "Ow, that hurt. What did you do that for?"

"Oh, I don't know. Maybe it was to put your tongue back in your mouth. Or maybe it was to keep your eye sockets from falling out or both. Oh, you're so busted. If I catch you looking at them again, then you'll know pain."

"Sorry. I didn't realize."

"Ya, right."

Finishing their Cokes, they ordered another until finally, Luke said, "Okay, now it's time for business. Fred, mind if I ask you a few questions?"

"If it's about that fella that you asked about before, the one that got killed, I don't know any more than what I told you already."

"It's not about him, but it is about the same killings."

"Killings? More than one?"

"Yes. At last count, there are five."

"Last count? Five?"

"Yes, sir, five. Maybe more. It's possible."

"Wow, I didn't know."

"No, sir, because we are keeping it from the public for now. But I told you because I need your help."

"Well, I'll try, but not promising anything. I actually thought you were coming back to bust the place up again."

"Yes, well I'm sorry about that. But the other guy brought that on. I'm here only to ask questions."

"All right, ask away."

"I'm going to show you a few pictures; you tell me if you've ever saw them before. Fair enough?"

"Ya, sure. Fair enough."

While he was fishing out the photo book, he asked, "Why is it so busy tonight? Every time I was here, hardly anyone was here."

"Well, they heard about your fight the other day, so they wanted to see if you would start another one. Hahahaha, just kidding. Every Friday and Saturday night is busy here. That's what keeps me going."

"That's right. It's the weekend. Duh, that was a stupid question."

By now he had the book in front of him with the page open to the pictures he wanted to show him. Pushing it toward Fred, he said, "Take your time. I need to know if you see anybody familiar in this book. Remember, these pictures are about fifteen years old. So like I said, take your time and be sure."

Fred started looking at the pictures but was interrupted by customers wanting more drinks.

"You'll have to excuse me," he said.

Luke told Claire, "This could take all night."

Claire looked back at him and said, "Well, you could always start a fight with someone."

She chuckled while he said, "Very funny." But he couldn't help himself and started laughing.

By then Fred came back. "Sorry about that. Just business. I'll start on those pictures now."

So it was the rest of the night, Fred being interrupted every so often by customers, who were starting to get rowdy because they had to wait a little longer to get served.

By then Luke and Claire had five or six more Cokes until finally, Fred said, "All right, guys, I'm finally finished looking at those pictures. Let me close shop, and I'll get to you with no more interruptions."

When Fred came back, Luke said, "I hope you have something for us because we've been here all night. It's past my bedtime."

"Well, sir, if you'll allow me to explain, it might be worth the wait."

"Okay, Fred, you've got my attention. Go on."

"Yes, well, you see these photos here?"

Both Luke and Claire looked at where he was pointing.

"Yes, carry on," he said.

"These pictures are fifteen years old, so I could be wrong."

"We'll take that into consideration. Go on."

"Well, these two guys came here maybe three times. Always came in together, always left together."

"When was that?" Luke wanted to know.

"Oh, I'd say maybe six months ago. Eight months tops."

"You remember that?"

"Sure. They always sat in the same seats. Over there." He pointed near the back.

"Wow, you have a good memory, Fred."

"Sometimes they got loud after they had a few. But the reason I remember them is because of how much they tipped."

"I take it they tipped well."

"Yes. Too well. Something like that sticks with you."

"Do they still come in?"

"No, I haven't seen them since."

Luke downed the rest of his Coke before asking, "Any other photos you remember?"

Fred pointed to two more on the bottom of the page. "These two over here."

"Any stories about those two?"

"Let's see." Fred closed his eyes and thought about it. "As I recall, they sat mostly by the back wall over there. But every now and then they would sit near the front row. Anyway, one of the two would always drink more than the other. The one that never drank much was always quiet. If he ever said two words, that's all he said. But he was always watching."

"Always watching? Watching what?"

"Oh, I don't know. The people I guess."

"Maybe he was watching the girls?"

"No, I don't think so. He never danced with them. He never left with them either."

"That's strange. What else could he be looking at?"

"Search me. But his friend, the one who drinks, danced with them the whole time. Sometimes he left with one of the girls but not always."

"Hmm, always the drinker but never the quiet one. That is strange." Luke seemed to be lost in thought. Then he said to Fred, "Anything else?"

"I'm not sure, but the times when the fella left with the girls, the quiet one was seething."

"Seething, how?"

"Well, I don't know. Like he was really jealous, but just like that, seemed to calm down and then forgot about it."

"Anyway," he continued, "it's funny I would remember those two since they only came here three or four times. After that, they never came back. Even those girls seemed to forget them."

Luke spoke, "How did you remember them?"

"Oh, that was easy. It was the tattoo. The drinker had a tattoo on the inside of his right wrist."

"Tattoo? He had a tattoo on the inside of his right wrist?"

"Yes, that's right. On the inside of his right wrist. That's the reason why I remember him."

"Well, please tell me, what was the tattoo?"

"It was a picture of the ace of spades."

If Luke was still drinking his Coke, he would have choked on it.

8

"Did you say the ace of spades?"

"Yes, sir. That's what I said."

After a few seconds to compose himself, Luke said, "What about the other fella? Did he have tattoos also?"

"None that I know of. I didn't see any."

"You said they only came here a few times?"

"That's right."

"You never saw them again after that?"

"Nope."

"Okay, Fred. I took up your whole night. But you've been very helpful. Thank you."

On the way home, Luke said to Claire, "Do you know what this means?"

"Yes, I know what it means. But it won't matter if you get us killed. Slow down!"

"Sorry. I was just excited. We finally got our break in this investigation."

"The bartender said the guy had a tattoo of the ace of spades. It has to be the guy. Is it just coincidence?" Luke asked in Willard's office the next morning.

"I mean, it's not even common to have a tattoo of the ace of spades. It must mean something."

"Yes, I'm sure it does. But until we find out what it is, I suggest we play it by the book."

XXXXX

Jake Wright and his wife, Brenda, were having a barbeque in their backyard. Beautiful day for it, sunny with a few clouds, but nothing to worry about. They invited their best friends, Brad and Monica Sparks. Spacious backyard, green grass with two big trees, and hedges surrounding the yard. Sitting out on the patio deck, in the shade of the trees, they were laughing at some joke that was said. Settling down a bit, Brad said, "Jake, remember in high school, that one class where you sat near window, and I was beside you?"

"I kind of remember, but I'm not sure. Why?"

"There were those two girls that sat directly in front of us. One time I put a rubber snake in their desks, and boy, did they scream. It was so funny, I nearly split a gut laughing so hard."

"I remember that. When they screamed, I nearly pissed myself. I never jumped so high." So the laughing continued.

XXXXX

The dark figure stood in the master bedroom, watching them through the window. What sheep. Look how they make fools of themselves. All that prancing and drinking and laughing.

Why go through all that? Don't they know they will be dead soon? Why waste all that energy? They should sit still and wait for death? That's all they're good for. How easy it would be to kill them all. Kill them now. But no.

The time was not right. Not yet. Soon. Very soon. Mother promised it would be soon. She better keep her word. If she didn't keep her word, she'd be sorry. Real sorry.

XXXXX

In the backyard, Brad stood. "Looks like I'll have to break the seal. Be right back."

Jake took another gulp and remarked, "That guy is always the first one to break the seal. Makes me laugh. Never changes."

Brenda spoke up, "Now, Jake, you know Brad always had those problems. He's going to be like that for the rest of his life. So lighten up a bit."

Brad went into the house and made it to the bathroom just in time. As he came out, he thought he heard a faint sound. Standing still, he waited a minute but didn't hear it again. He started toward the hall when he heard the soft noise again. This time he walked into the living room, but all was quiet. Next he went into the kitchen where he could see his friends still sitting around the deck. Coming out of the kitchen, he looked at the stairs leading up.

The dark figure was watching the sheep outside, through a closet door beside the bedroom. It was a perfect vantage point. Except now one of the sheep came in the house. It was below at the bottom of the stairs, wondering if it should come up.

If it does come up, it will be killed. It will be its own fault for being so stupid. Stupid sheep need to be killed. Stupid sheep have no purpose. Have no use at all. They should mind their own business and just wait to be slaughtered. That's why they were put on this planet. Just so they can be killed.

The sheep that was by the steps finally went back outside with the others. *Soon, maybe Mother would say the time is right. But until then, it would have to wait.*

When Brad didn't hear the noise anymore, he decided to join his wife and friends. Jake was the first to jump to his feet and say, "Brad, we didn't know you'd make it."

Brenda elbowed Jake in the ribs as he was sitting down. "Ow, that hurt!"

"I told you to take it easy. I meant it!"

"I was only joking. Brad knows that."

"Ya well," Brad said. "I kept hearing noises in your house. That's what took me so long. I was trying to find it."

Monica looked at her husband with concern. "Are you all right, sweetheart?"

"Ya, I'm fine. A little spooked."

"Maybe we should call the police," Monica said. "They could come here and check the house before we go in."

"Nonsense," Jake retorted. "There's nobody in the house, and there aren't any noises. You must have imagined it."

"No, I don't think so. But if you want, the two of us will go in and check."

"Well, okay," Jake said. But he didn't sound like the hero he did moments ago.

Just then a car, one they've never seen before, pulled into the driveway.

When Luke and Claire pulled into the driveway, they saw four people watch them. As they approached the group, Luke asked, "Does a Jake Wright live here?"

Jake cleared his throat and said, "That would be me."

Luke extended his hand and said, "Yes, I recognize your picture. I'm Detective Luke Myers, and this is my partner, Detective Claire Davis." They both produced badges. Once introductions were made all around, Luke said, "We need to ask you some questions—but in the meantime, the two of you"—he pointed at the two men—"may be in grave danger."

Jake cleared his throat. "What do you mean?" he asked.

"There have been a string of murders the last couple of months, and the killer is targeting all the classmates you went to school with fifteen years ago."

"What? I find that hard to believe."

"We also believe that he's one of your classmates."

"Whoa, this is too much. Who do you think it is?"

"We're not sure, but we believe that it could be Laurel Champ."

"Laurel Champ? Him? Are you sure? He was always friendly. Always laughing. I would never have guessed."

"Well no, don't jump to conclusions. We're not sure. I'm only saying that it's him because of his tattoo."

"Tattoo?" Brad spoke up.

"Yes, tattoo. The ace of spades on the inside of his wrist."

"You think he's the killer because he has a tattoo of the ace of spades?" Brad couldn't believe it.

"The killer always leaves the ace of spades on the victim's forehead. So it's only suspicion at this point."

Monica spoke up. "Excuse me, sir, but may I say something?"

"Certainly," Luke encouraged.

"My husband, Brad, went inside for a moment, and when he returned, he said he heard a noise but couldn't pinpoint it."

Luke turned toward Brad. "You heard a noise, sir?"

"Ya, but nothing came of it."

"Well, maybe it will because if we're right, that was probably the killer. Tell me, Brad, how long ago was that?"

"Just before you arrived. Maybe ten minutes before that."

Luke looked at Claire. "He could still be in there."

"Are the front and side doors locked?" Luke asked Jake.

"No, it's a friendly place. Only if we're gone, or at night we lock them."

"Everyone stays out here," Luke demanded. He looked at Claire and said, "You take the side; I'll take the front."

When Luke opened the front door very slowly, he waited a minute before he entered. The living room had a Persian carpet, coffee table, two end tables, and a love seat, but nothing seemed disturbed. Hiding behind his nine-millimeter handgun, Luke closed the door behind him. Getting a better look, there was a long couch against the far wall with a forty-two-inch television about twelve feet in front of the couch. The dark-green curtains made the room look dark. He skipped into the kitchen and saw movement by a door that was partially opened.

When Claire reached the side door, her handgun in front of her, she slowly opened the door. Walking in very slowly, she entered a small porch. Three steps up she would be in the kitchen; more steps lead down, probably to the basement. When she proceeded up the stairs, she distinctly heard a noise. It came from a door that was partially opened. She slowly made her way and jumped ten feet when Luke's shoulder bumped into her.

"What are you trying to do, scare the crap out of me? Well, it worked!" she said.

"Tried to scare you? You got that backward. You scared the shit out of me!"

Then they both jumped when a broom fell over in the closet.

"That takes care of that noise. Now that the main floor is secure, we still need to check upstairs," Luke said.

"Don't forget about the basement," Claire added.

Outside, Jake was getting restless. "What's taking them so long? They should have been done by now."

"Jake," Brenda said. "They don't know our house. They have to go slow and check every room. It'll take time. Don't worry."

Brad said, "I guess she's right, Jake. Let's just sit down and enjoy the rest of the afternoon."

Twenty minutes later, Luke and Claire emerged from the house. When they reached the group, Claire said, "Okay, guys, the coast is clear. There is nobody in there. We suggest you stay with relatives for a while until we can catch this killer."

"No way," Jake said. "Nobody is going to scare us out of our home. Nobody."

"Don't be a fool," Luke shot back. "Your ego is going to get you killed."

"I promise I'll lock every door and window at all times, but I'm not going!"

Luke said, "We can't force you, so we're going now. We have other leads to check out."

Jake, Brad, and the two wives watched the detectives go. Brad said, "Do you think we were wise not to leave?"

Jake looked at him and said, "Of course, nothing's going to happen. They even said nobody's here. We're safe."

"If you say so."

After Brad and Monica said their goodbyes, Brenda went inside.

Jake went to the backyard to clean the barbeque. While he was scrubbing the grill, he saw a little, gray kitty playing in the far corner of his yard. Slowly he went toward the kitty, trying not to scare it. When he got closer, he bent down on his haunches and said, "Here, kitty. You're a good kitty, aren't you? Yes, you are."

He crept a little closer, and still the kitty wouldn't budge. Jake crept closer still, and when he managed to reach kitty with his hand, he was startled. "What are you doing, Jake? What have you got there?"

Jake screamed so loud it scared the kitty, and it ran back into the bushes. Jake looked at his wife and said, "Jesus, Bren, why are you sneaking up on me like that? I could have had a heart attack."

"Ya, but you should have seen your face. Makes up for all the times you scared me."

"Well, it wasn't funny. There's a killer around here, you know!"

"You're right. I'm sorry. Let's just go in. Okay?"

XXXXX

The dark figure watched the sheep laughing and drinking. Two more sheep arrived went to talk to them. They kept pointing to the house. When they finished talking, the two sheep went inside by themselves. They came back and talked some more. Then they went to their car and drove away. The two other sheep finally went away, and only two sheep were left. The female sheep went into the house. The male sheep stayed outside. He was doing something when the little kitty emerged from the bushes and into the yard. The male sheep went to pick it up when the female sheep came out and scared the kitty away. They talked a little, and then both went back inside.

The dark figure watched the house until something broke a twig.

Kitty. Kitty was here. Very interesting. Very interesting indeed. The edge of the hunting knife felt very sharp. It was very sharp. Kitty felt how sharp it was when the knife plunged into its neck and through the throat.

The blade stuck in the ground. Kitty wouldn't know that. Kitty was dead.

9

When they left Jake's driveway, Luke said, "We need to go home. I need to check my computer on a couple things. You need to call our gracious captain and tell him we're continuing our investigation from this end. No time to go to the station. Also tell him we'll be in touch tonight or tomorrow."

As they pulled into Luke's driveway, Claire was just finishing her conversation with the captain and said, "Okay, that's done. What's our next move?"

"First, we need to find Laurel Champ. Once we find him, we'll have to have a little chat. Then we go from there."

"Okay," Claire said, "but what about your computer? What are you looking for?"

"I'm going to check Havenburg High. I want to see the names of the teachers they had. Somebody knows those kids. Probably even the killer. Who might know better than the teachers?"

"Not a bad idea. It won't hurt to try."

They walked to the house and opened the back door. As they entered the kitchen, Luke went straight to his computer and set to work. He punched in "Havenburg High 1997." More faces came up, students and teachers alike. Faces they never saw before. He was more interested in the teachers, so he began with that. Punching in teachers, he leaned back in his chair and waited for a response.

A few minutes later, four names came up. Two of them had passed away, one three years ago, the other just last year. But the other two were retired and lived in the area.

Luke said, "I can't believe it. I have two names of former teachers from fifteen years ago. I sure hope they can help."

"I'm sure they can, but first, you need to check your phone messages. The machine is blinking like crazy."

Luke looked at his phone. "You're right. I always forget about checking for messages. I usually get very few, if any."

He had four messages. The first two and the fourth ones were not important, but the third one was.

Claire saw his face and asked, "What is it?"

"I have to go see Dr. Karen Lamford."

"Who's that?"

"The one I told you about, the one for my dreams."

"That's great, sweetheart. When do you go?"

"I have to call for an appointment, but anytime that is convenient for me. Now that it's here, I might as well see it to the end. I wish there was another answer. I'm starting to panic."

"Panic, why?"

"What if she can't help? I might be worse than I ever was."

"Nonsense. You said yourself she's the best. I think it will do wonders for you. You'll finally get whatever this is off your chest."

"I guess you're right. I'm just reading into it too much. I've nothing to worry about."

"That's the spirit."

After calling to make the appointment, he looked at her and said, "It's official. I go in tonight. She wants me there for eight o'clock."

"Great. Now maybe you'll be rid of these dreams for good."

"Just get ahead of yourself. We hope it'll work, but nothing is guaranteed. In the meantime, let's get back to work."

"Slave driver!"

Luke went back to his computer to check the information on the former teachers.

"It says here that Adrian Miller was teaching at Havenburg High for thirty years and retired seven years ago. That means he should know all the students pretty well."

"Russell Haren was a teacher there for twelve years," he added. "So he won't be of any help."

Luke was surprised at how quickly the time had passed. "It's already six. Where did the time go? I have to get ready to go to the clinic."

"Do you want me to go with you?" Claire asked.

"No, you stay here. I shouldn't be too long, depending if my dream comes smoothly. Then we'll go check out our friend Adrian and see if he can help."

At ten minutes before eight, Luke was parked in the lot that was provided for patients only. The Havenburg General Clinic was a small building with only two stories. Luke walked in and followed the green line that would take him to the receptionist, noting how dim the place looked.

The fifty-something blonde behind the counter smiled at him and asked, "How may I help you?"

"I have an appointment with Dr. Lamford. She's expecting me for eight o'clock."

"Oh yes. She did mention that. She will be with you in ten minutes or so. In the meantime, please take a seat and fill out this paperwork." She smiled at him.

Taking the forms and thanking her, he took a seat with his back to the wall. On his left was a windowed wall with four seats along it. There was a six-foot-long coffee table with magazines placed neatly in the middle. Three seats were directly across from him on the other side of the coffee table, three seats on his right, and four more seats against the wall of which he sat. The carpet was a dark gray, giving the room an outcast look. He was the only one sitting in the waiting area.

Finishing his paperwork, he got up and returned it to the receptionist.

As he was about to take his seat, his name was called. He turned around to see the most beautiful woman calling his name. He was speechless at first, but finally found his tongue and answered.

The woman smiled and extended her hand. "I'm Dr. Lamford, but you can call me Karen. Everyone does."

"All right. I'm sorry but I wasn't expecting someone so—"

"So young?" Karen finished.

"Well yes." Luke blushed.

"I'm probably older than you. But at forty-three, I get that a lot. I'll take that as a compliment." Walking away from the receptionist area, Karen said, "I'll give you a tour first, and then we'll get started."

Two elevators were lit up in the lobby where they were standing. At this time of night, both elevators were stationed on the lobby floor. One elevator was able to go one floor lower than the other one, which would lead to the basement level. As they passed the elevators, they entered a long hallway. It was covered with dark flooring from one end to the other.

Luke asked, "I can't help but notice how dark everything is. Gray halls, gray carpets, lighting is dim. Why is that?"

"My, you are perceptive. It has a calming effect, helps the patients feel more comfortable, more at home, so to speak. Here at the Havenburg General Clinic, we believe those results are easier to achieve with the neutral colours. Have I answered your question?"

"Yes, thank you."

"Good. Now let's follow this hall to the patient lounge, as we prefer to call it, doesn't sound as menacing. There are three of those rooms, as you're about to see."

They arrived at three doors, two on the right and one on the left. She opened the first door on the right and showed him in. Inside, he saw a pull-out couch bed, a La-Z boy, and a desk on the wall opposite the couch.

"All three rooms are exactly alike," She said.

"What's on the top floor," he asked.

"There are only offices up there, mine and two other doctors. I'm the only one in tonight. We all take turns working the night shift. So, that's the tour. Not much to see but lots to get done. Any questions?"

"I was just wondering how long this will take?"

"I apologize. I thought when we spoke on the phone earlier, you understood. Let me explain our work here. This is a sleep clinic where patients come to get dreams and, in some cases, nightmares analyzed. Once we achieve that goal, we believe the patient overcomes that dream, allowing them to sleep peacefully at night. That's what our work here at Havenburg Clinic is all about.

"I work with two assistants. We hook up wires and electrodes to your head and then monitor your brain activity while you are dreaming. Once we analyze the results, you and I will sit down and discuss. This will establish a treatment plan to resolve your dream issues. Any questions?"

"No, not really. I was expecting to lie down and tell you about my dreams. You would be taking notes and offering explanations."

Karen laughed. "That's old-school. It's not done that way anymore. We get better results this way. Any other questions?"

When she saw none coming, she added, "If you have to make a call on your cell, you have to go in the reception area. When you are done, you must shut it off so it doesn't interfere with all the machines we have. But you need to go do that now. When you're ready, I'll take you to your room, where you will undress and put the gown on, which is in your room. All your clothes, including your cell, will be put away in a locker, and will be returned to you when you leave. Any questions?"

"No. I can't think of any."

He headed for the receptionist area to call Claire, then returned to where Karen was waiting. Once in the examination and on the stretcherlike table, Dr. Lamford gave him a sedative to make him relax and to help sleep. Then the two assistants came in the room to hook the wires onto his scalp. Soon Luke fell asleep, and Dr. Lamford viewed the monitor in which his brain waves beeped on the screen. One of the assistants brought her a coffee where she sat with the cup and waited.

XXXXX

Claire sat on the sofa with a drink and the television on. At the moment, the drink was untouched, and the television was ignored.

She kept going back to the phone call Luke made to her. He didn't sound comfortable or happy he was there. She knows he only went for her, but he needs help to get rid of his dream. Still, he sounded like something was fishy, out of place. But what could that be?

It could be his imagination, trying to see things that weren't there just so he can cancel. But Luke wouldn't do that. Once he promises to do something, he does it. So that couldn't be it.

So what then? She didn't know what to think. She knows one thing: sleep won't come to her this night.

10

Luke was trying to outrun whoever was chasing him. He hid between two houses when the black cat jumped the fence. Lightning lit the sky, and the thunder boomed same as always, but there was something else—something black, something that he couldn't describe.

Luke struggled to sit up, but his attempt was thwarted by the wires attached to his scalp. He lay in the strange bed, unable to move, wondering what to do next.

But just as he was thinking of what he could do, someone opened the door to his room.

XXXXX

Phil Blake was also awake. He couldn't sleep because of his headaches. They were pounding. He never had migraine headaches before. They were ripping him apart. For a week now, he was in pain. He just took his medication two hours ago. He still had to wait four hours. He looked at his watch. It was four fifteen in the morning. He got up and dressed.

Sleep was done for now. Not that he had any.

He went in the kitchen and put the coffee on. Then he headed into the living room and turned on the television. He sat down with the remote to check the channels. He was halfway checking when the remote fell from his hand onto the floor.

He put his hands to his head and screamed. He couldn't take the pain anymore.

Out. He needed to get out. He got up from the couch, went into the kitchen to grab his car keys from the wall hook, and left the house.

XXXXX

Even though she was tired and knew she should be in bed, Claire lay on the two-year-old leather couch, occasionally dozing. She fell into a deep sleep, the television blaring on deaf ears. Nothing could wake her up this night. Not even the hand that squeezed her shoulder.

XXXXX

Phil Blake was driving toward his office at the police station, rounding corners at excessive speeds and once running the red light. He couldn't shake the crazy headaches he was getting and really wasn't paying attention to his driving. If he had been paying attention, he might not have run through the stop sign and smashed into the lamppost.

XXXXX

Luke tried to turn his head toward the door, but it was no use. He couldn't see anyone. The wires restrained him from moving too much. Giving up, he relaxed and closed his eyes. When he opened them again, he saw Karen standing over him.

"Holy ch'meezie," he said. "You scared the crap out of me. I heard the door open and tried to see who was there but couldn't. I thought at least I would have heard you."

"You didn't hear me because I came in through the back door. Now, I will release you from these wires, and I want you to tell me about your dreams."

"Well, not much to tell. When I was little, someone was chasing me through the storm, so I hid between two buildings. Just as a black cat jumped a fence that was beside me, thunder and lightning erupted. That's when I always wake up. But this time there was something else."

"And what was that?" encouraged Karen.

"This time, at exactly the same moment the thunder and lightning strikes, there was a shape that looked like a man, but I'm not exactly sure. It had no features."

"Are you sure? I mean it's hard to believe a man with no features."

"I know that, but I don't even know if that was a man. This is so frustrating; this dream is driving me nuts. It must mean something; otherwise, I wouldn't keep having it over and over again."

"You're right that it means something. So this is what I want you to do. I want you to come back next week. We're going to get to the bottom of this dream. But for now, I'll get your things."

XXXXX

At the point of impact, Phil Blake became delusional. A giant, red creature he believed to be the devil rose out of the ground for him. Blake tried to cover his face, but the devil's claws were too fast, and he closed his eyes. When he opened them a short time later, the wisps of smoke from the engine had dissipated. Then he blacked out.

XXXXX

Claire woke with a jerk. What woke her? She could have sworn somebody's hand was on her shoulder. But when she woke up, there was nobody there. Maybe there was someone in the house?

She got up and pulled her gun from its holster. She went through the kitchen toward the front door.

Locked! She started toward the back door.

That too was locked. What the hell was going on?

Maybe she missed Luke so much that she was imagining things. She finished checking through the house, finding nothing.

It was 6:00 am. The phone rang.

XXXXX

When Luke pulled into his driveway, he saw lights on in the living room, but Claire's car was gone. When he entered through the back entrance, he found the door unlocked.

It was always locked, no matter what! He took his gun out and slowly entered the house.

In the kitchen, he saw a note on the table with his name on it. He picked it up and read it: "I'm at the hospital."

What the hell? What happened? Why was she there? Did she get hurt? Did something awful happen?

Luke raced back to his car and pulled out of the driveway with tires screeching.

Arriving at the Havenburg Hospital ten minutes later, he found a parking spot and rushed into the emergency doors, shouting, "Claire, where are you?"

"I'm right here, and keep your voice down! You'll get us kicked out."

"Sorry, but what's wrong? Are you hurt? Why are you here?"

"Sit down with us, and I'll tell you."

"Us?" Luke looked over and saw Willard in the seating area, looking deeply concerned.

Luke asked, "What's going on?"

Claire took Luke's hands in hers and said, "Phil Blake was in a terrible car accident. The doctors don't know if he's going to make it."

Luke was in shock. *What was she saying? Blake in a car accident? No, that wasn't true. Blake was home in bed. This is just another dream.*

"No," he managed. "It's not true. Phil's at home in bed. This isn't real."

"It is real, sweetie. He's not home in bed. He's in there," she said, pointing toward the operating room. "He's in there, and he's fighting for his life. We have to be strong for him. Be here for him when he wakes up."

Willard put his hand on Luke's shoulder. "Yes, son. We all have to be strong for him. Show him our support. He has no other family."

Luke looked up at Willard and asked, "What happened. Was anyone else hurt?"

"No, son," Willard responded. "His was the only car involved."

"Only his?" Luke was shocked. "What did he hit?"

"He hit a lamppost. He ran a stop sign and then hit the post, as far as we know."

Luke was sobbing. He couldn't believe it. Claire held him, comforting him. Willard went back to his seat.

When Luke calmed down a bit, Claire asked him, "How did your night go at the clinic?"

Luke was quiet for a minute, and then he said, "Okay I guess. The dream was the same except after the thunder and lightning, a black shape emerges. But I can't make out any details. Don't even know if it's a man or not."

"But that's good, isn't it?" Claire asked. "I mean, you never got to that part before."

"I guess . . . she wants me to go again next week again."

"Good. We are going to get to the bottom of this!"

At that moment, Willard cut in and said, "You guys go home. I'll stay here and wait. As soon as I hear anything, I'll call you. Now leave. Don't forget, after your sleep, you have to go see that teacher. I'll take care of things here."

XXXXX

The dark figure was watching Mother on her rocking chair. The chair was moving ever so slightly. She was quiet. But how long would that last?

The dark figure did not know. Mother was very unpredictable. When Mother was quiet, the headache was gone. When Mother was screaming, the headache pounded and would seemingly last forever.

Tonight was a good night. The headache was not here this night. Mother was very still. You'd think she was dead. Maybe she was. Who knew?

The hunting knife that was used so often was getting sharpened. It was really sharp.

XXXXX

Something woke Jake Wright. A faint noise. Very faint.

He looked over and saw Brenda still asleep. She didn't stir. He checked his watch. Three o'clock.

He heard the noise again. But he couldn't tell what kind of noise. He got up and put his robe and slippers on. He left the room and went downstairs.

Quiet. Too quiet. What was going on? Then he heard it again. A low growl. Towards the window.

He looked out the window facing the backyard. The barbeque. The noise was coming from the barbeque. That's strange. Why would it come from the barbeque?

One way to find out.

He went outside to the backyard toward the barbeque. Did he see something move? He wasn't sure. Maybe he should turn around and go back inside. Maybe not.

He continued walking forward toward the barbeque. He stood in front of the barbeque and slowly opened the lid. Then from underneath the barbeque, a racoon scurried past. He jumped ten feet it seemed.

He caught his breath in a sigh of relief. The low growl again. Then he caught a very sharp knife in his neck. He never even felt the ground.

XXXXX

The dark figure was watching the house from the bushes out back. The raccoon trying to get underneath the barbeque finally succeeded. The raccoon made enough noise to wake the dead.

The sheep emerged from the house, walked toward the barbeque, then stopped.

Didn't look promising. He continued onward and stopped just before the barbeque.

The dark figure moved forward.

As the raccoon ran toward bushes, the sheep jumped, then relaxed. When the sharp knife struck, the sheep was still—quiet.

The sheep did not see the ace of spades.

11

A SHARP PANG IN Luke's head kept pounding. This must have been a different dream. Even though it was a consistent pounding, it wasn't hurting his head.

He opened his eyes and looked beside him. Claire had her back to him, sleeping soundly. The pounding in his head was still there. He looked at his watch. Nine fifteen. Only two hours sleep. No wonder he felt like crap.

Might as well get up and put the coffee on. When he entered the kitchen, the pounding was at its loudest. Then he knew. Someone was at his door.

The captain looked grim when Luke opened the door. "I thought you'd never answer!" growled Willard.

"I was sleeping, sir, and I thought it was a pounding in my head."

"Well, never mind that. Where's Claire?" he asked.

"Still sleeping. Any news on Blake?"

"That's why I'm here, son. I have grave news. Doctors told me they did everything they could—"

"No, he can't be dead!" Luke interrupted.

"I wasn't finished, son. They did everything they could, but Blake slipped into a coma. That makes things more complicated. They don't know how long he will be like that, but if he doesn't regain consciousness soon, he will die."

"Oh my God," Claire said. Joining the men around the kitchen table, she added, "That's just awful."

"Anyway, they put him in a private room, and they're monitoring him around the clock. They'll let me know when something develops."

Claire poured three cups of coffee and brought them to the table.

Willard broke the silence, saying, "So how about you guys? Are you planning to talk to that teacher today? I'll understand if you're not up to it. I can always give it to someone else."

"No, that's okay, Cap," Luke managed. "Our case, we'll get 'er done."

"Thanks, guys. I was hoping you'd say that. Well, I hate to drink and run, but the paperwork is piling on my desk. It's not going to get itself done."

"Well, thanks for keeping us informed about Blake. We'll let you know how that parent-teacher interview comes along."

About eleven thirty that morning, Luke and Claire found themselves in a very quiet neighbourhood. Not a single soul in sight. Nobody walking on sidewalks, nobody tending their yards, no kids screaming, nothing.

"That's strange," Claire was saying. "It's so quiet here. I wonder why."

Luke was pulling into a driveway and shut the engine off. "Even here," Luke noted. "This house looks deserted."

As they got out of the car, Luke looked straight down the driveway and saw a garage. The door was partially open. Trees outlined the edge of the driveway on both sides, and a little sidewalk led to a small door.

"After you, sir." Claire motioned.

"No, I insist, ladies first." Luke chuckled.

"Oh fine, be that way, chicken," Claire shot back.

"I'm not chicken. I'm a gentleman."

"I'd like to differ." Claire was smiling.

Reaching the side door, Luke rang the doorbell. There was no answer. Ringing it again, there was still no answer. Suddenly there was a loud racket.

Luke said, "Coming from the back. Maybe the garage. I saw a door partially open when we got out of the car."

"Let's go then," was Claire's reply.

As they proceeded down the rest of the driveway, they came closer to the noise. It was indeed coming from inside the garage. The garage, from the outside, was not much to look at. Shingled all around with one window on the side and a double door in the front were all there was. But when you look inside the garage, new shelving was put all around the walls. Except the front where the door was, the walls were all plywood. The bench where most of the work found itself being done was a little messy at the moment. The floor around the bench area were littered with sawdust. Other than that, the floor was spotless.

There was an elderly man with his back to them. He was using an electric saw, cutting up some wood at certain lengths.

That was the noise they heard.

Luke waited until he was finished cutting. When the old man saw them, he stopped what he was doing and strode toward them.

"Wow," Luke was saying. "You do this all yourself?"

The old man beamed from ear to ear. "Yes, sir. I sure did. It helps pass the time now that I'm retired. Now, what can I do for you?" he asked.

"Well, that would depend. Are you Adrian Miller, former Havenburg High School teacher?" Luke asked.

"Well yes, that would be me. Why? Who are you?"

"I'm Detective Luke Myers; this is my partner, Claire Davis." They both showed identification.

Adrian Miller was about two hundred pounds, brown eyes, thin lips with almost pointy ears. Sweat was pouring down his bald head onto his thin, white beard. He needed a towel to dry himself with. At that moment, he showed all his sixty-two years.

"We'd like to ask you a few questions regarding some former students."

"Former students?" Miller asked. "I don't understand."

"We're particularly interested in the men. Think back. Do you remember a student named Laurel Champ?"

"Laurel Champ?" Miller asked. He was stroking his chin in thought. "Oh yes. I do remember him. What did you want to know? He was one of the nicest boys in class. Is he in trouble?"

"Well, we don't know. But we need to find him. Ask him a few questions. Is there anything else you could tell us about him?"

"No, not much. But he was always kind and polite. He always opened doors for the girls and always did his homework. Never late. Don't know what else to tell you."

"What about his tattoo?"

"Tattoo?"

"Yes, tattoo. He had the ace of spades inscribed on the inside of one of his wrists."

"I do remember, but it's been so long ago. I almost forgot. It was the inside of his left wrist. I know because he's right handed. It was the opposite wrist."

"Would you know his whereabouts?"

"No, I'm sorry. I haven't heard about or seen any of the kids since I retired. I can't help you there."

"That's okay. You've helped enough." They shook hands, and then they left.

In the car, Claire asked, "What's our next move? Find Laurel Champ?"

"My, you are a pretty bright detective, aren't you? We may also have to find Angelo Martin, the quiet man. Maybe he knows something."

"It's going to be difficult. We don't even know if any of them are still around," Claire pointed out.

Luke tallied back. "If Laurel Champ is responsible, he's here somewhere." Then his cell rang.

When he shut off his phone, he was quiet for a few minutes. His veins were throbbing on his forehead. Claire was worried. Whenever she saw that look, she knew something was very wrong. Finally, she broke the silence.

"What's wrong? Did Blake take a turn for the worse?"

"No, it's not Blake. That was the captain. He just told me they found Jake Wright's body."

"What! Oh my God. That's just terrible," Claire cried. After she composed herself, she asked, "Where?"

"In his backyard. Right beside the barbeque. His wife, Brenda, found him this morning at around nine. She has no idea why he was even outside. He was dressed in his robe and slippers. We have to go there."

Willard was already at the Wright house when Luke pulled in. He greeted them as they got out of their vehicle.

"Man, this is getting crazier every day. This psycho attacks whenever. He has no pattern. Why does nobody ever see him? Is he a phantom?"

"Well, phantom or not, we have to find Laurel Champ and soon. We could bring him in for questioning. But where is he?" Luke wondered.

They walked to the backyard by where the body was found. An outline was drawn on the ground so they could see his positioning. The barbeque was directly in front of it.

"Why would he be out here in his robe and slippers?"

"Who knows?" Willard replied. "His wife didn't know either."

"So my question arises again. Why was he even out here?"

"Hard to tell. Maybe he heard something."

Luke looked around the yard. He couldn't find anything out of the ordinary.

They both went into the house by the side where they saw Brenda Wright crying. Her face was tear streaked, and her eyes were all red.

Brad had his hand on her shoulder while Monica was holding her.

When Claire saw Luke and Willard come into the room, she walked over to them and said, "There's nothing we can do here. We'll have to talk to her later."

"I absolutely agree," Luke answered as he waved Brad over.

Claire, seeing that, said, "Luke, how could you?"

"Relax. He might be the person we need."

When Brad got there, Luke gave his condolences and apologized for the timing. Then he asked Brad if he could speak to him outside.

Brad was a little nervous, and his palms were sweaty. Luke, seeing that, said, "Relax. I only want to ask you a few questions. You're not in trouble."

Brad took a deep breath and said, "I thought you suspected me because I was here yesterday."

Luke looked at him and said, "No—just want to ask you something. Hopefully you can help me. I didn't want to ask you inside in front of the girls.

"Okay," Brad said. "I'm listening."

"Do you know a fella named Laurel Champ?"

"Laurel Champ? Vaguely. I remember him being quiet."

"Well," Luke continued, "he also hung out with another quiet fella. His name is Angelo Martin."

"I do remember Champ hanging out with someone. It must have been Martin."

"Well, Brad, you went to school with both of them fifteen years ago."

"That's where I remember them from. Okay, what about them?"

"Did you know that Laurel Champ has a tattoo of the ace of spades on the inside of his left wrist?"

"No, I didn't know. We weren't close. Champ and that other guy stayed to themselves most of the time. Hey, wait a minute. There was an ace of spades on Jake's forehead. Is there a connection? Do you think maybe Champ is responsible?"

"I don't know, son. I don't want to speculate. At least not until we find him and talk to him. Now, as you were saying, they never hung out with anyone else?"

"None that I'm aware. Not at school anyway."

"Do you know where I could find either one of them?"

"No, sir. We were never close, like I said, but I've never run into him since. I'm sorry."

"That's okay. We'll just have to keep looking. Now I'm sorry for taking you away from your wife and friend to talk to you."

Later that afternoon, Luke and Claire were sitting in Willard's office. The captain was saying, "We still don't know anything about Laurel Champ or where to find him."

Luke answered him, "I wonder if the school's library would know anything. Maybe the librarian would know something."

Claire was pondering that thought. "It definitely wouldn't hurt. We have nowhere else to go."

So within the hour, they were in Havenburg High School's parking lot.

Killing the engine, Luke looked at the building and said, "Does that school ever look menacing."

"Menacing?" Claire asked him. "How?"

"I don't know. Nothing I could put my finger on. Oh well, let's get this over with."

When they entered the building, they were in the familiar hallway that led to the office. As Claire was leading that way, Luke grabbed her arm and pulled her to him.

Taken back from his movement, her hair falling over her eyes, she asked him what was wrong.

"I'm not sure," was his reply. "Walk toward the end of the hallway instead."

Claire did as she was told, and when they arrived to the end of the hall, they saw a sign that read "Library—Basement Level." It had an arrow pointing down. They could see two flights of stairs leading downward.

"You knew that sign was there?" Claire asked him.

"Had a feeling. Saw that sign the last time we were here. But I paid no attention to it. Besides, I didn't want to go to the office."

"Why, was Luke a bad little boy." She was making faces the way grown-ups talk to kids when they are teasing them.

"No, Luke wasn't a bad little boy," Luke responded. He answered back in the same teasing tone. Being more serious, he continued, "It's just something weird. Maybe it's just me, but I think something's not right."

"Okay," Claire said. "We'll play it your way for now. Let's go find that library."

They went down the stairs until they hit bottom.

"It's ever creepy down here," Claire mentioned. "I wonder how many people use the library."

"It's probably used more in the earlier hours when the students are here. I think we came a little too late. Look up ahead."

Claire looked and saw a door that was closed. It was marked Library.

Luke put his hand on the handle and turned. Nothing happened. It was locked.

12

"The door's locked," Claire said in despair. "What'll we do?"

Luke was thinking. "I guess we'll have to go to the principal's office after all."

Luke was leading the way up the stairs when he heard footsteps coming toward him. When they reached the top, Kim Lacy was there waiting to greet him.

"Detectives Myers and Davis. Is that correct?"

"Yes, it is. Principal Lacy, that's correct—is it not?" Luke challenged in the same tone.

"My, you do have a good memory. Now, is there a reason why you are in the basement?"

"Well yes. We were going to look for information in the library, but we didn't know it was closed."

"Mr. Myers, our library is open from nine in the morning until four in the afternoon. Just long enough for the students to use. Mind you, they very seldom do. How is your investigation coming along?"

"It's coming along not as quick as we'd like, but it's coming. There is someone we need to find, so we thought we'd look in the library for help."

"If it'll help, I'll let you in. Would that be all right?"

"That would be great. Thank you."

"No need to thank me. I always like to help anyway I can."

Backtracking their steps, Kim Lacy unlocked the door. She turned the lights from the switch on the wall directly beside the door.

"I'm here until nine this evening. That gives you four and a half hours. Would that be all right?"

"Oh yes," Claire responded. "Thank you again."

"Like I said earlier, no need to thank me; just let me know when you're done."

After she left, Luke looked at Claire and said, "Wow. I never expected that. Never would have in a million years."

Claire said, "That was exciting about the way you challenged her about the names. What brought that on?"

"I don't know. Mainly because I don't like the vibes she gives. Call it a hunch."

"Do you still have something against the office?"

"Probably even more so. She really gives me the creeps. But let's get started. Let's see where to begin."

Luke looked down the aisles of the library. There were six rows of books about twenty feet long and seven feet tall. There was a stool every second row so the top shelf could be reached.

Books were packed together so tight, even a mosquito would have a hard time getting through. The walls were white, but through the years it had grayed. The ceiling was about ten feet high with fluorescent lighting the whole length, two feet apart. The floor was a dark terrazzo, which made the library look dark, even with the lights on.

Luke started walking up and down the aisles, looking at the different types of books. One shelving area had books about history. Another section was geography, another about religion, and so forth.

Luke went back to the front aisle to see what Claire was up to. She was looking at books up and down the aisles opposite of where Luke was looking.

He got her attention to join him.

When she was beside him, she asked, "What should we be looking for?"

"I'm looking for a bibliography archive. If we find that, we may be able to locate Laurel Champ's address. We might also look for Angelo Martin's address while we're here."

"That's a good plan. I imagine we should look toward the back of the library. A section away from everything else."

"That's a good idea, Detective. I told you I needed you."

They went to the back of the library. Toward the right side, the wall stopped just past the first aisle. Nothing on that side. Straight ahead where aisle 2 began up to where aisle 5 finished, there was the back wall. Nothing there. Towards aisle 6, or the last row on the left, led to another small room. Just looking at it, they knew they found what they were looking for. *The archive room.*

There were dozens of filing cabinets about ten rows wide and about twenty feet long. They were amazed at how many students had come and gone to this school.

The floor of the archive room was all plush carpeting. The walls here were beige with no windows.

He went up to the closest cabinet and saw by class years that they were in alphabetical order. He went to the earliest, which read Class of 1990—twenty two years ago.

They started numbering these bibliographies twenty-two years ago.

Perfect. They should be able to find what they need here.

"Are you ready?" Luke asked Claire.

"As ready as I'll ever be," she answered back.

"Good," Luke replied. He looked at his watch and noted the time. "Five ten. That gives us just under four hours to find what we need. It really shouldn't take us too long."

They started checking the files. Flipping through them quickly, he noticed that some files have been moved around for some reason, so a bunch of them were in wrong order. He quickly went through the files one cabinet after the other.

Claire was in the aisle beside him and started looking at the files from that side. Not until they were working the seventh aisle about halfway down that their break came to them.

Luke saw the files that were marked in the nineties, and he shouted at Claire, "I see them, finally. Come over here and help me."

She came over and quickly saw the files marked Class of '94, Class of '95, Class of '96, Class of '98.

"Wait a minute. Where's the class of '97?" Luke wondered. He started flipping back, back some more, but there was nothing. So he reversed and started flipping forward. Kept flipping and suddenly he stopped.

What was that? He started pulling the file out and saw that indeed it was the one he had been looking for. The file read Class of '97.

"This is it," he exclaimed! "The one we need to look at."

So they began checking page after page until Luke finally said, "Wow. Would you look at that? Every student is in here, everything about them. Dates of birth, addresses, how long they've been at Havenburg High. Now let's see. Laurel Champ, where the heck did you live?"

"I didn't know so many students came to this place," Claire was saying. "I didn't even know there were that many kids in Havenburg."

"It does seem a lot, doesn't it? I would have to agree with you."

Then Claire said, "I found it. I found Laurel Champ's information. Let's see, it says here that Mr. Champ lives at 32 Brook Road."

"Good work. Now we need to find Angelo Martin's address."

They kept looking, and finally, Luke pulled out Martin's file. "Here it is," he said. "According to this, Martin lives at 847 North Avenue."

Luke continued, "Those two addresses are so far apart, yet they remained best friends. Go figure."

Claire looked at Luke and asked, "How do you want to play this?"

"I think we should go see Martin first. Hopefully, he'll give us some information about Champ. It's always nice to know something about the person when asking them questions. Catch them in a lie."

Claire said, "But don't forget. These addresses are fifteen years old. They might not even be living there anymore."

Luke answered, "I realize that. But right now that's all we've got to go on."

As they shut the lights and door on their way out, they stopped in the office to tell Kim Lacy that they were done for now and to thank her once again.

When they were in the car, Claire said, "So, do you still feel the same about the office as you did earlier?"

"I don't know," Luke said. "I don't know how I feel."

Luke started the car and headed toward Martin's place.

XXXXX

Angelo Martin was pacing back and forth in his living room.

Where the hell is Laurel? He was supposed to be here an hour ago.

But Martin hadn't heard a word. Not even answering the phone. That made Angelo Martin nervous. Very nervous.

He kept peeking out the window curtains, but the driveway was empty. Maybe he should try calling him again. He tried but still no answer.

What if something had happened to him? That would explain why he wasn't here.

What if he needed my help? Even if that is true, without him answering his phone, I'd never be able to help him. He could be dead, lying in a ditch somewhere. But I would never know. Where is he? Please show up soon. I will just have to wait until he shows up. I have no other choice.

XXXXX

The dark figure was watching the house. There was movement inside. Someone kept looking out the window.

Sheep are a funny breed. They never stay still. Always have to be doing something. Otherwise, they get bored. That's another reason why they need to be killed.

Watching the sheep looking out the window was amusing. The kill would be more enjoyable.

The sheep moved away from the window. It was dark inside. Only one light. Toward the back of the house.

The dark figure was holding the hunting knife in one hand. Felt how sharp the blade was.

Yes, indeed. It would be very enjoyable. Mother would be happy this time.

Instead of being upset and yelling at him, this time Mother would be proud. That would make everything all right.

Finally.

XXXXX

When Luke and Claire parked in Martin's driveway, they noticed how quiet it was. Luke looked at the surroundings and marvelled at how well kept the yard was.

It was a small house with white siding, almost looking brand-new. Even the roof shingles look like it was redone recently. The front door was new also and appeared to be a metal material of some sort. One picture window, not so wide or tall, had thin curtains hanging from it.

Luke looked at the house and noticed someone peeking out from behind the curtain. Martin perhaps.

As quickly as he had seen it, it was gone. He looked at Claire and asked her, "Did you see that?"

"See what?" she said.

"There was someone peeking out the window."

They got out of the car and looked around. They walked up the steps that led to the front door.

Luke rang the bell and waited. A minute passed and nothing. He rang the bell again. Still no answer. "Stay here. If he doesn't answer, ring it again."

Claire looked at him and asked, "Where are you going?"

"I'm going to peek around back. I won't be long." Then he was gone.

Luke went around back but didn't see anything amiss: a door at the back with windows on it and a curtain hanging from them. He decided to knock on the door. When nothing happened, he put his ear to the door and listened. Still nothing.

Giving up, he went to the front to see how Claire was making out.

She was still in the same spot as before. When she saw him, she said, "Nothing. If he is here, he's not going to answer."

Luke said, "He might not answer, but someone is here!"

They both went to the car and got in. Luke was backing out of the driveway and onto the road when he saw the face at the curtain again.

"There!" he shouted. "Did you see him that time?"

"No," Claire said. "I didn't see anything."

Luke drove down the street and turned the corner, the same side as to where Martin's house was.

"What are you up to?" she asked.

"When I was in his backyard, there was a small clearing, and from there, I saw a road. I bet it's this road. If I'm right, we could watch his place for a while and see what happens."

As he drove a little farther, he slowed down a bit. "There," he said. "Look over there. I was right."

He was pointing at an opening to which you could see the house.

"Now the waiting begins."

XXXXX

When Martin heard a car in the driveway, he thought it was Laurel Champ finally showing up. He looked out the window but saw it wasn't Champ. A different car.

Who the hell was that?

He saw two people getting out and looking at the house. Man and woman.

Martin was starting to sweat. Why were those people even here? What did they want?

The sweat was coming down his face, around his glasses, onto his chin, and onto his chest. His black hair was all damp from his sweat.

He was about one hundred and fifty pounds soaking wet. When the doorbell rang, he must have jumped ten feet. He stayed still, hoping they'll stop and go away. But the doorbell rang again.

Go away. Leave me alone.

He was shaking like a leaf. It was Champ's fault.

If he would have been here when he was supposed to be, this wouldn't be happening. Wait. Now what's going on?

The man was going around the back. Trying to trick Martin. But it won't work.

I'll just stay put right here until they leave. They can't make me open the door. I'll just wait them out.

The front door rang again. Finally it stopped. Now there was a knock on the back door. That startled him. Made him jump.

Leave me alone. Go away.

He closed his eyes to shut the noise away. When he finally opened them, they actually were gone.

When he checked out from behind the curtain, they were just leaving.

XXXXX

It was starting to get dark. The house was quiet. She finally went to sleep. Now he had time for himself. Do what he wanted. He went to the refrigerator to grab a brewski. He opened it and took a big swig. Then he looked at the kitchen.

What a mess. Did he do that? He couldn't remember. He took another swallow and put the bottle down on the counter. He started picking things up and put them in their proper place. Then he started on the garbage.

He filled bags and tied them. He had two garbage bags ready to be thrown out. He opened the front door and threw them out. He closed the door and went to pick up his beer off the counter.

He finished the rest of it in two big gulps.

Man, that was good. I'll have one more. He opened the refrigerator again to get another. This time he spotted some leftover chicken they had the night before. He took that out and leaned against the counter. He started eating out of the container and took a long swallow. *Was this ever good.*

He ate most of the chicken and had two more beer. Now he felt better. He took more garbage out the front door with the other two. He better bring them to the bin beside the house.

He grabbed his jacket that was hanging, opened the door, and went outside. He grabbed two bags and brought them to the big bin. Then he went back to grab the other one. As he went to pick it up, he thought he heard a noise. He looked up but couldn't see very well, partly because it being so dark, but mostly because he had been drinking. He stood still a while longer but still couldn't hear anything. He continued his chore, and as soon as he rounded the corner, he heard it. It was a low growl. What the hell could make a noise like that.

At that moment, a knife went into his neck and pushed all the way in. As he fell, he saw the horror that was standing behind him.

13

"It's starting to get dark. How much longer are we going to stand watch?"

"Not too much longer. I just want to see if he leaves the house."

Claire said, "I don't think he's leaving any time soon."

"I agree," Luke added. "Let's go."

Just as they were about to leave, a car pulled into Martin's driveway.

As someone was getting out, a light in the house came on.

"Very interesting," Luke commented. "Things are beginning to boil!"

Claire asked Luke, "Did you see who that was getting out of the car?"

"I couldn't make out who it was, but it was a woman."

"How would you know that?"

"Unless guys have started carrying purses, that was a woman!"

"Nothing escapes those hawklike eyes of yours, do they, beloved?"

Luke laughed at that. "We should drive a little closer to the house. Try to see better."

He made a quick U-turn and drove around the block. He stopped on the side of the street, but not quite enough to be spotted from the house.

A few minutes later, a woman came out and got in her car. She backed out and drove away. When she sped past the two detectives, she didn't even give them a second glance.

Making a quick decision, he made another U-turn to follow her car.

"Why are we going after her?" Claire wanted to know. "Why not go see Martin instead?"

"If we go knocking on Martin's door, a good chance he won't answer it again. So, we go after the woman. Maybe she'll answer our questions. Besides, we know where Martin lives. We could come back anytime."

"Good logic to me," Claire answered.

They followed her from well behind, never losing her. About twenty minutes later, she pulled into a driveway and drove to the back.

Luke drove past the house but took a quick look at the address.

"Do you know where we are?" Luke asked her.

"I can't put my finger on it, but I've been in this area before."

"I'll place your finger for you. Do you remember Darren Peters?"

"Now I remember. He lived one block over, near the woods. I wonder how those poor kids are."

"They're in good hands. But now we have to concentrate on the task ahead. Now, back to topic. That yard in which our lady friend drove in was our other friend Laurel Champ's house."

"My God, Luke, he sure likes to work close to home!"

"You know what they say. Home is where the heart is. I mean, where the knife is."

"Oh, that's just nasty, Luke. Where do you come up with these?"

"I'm just talented. Call me Luke of all trades."

"Whatever."

Luke just smiled at her.

"Are we going to watch this house now?"

"No. We're going to knock on the front door and introduce ourselves."

"Pretty bold, don't you think?"

"We'll find out how bold, after we talk to her."

They parked on the shoulder of the road in front of the house. They got out and looked around. Like everywhere else they've been, very quiet. The front doorbell sounded loud compared to how quiet it was. They rang it one more time when the door opened.

A brunette woman with bangs over her eyes was at the other end of the door. "Yes?" she asked.

"I apologize for any inconvenience, I'm Detective Luke Myers; this is my partner, Claire Davis."

They showed their identification. "We'd like to ask you a few questions, ma'am? If that's okay?"

"Questions?" she asked. "Questions at this time of night? About what?"

"Your name for starters."

"Have I done something wrong, Detective?"

"I don't know. Have you?"

"No."

"Good. Now that that's out of the way, I'll repeat my question. What is your name?"

"Margo Henderson."

"Okay, Margo, much better. We're looking for a gentleman named Laurel Champ. Would you know a person by that name?"

"No, why would I?"

"Well, for two reasons. One, you know Angelo Martin. Two, for a more obvious reason, Laurel Champ owns this house. So, by you being here, you either know him and you know him well, or you're breaking and entering into his house. So, would you like to change your answer, or do you want to go downtown?"

"Well, if you must know, I don't know whatever his name is, and I've lived here the past four years. Maybe that fella lived here before, but I do now. Any more questions?

"Yes, how do you know Angelo Martin?"

"Who?"

"Angelo Martin. How do you know him?"

"I don't know him."

"You don't know him?"

"No, I don't."

"You're sure?"

"Positive."

"You don't want to change your story?"

"Not a chance."

"Suit yourself!"

With that, Luke and Claire left and went to their car.

"Apparently Ms. Henderson didn't know we saw her at Martin's. Otherwise, she wouldn't have stuck with that answer," Luke said.

"I agree. But what should we do now?"

"Do? Nothing, except go home. Tomorrow we visit Martin again, find out where Champ really lives, and get to the bottom of this."

When Luke woke up the next morning, he could smell coffee brewing. After dressing, he went into the kitchen and heard Willard saying, "Was still no change in his condition."

Luke poured three coffees, saying, "Phil's still in a coma? My God! I hope he pulls through okay."

"Well, son," Willard went on, "we all do. Everyone at the department and hospital are praying for him."

Looking at Luke, Willard continued, "Claire tells me you guys had some excitement last night."

"If you mean by nobody opening doors or wanting to talk to us being excitement, then we had plenty of that last night."

Willard smiled at that. "But I know you, Luke, and you won't let that stop you."

"You're right about that," Luke was saying as he was taking a sip of his coffee. "Now that we know where Martin lives, we're going to pay him a little visit."

At that moment, Willard's cell rang. He growled into the phone and then went quiet. When he cut the connection, he looked at the two of them and said, "They just found number 7."

Driving toward the murder site where they would meet up with Willard, Luke was trying to figure things out.

"I wonder what our friend Champ was up to last night."

"When we pull into the site, your question might just be answered."

They parked on the side of the road, so they'd be out of the way. Looking around as they were getting out, Luke recognized the familiar place.

"Well, I'll be damned. I never thought we'd be coming around this place so soon."

Claire walked around the front of the car to join him and said, "Who would have thought?"

Luke ended up to where the body lay and looked at it.

"Something's weird about this one."

The medical examiner of the county that was called to replace Phil heard him and said, "Weird? How?"

"I'm not sure yet, but something is." He went looking for the photographer and told him, "I want pictures from every angle, I don't care how many, and I want to see every one of them! Understand."

"Yes, sir," was the reply.

He caught with Claire and told her, "Something's wrong with this one."

"What do you mean?"

"Not sure yet. When I study the pictures, maybe it'll come to me."

Claire nudged him and pointed toward the house. "Hope we find some answers in there."

They went to the front steps, where a policeman was guarding the door. Recognizing them, he tipped his hat, exchanged pleasantries, and let them through.

Entering the house, they saw Willard sitting on a chair in the living room. When he saw the two, he got up and intercepted them at the entrance. He motioned for them to follow him into the kitchen. They sat at the round table before Willard said, "The wife told the officers that her husband was in a terrible mood all evening, so she went to bed around ten. She usually goes around midnight."

He looked at Claire and said, "You had a connection with her in one of our earlier interviews. Maybe you should go keep her company for a while, see if she'll talk to you, if she's up to it."

"Okay. I'll go see her. But one of you should go grab us all a coffee." She got up and started toward the living room.

When she left the room, Luke turned toward Willard and said, "There was something different about this body. I'm not sure what yet, but have the photographer take some shots from every angle, and then give me a copy. I want to study them."

"That's a good idea," Willard agreed. "I wonder what was so different."

Claire entered the living room where a lone officer stood by. Claire nodded for him to leave. Now alone with the widow, she didn't know what to say. She sat beside her on the gray leather couch and took her hands in her own.

She said, "Mrs. Haswell, I mean, Diana, I'm so sorry about Larry. I don't know what to say. Is there anything I can do for you? Anything I can get for you?"

"N-no," she sniffed. "I don't need anything right now. But thank you." She started crying again.

"You poor dear," Claire said. Then she was hugging her. Claire held her for some time before she let go and said, "Diana, I know this is hard, but when you're up to it, I need you need to answer some questions. Not now, but sometime soon. We'll come back and talk. Is that okay?"

After Diana finished sniffing, she said, "That will be fine."

Just then Luke came in with four coffees and some muffins. He brought in four paper plates and spread them out on the mahogany coffee table.

They made small talk for a bit, but clearly Diana was in no mood.

Luke got up from his chair and said, "We have to be going now, Diana, but we'll be back to see if you need anything. Again, I'm sorry for your loss."

When they got up to leave, Claire went to Diana and gave her another hug.

"Hang in there. I know it's tough, and my thoughts are with you."

Then they left.

Luke told Willard they were going to head out to Martin's place to see what they can manage to find. Hopefully, they'll be close to end their investigation. While they were driving to their destination, Claire said, "She'll come around. Larry never treated her good, so maybe she'll be over it soon."

Luke answered back, "Let's hope so. The sooner we get her statement, the sooner we can continue our investigation."

They were close to Martin's place.

"Okay," Luke said. "We're a minute away. Let's be sharp. We may need it."

They parked on the road halfway down the street. As they shut off the engine, the same car that Margo was driving the night before came out of Martin's driveway. As it rolled down the street past them, Claire noticed that it was a male driver. In the passenger side was Martin. More importantly, the driver looked to be Laurel Champ.

14

They followed the car at a safe distance, but never losing sight. Claire broke the silence, saying, "They're headed in the same direction as Margo did last night. I bet it's close by."

"That same thought came to me. I wonder why Margo would lie to us. When we catch up to these guys, everything should come to light."

True to form, the driver pulled into Margo's driveway. They got out of the car and went into the house by the front door.

Luke drove by and parked farther down the road. Then he crept slowly forward until he was one house away. He shut the car off and waited. He was watching the house when he decided what to do. He told Claire, "Take a position in the back. I'm going to knock on the front door and see what develops."

As he approached, Claire was already headed for the back with her gun drawn. He gave her two minutes to get set, then knocked on the door.

A man with curly, black hair with glasses on answered the door. "Yes? May I help you?" he asked.

"I hope you can. My name is Detective Luke Myers, and I need to ask a few questions. He paused to show his badge; then he continued. "First, what would your name be?"

"Angelo Martin."

"Yes, Angelo Martin. I was wondering if you can help me locate a man named Laurel Champ."

Martin looked thoughtful for a moment before he replied, "Laurel Champ? No, I don't believe I've heard of that name."

"You're sure you never heard of Laurel Champ?"

"No, never."

"Let me refresh your memory. He was the man that you were sitting beside in that car"—he was pointing in the driveway—"when you arrived home ten minutes ago."

At that, Martin slammed the door in Luke's face and heard Martin shouting, "It's the cops. Let's get out of here."

Luke kicked the door down and, drawing his gun, started toward the back of the house.

Claire stiffened when she heard Martin yell "It's the cops, let's get out of here." She watched when the back door opened, and Margo stepped out, right in front of the detective.

"Margo, my friend. Long time no see. Care for a cup of tea?"

Seeing the detective, Margo lost it and charged Claire like a savage animal. With her hands up high and fingers curled, her hair all over her face, it was a wonder she could see anything at all.

Getting closer and closer toward Claire, who was holstering her gun, she was too slow, and Claire managed to grab both of Margo's wrists and pull her down on top of her. Getting both feet in Margo's stomach, Claire was able to let the momentum continue to throw Margo over her head. Margo landed on her backside and was dazed for a moment before getting up.

Just as Claire was getting up, Margo rushed her and put her shoulder in Claire's side. She went falling backward, but got on her feet quickly.

Margo rushed her again, but Claire moved and planted a foot to the small of her back and gave a shove. She went flying into Martin, just as he was coming out the door. The impact threw them both on the ground.

Claire was standing over both of them, covering them with her gun, and said, "I guess this means no tea?"

When Luke came out the same back door that Martin came out a few minutes earlier, he saw the fight happening. He also saw Laurel slip past the women and went toward the far end of the yard and disappear into the trees and bushes.

Luke followed. He entered the same spot he saw Laurel take.

Wow!

It was a forest back here. He drew his weapon and proceeded slowly. It was hard to cover his back in such a wide-open space. The best he could do was to stay with the trees and hope for the best.

He thought he heard a twig snap toward his right. He looked that way, but he couldn't see or hear anything. He was about to move on when he heard another twig snap to his right. He continued in the same direction, for the noise was up ahead. Two steps more and he heard it again.

The sound came from about twenty feet up ahead. He crouched, staying perfectly still. He waited a minute before raising himself to his feet and about to step forward when he was attacked from behind.

He was hit so hard that when he hit the ground; his gun fell from his grip and rolled somewhere ahead and out of reach. The attacker continued his assault. Not letting Luke recover, he grabbed a handful of hair and smudged his face into the earth.

Finally, pulling Luke on his feet, the attacker punched the detective in the face. Down on one knee, Luke realized his gun was missing, so he grabbed a handful of dirt and targeted the attacker's eyes.

Bull's-eye!

The attacker was screaming, trying to clear his eyes, but the fist that met his jaw wouldn't let him. He went down but got up again.

Luke, trying to regain his composure, said, "Did you have enough, Laurel, or do you still need some more?"

At the sound of his voice, Laurel Champ rushed Luke and knocked him backward. He fell over a fallen tree and lay firmly on his back. When Laurel reached him, Luke put his feet into Laurel's gut and pushed. He went backward, but not too far. He gave a yell and ran toward Luke. This time, because of Laurel's momentum, Luke put his feet in Laurel's gut again; he was able to flip him over his head.

Laurel landed among bushes and broken twigs, but lay still. When Luke got up and saw Laurel wasn't going anywhere, he retrieved his gun.

Going back to Laurel who was just moving to get himself up, he told him, "That's enough, Laurel. You're under arrest."

By the time Laurel Champ was brought back to the house, police were already buzzing around. They came and grabbed Laurel and brought him to the waiting squad car. The other two were already on the way to the police station.

When it was just the two of them left, Claire said, "You must enjoy getting the crap beat out of you."

"Yes, I do. I really love it when they grab my head and shove it in the dirt. That's the best. What about you? You got into it with Margo."

"I did. One thing I did find out about her though."

"What's that?"

"She doesn't like tea."

When they were in the car, Luke's cell rang. It was Willard.

"Are those three on their way here yet?"

"Yup. They left ten minutes ago."

"How do you want to do this?"

"Get them set up separately. Don't do anything until we get there." Then he hung up the phone.

When Luke was on the highway and headed toward the heart of downtown, he said to her, "You never did give me an answer about my proposal."

Claire looked at him and said, "We were just too busy lately. I haven't had time to think. I still don't know. But I promise you, I will give you an answer. In my own time, okay?"

"Fine. I just thought you would have known by now."

When Claire saw the route Luke was taking, she said, "This isn't the way to the precinct."

"I know. Stopping at my place first. Get this makeup off."

She started laughing. "But dirt and mud do you justice. You should leave it on."

"Hundreds of thousands of comedians in this world and I'm stuck with you. Talk about justice."

Thirty minutes later, they were pulling into the police station. Entering the building, they headed straight for Willard's office. When they opened the door, Willard growled, "Get in and have a seat!"

"Nice to see you too, Cap," Luke replied.

"Don't get cute with me. Where were you? You were supposed to be here an hour ago!"

"I had to go home to think strategy."

"Strategy?" Willard repeated.

"Yes, sir," Claire responded quickly. "He had to think if he should use a rough towel or a soft one to take his makeup off, sir."

"Makeup?" the boss asked. He looked at Luke and said, "Since when do you wear makeup?"

"Since his face was introduced to the ground earlier today, sir," Claire finished.

Luke looked at Claire and gave her a look that read "You're dead meat."

"Anyway," Willard continued. "We have all of them separated. Just like you wanted. Now, how do you want to handle it?"

"We'll talk to them, Cap. Claire will go see her new friend Margo. Maybe they can play dolls or something. I'll do the grown up thing and visit with Martin and Champ."

"Okay, guys. Get to it." And they were dismissed.

When they left the office, Luke and Claire went to see what reaction they were giving from the observation room. Margo was cool as a cucumber, Champ pretended to be sleeping, and Martin was sweating profusely.

Luke watched him closer than the others. He turned to Claire and said, "I'm going to get the folder with all the victims. Then I'm going to make Martin squirm even more. You stay here and watch."

"What about Margo?"

"Wait until my interview is over. You might be able to use some of the information I get out of Martin on her. Then I'll watch your interview."

"Makes sense."

He left the room, and a few minutes later, he entered the interrogation room with Angelo Martin waiting very impatiently. Luke stopped at the table and threw the folder down hard. Martin jumped at that, and if his black, curly hair and face wasn't drenched in sweat, it most certainly would have been at that moment.

Then to make matters worse, Luke turned his back on Martin and ignored him again to get a coffee out of the maker.

Taking a sip and making a face, Luke was wondering why he was drinking this shit. Anyway, back to the problem at hand.

He headed toward the table and stopped. For the first time, he looked at Martin.

If looks could kill, Martin surely would be.

Luke continued to stare at him for an eternity it seemed, but it only lasted a few seconds. Then he pulled out a chair, turned it around, and sat.

He took another sip, then slammed the coffee down. He had Angelo Martin right where he wanted.

"Angelo Martin. That is your name, correct?"

"Y-yes," he stuttered.

"Angelo, my friend Angelo. Why did you lie to me earlier today?"

"I-I don't know," he continued to stutter. "I was hoping y-you'd go away."

"Did that work?"

"N-no," was all Martin could muster.

"I don't like you, Martin. Do you know why I don't like you, Martin?"

Martin shook his shoulders. But then said, "I lied to you."

"Do you know why else I don't like you, Martin?"

"N-no."

"Remember last night, when I came knocking on your door? You wouldn't even answer. I had to go to the back door and knock. You still wouldn't answer. Why wouldn't you answer?"

Martin was stuttering uncontrollably now. He was stuttering so bad, Luke couldn't make out what he was trying to say.

"It's okay," Luke told him. "It was a hypothetical question. You weren't supposed to answer. But now I'm going to tell you a game we're going to play." Luke was in his glory.

"I'm going to ask you some questions. All you have to do is answer them. I'll know if you're lying, so you need to tell the truth; otherwise, I'll get angry. You don't want that, do you?"

"N-no," was the reply.

"Good."

Luke got up and walked toward the coffeemaker to refill his cup. Then he turned around and faced Martin.

He went back to his chair and sat down. Luke was ready.

"Martin," he began. "Tell me what your relationship with Margo Henderson is."

"Margo Henderson?" he asked.

"Yes, Martin. How do you know her?"

"I don't know her at all. I've seen her a few times. I don't know anything about her."

"Really?"

"Yes, really."

"That's funny, Martin. Do you know why that's funny?"

"No."

"It's funny because my partner was already talking to her. Would you like to know what she said?"

"N-no," he started stuttering again.

"She sung like a canary, Martin. She told everything about you. About how you helped with all the killings going on around here."

"WHAT! What are you talking about? I never killed anyone. Let alone help."

Luke finally opened the envelope and spread seven photos in front of Martin, making him squirm. They were positioned right side up so Martin would have to look at them.

"Do you recognize any of these victims?"

Taking a closer look to study them better, he said, "Sure. We all went to school together. But I didn't help kill them."

"Are you saying that you never helped kill at least seven people?"

"Of course that's what I'm saying. What kind of person do you think I am?"

"I don't know, Martin. Maybe a cold-hearted killer."

"You really are crazy if you think I did that. You have no evidence."

"Then why would your friend Margo Henderson say that about you?"

"I don't know why."

"What about your other friend? Laurel Champ?"

"What about him?"

"Well, what can you tell me about him?"

"Not much. We went to school together. Started hanging out."

"What were you guys up to the last few months, Martin?"

"We weren't up to anything. Like I said, we just hang out together."

"Martin, I'm going to tell you something. All those killings I just mentioned moments ago, we believe that Champ was involved. If we're right, which I think we are, would mean it would put you right there with him. You will spend the rest of your life in jail. So if you have something to tell me, now would be the time."

"Listen, Detective, I told you I didn't kill anyone. Never helped kill anyone. You're barking under the wrong tree."

"Then why did you slam the door in my face? What are you hiding?"

Martin's face flushed, and he was starting to sweat again. But he didn't say anything else.

Joining Claire in the observation room, he said, "I think he's telling the truth about the killings, but he's holding something back."

"How do you know that?"

"All of a sudden he stops talking. He looked more nervous or scared as to why he slammed the door in my face. More nervous than you should be if he was involved in the killings."

Claire finished her coffee, then got ready to go see Margo.

"Wish me luck."

"Break a leg, kid. You can do it?"

When Claire opened the door, Margo feinted disinterest. Not even looking at Claire, as though she wasn't even there.

"You're not a bad fighter," Claire said as she was getting another coffee. Standing in front of the table, she sat her coffee and herself down. Facing Margo, she placed the envelope in front of herself and took a sip of coffee.

When at last she was done, she asked Margo, "Why did you lie to us?"

Margo still didn't meet Claire's gaze or answer her.

Claire continued, "How long have you known Angelo Martin?"

Nothing.

"How about Laurel Champ? How long have you known him?"

Nothing.

"That's okay. My partner got Martin to talk. He mentioned a few things. We'll check them out, and if he's telling the truth, jail term will be less for him."

At the mention of jail, Margo briefly looked up, but for only a moment.

"Anyway, that's another story."

Claire picked up the envelope and took out the photos.

She placed them in front of Margo so she could see them clearly.

Margo glanced at them fast but did not linger on them. Her short, brown hair wasn't even mussed. Her face was expressionless. She was a cold-hearted person.

"Do you recognize any of these victims?"

Nothing.

"Fine. We have proof, and Martin's statement that puts you, Martin, and Champ at all the scenes of the crimes. So I hope you don't talk because when the jury hears all the evidence, you'll be going to jail for the rest of your life. Personally, I can't wait for that day."

Still nothing.

Claire picked up all the photos and put them back in the envelope.

Getting up, she turned around to leave. As she put her hand on the doorknob to twist it open, she heard, "WAIT!"

Claire waited a moment, then turned around.

She just looked at Margo but said nothing.

Margo said, "I didn't kill anyone. Neither did Laurel or Angelo."

Claire came back and sat down again. "Seven murders in the last couple of months, always with the ace of spades on the victim's forehead, and Champ having a tattoo of the ace of spades. You see why we're having a hard time not believing you?"

"We still didn't kill anyone."

"Then why were you so rude with us? Running away if you have nothing to hide?"

Margo was silent.

Claire looked at her and said, "You are hiding something, aren't you? That's why so vague. Everything makes much more sense now."

She was quiet for a moment but then said, "How long have you known Martin and Champ?"

She thought Margo wasn't going to answer, but then she said, "I've only met Martin two or three times."

"Okay. But what about Champ?"

"I've known him for a few months."

"Where does Champ live?"

"You've been there."

"You mean the house where we had the fight? The house where you said that you lived?"

"Yes, that house. I live there too. I'm his girlfriend."

"You're his girlfriend? Wow, I never would have thought."

Claire sipped more coffee then said, "So, Margo, what are you hiding?"

"I'm not hiding anything."

"You're lying again. But that's okay. We'll find out."

Then she got up and left the room.

Back in the observation room, Luke told Claire, "Wow you really can do it. You should have seen her face when you mentioned the jail part. You really got to her."

Claire smiled. "Elementary, my dear Luke. But seriously, I'm not convinced she or Martin had anything to do with the killings. So I hope you have better luck with Mr. Champ."

"Yes. It's time to go for a little chat." He took a deep breath and then left the room.

15

THE DARK FIGURE WATCHED the two female sheep in the backyard fight. It was amusing to see them beat the crap out of each other. Why not finish and kill each other? That's all they're good for. One of them even has a gun, but she won't use it.

Why? Are they all useless?

Just as the fight was finishing, two more male sheep came out of the house. But they didn't come to watch the fight. The first male sheep was running away. The second male sheep was trying to catch him.

He had difficulty because the first male sheep ran into the woods. When the second male got there, he slowed down almost to a crawl.

That's when he pulled out a gun. Another one with a gun. The dark figure had seen this sheep before. Recognized him. Couldn't remember from where. That sheep might be trouble later on. So while he proceeded slowly with the gun, the second sheep attacked him from behind. The gun fell and rolled a few feet in front of them.

Out of reach.

Now the dark figure saw the second sheep more closely.

Tattoo. He saw a tattoo on the sheep's wrist.

He remembered a tattoo from a long time ago.

The dark figure drifted back fifteen years ago. When there was a school. There was a boy who had a tattoo on his wrist.

A mean boy. A mean boy who always made fun of smaller boys. He remembered another small boy who was weak. Scared of everyone.

One day when . . . hahahaha, and he's so ugly that every day just before he gets home from school, his mama has to put a bag over her head—hahahaha

The small boy yelled, "SHUT UP! LEAVE MY MOTHER ALONE! And then fell quiet.

At that moment, the door opened, and the teacher yelled, "Who made a mess of my classroom?"

The bully answered, "It was Earnest; he's the one who did it."

Teacher walked up to Earnest and said, "Is that true Earnest?"

Earnest was so scared that he didn't say anything. He was sent to the principal's office and received the strap.

When school was over, the bully was chasing Earnest down the street. When Earnest fell, the bully reached him and kicked him in the ribs four times really hard. Earnest thought he was going to die.

It wasn't his fault that he was ugly. Not his fault he was born with scars on one side of his face. Not his fault that he has a twitch.

When he looked up, the bully showed him his tattoo, and the bully said the ace of spades is power. "My father said to have the ace of spades tattooed, is mightier than the sword. So, don't ever get in my way again or you'll be sorry," said the bully.

You'll be sorry.

And the dark figure was back in the present. That tattoo was still there.

The fight was over. The one with the gun was victorious, leading the other back with his gun.

If the one with the tattoo will survive, the dark figure will come back.

Revenge.

XXXXX

Luke entered the interrogation room and went straight to the table. He pulled the chair around backward and sat.

He was looking at Champ, who was wearing a big grin. His spiked blond hair wasn't even mussed. He had thin, blond eyebrows to match his hair. His shirt and pants were clean and neat. You would never know he was just in a fight. This wasn't going to be easy, he thought. Took a moment to collect his thoughts then said, "Laurel Champ. My, you're a hard one to track down. That's a mighty fine tattoo you have there. How long now have you had that?"

"Is that why I'm here, Detective? To talk about my tattoo?"

Luke thought about that as he replied, "In a manner of speaking, yes. That is why you're here."

Champ just looked at him but said nothing. Luke picked the envelope up and put photos on the table. Turning them around so they faced Champ, he asked, "Do you know any of these victims?"

Not bothering to look at them, Champ said, "Nope. Not a single one."

"Are you sure you don't want to look at them again?"

"Nope."

"That suits me fine. When the jury reads about the ace of spades on each of the victims, then sees your tattoo of the ace of spades, it won't be a long trial. Also won't be in your favor."

Champ was chewing his lower lip and said, "Do you think I killed them?"

Luke looked at him and said, "Doesn't matter what I think, but the way you're acting so mysteriously, avoiding answering questions, I would have to believe you did. Who else would use the ace of spades and you happen to have a tattoo of the ace of spades? What are the odds of that?"

"Well, I didn't kill them."

"Doesn't matter. If we can't catch the real killer, and you can't prove it otherwise, it's a done deal."

Champ was starting to look uncomfortable. Luke continued. "Even if you didn't kill anyone, we believe that you and your other two friends are hiding something. Do you care to tell me what it is, or do I have to find out on my own? Remember, if you don't tell us what it is, you get no breaks when we do find out. Which, by the way, we will."

"I don't know what you're talking about."

"Of course you don't. So now, do you want to tell me if you knew any of the victims?"

This time Champ looked at them and said, "They all look familiar. But I don't know from where."

"Let me refresh your memory. You went to school with all of these people. From fifteen years ago."

"That's where I know them. But why would my old classmates be getting killed?"

"I don't know, Champ. But we speculate that the killer is someone from your class."

"The killer is one of my classmates? I find that very hard to believe!"

"Regardless, is there anyone in that class who would want to kill your friends? Anybody that didn't get along with some of the others?"

"None that I know."

"What about people that you didn't like? Someone you might have been mean with? Someone maybe looking for revenge, so to speak."

On that question, Champ looked guilty, but Luke couldn't figure it out. Instead Champ said, "No. I got along with all my classmates. So it has to be someone else."

Luke looked at him and said, "Are you positively sure? I don't know if you know the seriousness of this situation, but this is very important. He's already killed at least seven people. We are almost positive that won't be the end of it, so I'm asking you again. Are you positively sure that there is somebody out to get you?"

"No. None that I'm aware of."

"Well all right. I guess we're done here."

Luke got up and left the room.

When Luke got back to the interrogation room, Claire had a coffee waiting for him.

"Thanks," he said. "I needed that."

"So," Claire was saying. "Do you think he was lying?"

"I'm not sure. With him it was hard to tell. But I do think he was a bit of a bully back at school, and if I'm right, he might know who it is."

Just then Willard came in. He looked at the two detectives and said, "The photos you asked from the photographer are on my desk."

"Let's go," Luke answered.

Seated in Willard's office, the captain had all the photos spread on his desk. Luke got up to get a better look.

"There's still something about these photos that look out of place. But I don't know what."

So they kept looking. They were at it for a good hour or more when Claire announced she was hungry. They ordered in Chinese, then continued to study the photos.

"It's right there in front of us, just waiting to bite us, but I still can't see it."

The Chinese came at that moment, and just as they were getting ready to eat, Claire said, "I got it!"

Both Luke and Willard looked at her in excitement. "You got it?" Luke asked.

"Yes, I got it. The soya sauce all over my chicken fried rice. Delicious."

Luke and Willard frowned. "Is that all? I thought it was something important." Luke went back to the photos.

Forty-five minutes later, Claire shouted, "I got it."

This time Luke paid no attention.

When Claire saw she was being ignored, she got up from her chair, went to the desk, and slammed her palm down. Then repeated, "I said I got it."

This time Luke and Willard paid attention.

"Well," Luke said.

She picked a photo showing Larry Haswell's eyes clearly.

"Look here," she pointed. "What do you see?"

Both Luke and Willard looked at the eyes, but still couldn't make the connection.

"His eyes. His eyes are wide open. He saw the killer. He's the only one to have seen him."

"My God!" exclaimed Luke. "You're right. That's what was bugging me. All the other eyes were closed. His is wide open, and he saw. From the expression, he knew his attacker. Which means we're on the right track about the possibility of a classmate."

Luke looked at Claire and said, "See, I told you I need you."

Willard chimed in. "But we've known that for a while and still not getting closer."

"That's why we stick with Champ and his friends."

"You think they're involved?" Willard asked.

"Don't know. But they are up to something. We have to figure what that is. Speaking of which, what did you do with them?"

"They left a few minutes ago. We didn't have anything to stick them with."

That night at Dan's Cooler, Champ, Martin, and Henderson were drinking at a table in the back far corner.

Martin took a sip of his beer and said, "That detective guy knows we're up to something. What if we get caught?"

"We're not going to get caught, Marty. We just have to be careful."

Margo Henderson added, "Extracareful. I think the lady cop is going to be a problem for me."

"Okay," Champ answered back. "Enough of that. Back to business at hand."

They ordered another round of drinks before Champ blurted out. "We'll lay low for a few days until the heat dies down. We can afford to take our time anyway. So, when we leave here tonight, Marty, you won't hear from me until I feel the time is right. Do you understand?"

"I understand, and I think that's a good idea," Martin said.

After another couple of rounds, enough laughing and talking beginning to take its toll, they left and went their separate ways.

16

That same night at Luke's place, Luke and Claire were sitting around the kitchen table having a night cap.

Claire asked him, "What are we going to do about Champ and his friends?"

"I would think they'll lay low for a while. They might suspect we'll be following them, which is what I want them to think."

He took a gulp from his bottle before continuing, "In the meantime, I'm going to make an appointment for tomorrow night at the Havenburg General Clinic."

Claire was delighted to hear that. "I can't wait for your dreams to be over with." She took a drink of her gin.

When they finished their drinks, he said to her, "Do you want to go to bed?"

"I'm not tired," she replied.

"Neither am I," he answered back.

"Are you ever bad."

When they both got up and she walked by him, he slapped her butt, which registered a giggle, then went to the bedroom.

XXXXX

Jim Parent was sitting on the deck in his backyard when he thought he heard a noise. He cocked his head to listen, but it never returned. He continued drinking and listening to the easy-rock channel on his ghetto blaster.

He needed to go to the bathroom, so he used his backyard. His backyard stopped where the edge of the woods began.

When he was not quite finished, he looked straight ahead. Being so dark, he couldn't see anything when he was finishing and zipping up.

Something hit him on the side of his left leg. He almost went down, but kept his balance. Must be a cat or maybe a raccoon.

He was a little dizzy when he got back to the deck.

He gasped as he looked down. At point of impact, there was blood all over his leg, just below the knee. His pants were torn at the same spot, and there was a needlelike prick where he was bleeding.

What the hell just happened? I'm not drunk. I'm not imagining it. Something actually did hit me. But what?

He decided to go inside and get cleaned up. After a good-night sleep, he would feel much better. Then he would come back outside to see if he could find what hit him.

XXXXX

If the dark figure could smile, there would be one now.

The poison arrow that nicked Jim Parent in the leg worked like a charm. Never thinking that the arrow would be used, what a great feeling it was just to have it. Waiting for the poison to take effect, the dark figure would take it slow.

For if there was one thing the dark figure had, it was time. Even Mother agreed to let him go out and have some fun.

Killing sheep was fun. Killing one sheep at a time was fun. To see them scared when they knew. To hear them scream when nobody could help.

Yes, the dark figure was having lots of fun.

Now as the house turned black; the dark figure waited.

Then moving slowly toward the house, the back door would do just fine. The dark figure advanced.

XXXXX

About an hour after he went to sleep, Jim Parent woke in a sweat. He had the blankets covering from his neck down, but he was still frozen. Even his teeth were clacking.

His pajamas were sticking to him like leeches. His dark hair was all matted, and sweat was trickling down his face and onto his neck.

The sheets were soaked. He tried to get up but was too weak.

Feeling very sick, not able to get out of bed, he vomited all over himself.

Some of the vomit missed him entirely and made a puddle on the floor.

A dark shadow covered the puddle, and Parent could see the shape of a knife arc in the air. Then he could see no more.

XXXXX

The following morning, Luke and Claire stopped by the hospital to see how Blake was doing. "Not so good," the doctor replied. "He's still in a coma, and the longer he stays that way, the worse his chances are."

They thanked the doctor and left.

The rest of the drive to the precinct was quiet. Neither one of them had anything to say. When they arrived at the station, Willard noticed how quiet they were.

He asked, "What is it? What's wrong?"

"We just came from the emergency centre, and Phil is still in a coma," Luke said. "Doctor says if he doesn't come out of it soon, he won't make it."

Hearing that, Willard was quiet for a moment before he said, "If you're in a bad mood, it's not going to get better. They found number 8 early this morning."

"They did?" Claire asked. "Where?"

"Near the same place you've been hanging out lately. Couple of blocks from Champ's house."

"Wow," Luke finished. "Do you know who it was?"

"Do you remember Jim Parent? He was one of the classmates that came by to help with the photos."

"Yes, I remember. Seemed like a nice guy."

"Yeah. Well, not anymore," Willard said grimly.

At the crime scene, Luke and Claire showed their badges to the policeman guarding the front door. He let them pass and pointed the way up.

Upon arriving to the bedroom, they both had to take out handkerchiefs to cover their nose. The smell of vomit was sickening. At the sight of the body was disturbing in itself.

His head down to his waist was hanging on the floor, and from the waist down lying on the bed. It was like the killer grabbed him and threw him on the floor, then put his legs on the bed at an awkward angle.

There was also puddles of vomit on various parts of the floor.

The knife wound in his back was in plain sight, but there was also blood on his left leg by his knee.

After a few more minutes of examining the body, Luke pulled Claire by the elbow out of the room.

Being free of the smell and taking a couple of deep breaths, Luke asked Claire, "Don't you think this is becoming a little weird?"

"What do you mean weird?" she asked.

"Well, all the murders have been from behind. Nobody ever saw anything. Now the last two are entirely different. Larry Haswell saw him. Maybe the killer let him. Jim Parent's death seemed sloppy. It's bad enough he kills from behind, but now he made a big mess of it. The question is why. Is he just getting careless, or is there more to it?"

He took a minute to wipe his forehead. It was getting stuffy inside the house. They went for a walk outdoors.

Claire said finally, "Let's just wait for the autopsy report. It'll explain why there was blood on his leg. Then we'll go from there. In the meantime, you have a busy night yourself, so let's go home and get you ready."

17

Later that evening, Luke was met by Dr. Lamford at the reception desk. "Glad you made it, Luke. I thought you might change your mind."

"No, I want to get to the bottom of my dream, but I hope this is the right place."

"It is, Luke, but a little at a time. Would you like the same room as before?"

"Yes, please. If it's no trouble."

"No trouble at all. Now remember, make your phone call now, here in the reception lounge like before. When you are done, I'll take your phone and lead you to your room."

"I'm fine. I don't need to make that call. I'm ready."

"All right. Follow me please." And she led him down the corridor until they reached his room. "Here you go," Karen said. "You remember the procedure?"

"Yes, I do."

"I'll be back in a little while to get you set up."

When Karen returned, Luke was lying on the table, ready to get started. She came over to him with a smile and said, "My, you're anxious to get started, aren't you."

He smiled back and said to her, "I am. I can't wait for this to be over. Let's get it done and over with."

Her two assistants came in the room.

The assistants. He had almost forgotten about them. They sure acted creepy. He sure as hell didn't care about them.

They started putting the wires on his scalp as they did before, and when it was completed, he couldn't move his head a whole lot.

When the two assistants left, Karen came back into the room to see how he was making out.

"I'm fine," he assured her. "Except it's so early still that it'll take awhile before I fall asleep."

"You've forgotten already. I will be giving you a sedative to make you drowsy, then fall asleep. So here goes nothing."

It only took a few minutes for his eyes to feel droopy after the sedative was ministered. When he was close to sleep, she said to him, "Let the games begin."

Then she was gone.

XXXXX

Dan's Cooler was booming this night. Ever since Fred Dwyer bought his meat locally, he was able to afford more different kinds of meat.

He couldn't get enough moose and deer. They were the favorites, it seemed. But they also did well on chickens and rabbits. A little partridge and other wild birds didn't hurt either.

All this week he was doing well. If this was to continue, he could make this bar bigger. Hire a few more waitresses.

Maybe he could talk to the owner about giving him a raise. After all, he deserved it.

All the bullshit he had to take every weekend from the customers because they're so drunk and high. They become violent, sometimes.

But that would come later. When the time was right. But for now, all he could think about was the meat they kept bringing in.

What a turn of events this turned out to be. For the first time, in a very long time, Fred Dwyer smiled.

XXXXX

Just finishing her shower, Claire turned the television on to the news. Not concentrating, her mind was elsewhere.

She worried about Luke being at the clinic. She couldn't help it. She knows he's in good hands, but she did force the issue. If it wasn't for her, he wouldn't have bothered. He was doing this for her. Now she feels like a heel.

She hoped that the clinic could finish the dream so he won't have to go anymore, but only time will tell. Maybe when he comes home, he'll have some good news for her.

Maybe.

If her mind wouldn't have wandered away, she might have heard the story about some remains of animals were found in the woods. How the heads and intestines were scattered about. All different kinds of animals.

No one seemed to know anything about that.

In other news, Claire fell asleep.

Karen was in her booth drinking coffee watching the monitors.

Nothing happened. Everything was normal. So far.

As she was sipping her coffee, a pounding in her head began. It came all of a sudden. Her cup fell from her hand and smashed on the floor.

Coffee was everywhere. She didn't notice. She also didn't notice the monitor racing to beat the band.

She thought she heard a voice whispering. "Not yet, child. Soon, child, but not yet."

Then she snapped out of it and her mind was clear. She noticed the broken cup but no recollection of what happened. Karen looked up and saw Luke squirming on the stretcher.

His brain waves were going crazy. What the hell kind of dream was he having?

XXXXX

Margo Henderson and Laurel Champ were drinking beer with the tube on. After Margo took another swig, she said, "I wonder when your contact is going to call you. I mean, with the police suspecting you of murder, they'll probably keep an eye on this place."

"It won't last," Champ complained. "They'll see us here all the time. When another killing is revealed, it'll prove my innocence. Then they'll have to leave me alone."

Margo, almost drunk, responded. "I hope you're right."

XXXXX

When Luke was dreaming, his body was covered in sweat. He was twisting and turning on the table. He could only move his head so much because of the wires, but still he slithered about.

In his dream, when the black cat jumped over the fence, there was the thunder and lightning along with the black shape. This time the black shape raised his arm and pointed directly at him. The shape's mouth opened, but nothing came out.

Or maybe it did, but Luke couldn't tell. The shape came closer and closer.

He reached out and tried to grab Luke. Then he whispered something. Luke opened his eyes.

XXXXX

With a start, Claire woke up. For a moment, she was confused of her surroundings. Then her mind cleared, and she was in Luke's living room, with the television on.

She checked her watch. Five fifteen. She slept almost all night. That very seldom happens. She must have been dreaming.

XXXXX

The two attendants were in Luke's room in a flash. They began to undo his wires, but he was sweating so much, it was a slow process.

When they were finally done, Karen left her booth to check on Luke. When she reached him, he was sitting on the edge of the table with a blanket draped around him. His hair was matted and tangled so much, it looked like a nest of snakes.

She had no idea what he was going through at this moment, but whatever he dreamed, it unraveled him.

"What did you dream about?" she asked him. "It looks like you went farther tonight."

"What time is it?" he asked. He looked around like he didn't know where he was.

She looked at her watch. "Seven fifteen."

"Really. It feels much later than that. I'm sorry, were you asking me something?"

She looked at him. "Yes, I asked you what you dreamed of. It must have been something. I've never seen your eyes this big before."

"I'm not sure what I saw in my dream, but maybe it wasn't real."

"Tell me. Then we'll see."

"Well, the man chasing me caught up. In between the two buildings, he pointed at me and tried to say something."

"Tried to say something? Like what?"

"I don't know. I couldn't hear him. Maybe I didn't want to hear him."

"Why wouldn't you want to hear him?"

"I don't know. Maybe I won't like what he has to tell me."

"Luke. You were a little boy when this happened. Surely it can't be bad. You're here now."

"Maybe I know what happened, and I blocked it out."

Just then, Karen's headache returned. She rubbed at her temple; then her knees buckled. Luke had to grab a hold of her so she wouldn't fall.

After she composed herself, Luke asked, "Are you okay? What happened?"

"I'm not sure. It's the second time this morning I had a headache."

"Second time? When was the first time?"

"While you were sleeping. It must have been a migraine because I dropped my coffee cup and broke it, but I don't remember doing it."

"Did you cut yourself?"

"No, nothing like that. I'm fine, but there was something else."

"Something else? Like what?"

"I could have sworn I heard a voice in my head."

"Heard a voice? Really? What did it say?"

"I'm trying to remember. Let's see. Something like 'Not yet, child, but soon'—something to that effect."

"Wow," was all that Luke could say. But then he added, "Too soon for what?"

"I don't know. I don't know what any of it means."

"That sure is strange. Let's hope nothing more comes of it."

"You and me both."

XXXXX

Claire was having breakfast at around eight thirty that morning when she heard a car pull up in the driveway. She got up to go to the door as Luke was coming in.

"How did it go?" she asked.

"I'm not sure," was all he said.

"Not sure? I don't understand?"

He told her about the dream, about Karen getting headaches and hearing voices.

"Hearing voices? What can all that mean?" she asked.

"I don't know. It's too early to tell. But it doesn't sound like anything good if she's going to continue to have them."

He went to the coffee pot and poured a cup. He refilled hers at the same time.

"So what's on the agenda for today?" she finally asked.

"Don't know yet. I'm going to get cleaned up, then figure it out."

"Just so you know, Willard called me about half an hour ago."

"Really? What did he want?"

"He said the phone's been ringing steady off the hook. Something about animals showing up dead in the woods. The carcasses gone, but the pelt's left behind."

"Really?"

"Yes. Also the callers are asking what we are doing about it."

"Us? We're homicide. That means when people are murdered. Not when animals die."

"I know," she said sadly.

He looked at her and said, "Let me get cleaned up, then we'll go see the captain. Okay?"

She brightened up a little.

Later that morning, Luke and Claire were sitting in Willard's office. The captain looked at them and said, "Well?"

"Well what, Cap?" Luke answered.

"Don't get funny with me. You know damn well what I mean. I haven't been off the phone all morning about those animals. Somebody, or a group, is going through a lot of trouble killing them. The woods are full of their pelts. They want to know what we're going to do about it?"

"Well, Cap, I don't know if there is anything we can do."

"Why not?"

"For one thing, like I told Claire, we're only homicide. We deal with murders. On the human variety, not the animals. Number two, we don't have enough staff to cover it."

Willard looked at him but remained silent. Then he said, "What about your case? Where are you with that?"

Luke cleared his throat before saying, "We're still going to keep tabs on Champ and his friends. I'm very certain they're up to something. I want to know what."

"Okay, that's fine. I just wish the damn phone would stop ringing. Keep me posted."

XXXXX

Mother was agitated. Very upset. Her rocking chair wouldn't stop moving.

The dark figure stayed clear of her. Even that wasn't safe. She could reach out anywhere and grab your mind. No one was safe.

The dark figure left the shack. Into the clearing. Started walking into the woods.

It was very quiet.

The dark figure headed north. The area was familiar, as all the woods were. Farther down the trail and to the west was a huge swamp. At least a twenty-five-foot drop, from the shore alone. Probably at least thirty-five to forty feet deep in the middle.

It must be a few miles wide and maybe four hundred feet long.

The dark figure stood about ten feet from the swamp and just stared. Stared for a very long time.

Who knows what things would go through the mind of something insane. If indeed it has a mind.

Finally, edging closer to the swamp, about to put one foot in the water. Then stopped. Stopped and turned around.

Headed back toward the shack. The clearing. Approaching it, kept going past. Crunching through the path.

A couple of miles later, the dark figure finally stopped walking. A familiar building loomed ahead.

18

Laurel Champ and Margo Henderson were sitting around the small, round wooden table, matched by four chairs having a little brunch.

While he was eating, Champ had an uneasy feeling.

"What's wrong," asked Margo.

"It doesn't feel right," he said.

"What doesn't?" she asked again.

"I don't know. Like I'm being watched or something."

"The police might be watching you."

"No. Another kind of being watched."

"Like what?"

"That's just it. I don't know."

Margo stopped pressing. She saw how Laurel was starting to get upset.

"Let me clear the table," she said.

As she was doing so, Laurel got up to check the living room window facing the street.

Nothing.

He decided to check the back window.

Nothing.

But that was where his gut feeling told him.

But nothing looked out of place.

Normal.

Maybe he was wrong. He sure hoped so.

XXXXX

Luke and Claire were weighing their options. Back at Luke's place, with a coffee in his hands, Luke was saying, "Since I don't believe that Champ and his friends are involved with the murders, they're also not clean. I would like to know what they're up to."

"How are we going to do that?"

"Not much we can do. Just stake out their place and hope for something to happen. Don't forget. We had their phones tapped while we interrogated them. That should help."

"Hope it happens soon. In the meantime, why don't I fix us up some lunch."

"I was hoping you'd ask."

XXXXX

The dark figure continued to look at the building. It was more of a barn than anything.

It looked quiet. Nothing was moving. From the outside.

However, there was movement on the inside. Lots of movement. Many sheep. Talking loudly. Like they didn't agree to what was being said.

The door to the barn was open. Sheep were still moving about. They were visible when they walked by the door.

How the dark figure hated every one of them. How the sheep believed they belonged. The only place they belonged was in a deep pit. Dead and buried.

Watching the barn, a male sheep came outside and hurried to his old beat-up, black pickup truck.

As he was backing up, a much wider door on the same side opened up. The truck backed right up to the opening and into the barn itself.

Then the engine was shut.

It was plain to see about a dozen of dead animals hanging from the rafters. Moose and deer were the majority, but a few rabbits and partridges were mixed in there as well.

Already cleaned, the pickup truck was directly underneath a couple of them.

Cutting the rope, they fell into the truck. Moving the vehicle out, another one moved in and so forth until all the animals were picked up.

The dark figure watched everything from start to finish. Finally losing all interest, the dark figure left the barn.

Turning around, heading toward home, it remembered another building much smaller than the barn.

A house.

The sheep inside the house was the cause of everything. If that one gets killed by his knife, maybe all the headaches would stop. Stop and never come back.

Maybe Mother would be proud.

Finally.

The dark figure could be free of her. Forever. Maybe.

XXXXX

When the call came in, Champ listened. After a couple of minutes, he asked, "When?"

He kept listening, then finally hung up the phone.

Champ turned around and said to Margo, who was directly behind him, "That was the Boss. He says we strike tomorrow at midnight. He doesn't think we'll have problems with the police. We meet at the same place. I'll call Angelo and tell him the news."

Angelo Martin was having a beer with the music blaring when the phone rang. It kept ringing, but the music was so loud Martin never heard it.

When the song was finally over, the shrill of the phone made him jump.

Turning down the music, he finally picked it up. "Hello," he answered.

"Where the hell were you?" Champ demanded. "The phone must have rung twenty times!"

Martin apologized. "The music was loud. I didn't expect you to call so soon. What's up?"

"I'll tell you what's up. The Boss just called, and he wants us at the same spot midnight tomorrow."

"Wow, that's fast. But the police, they'll probably be watching us. Won't it be risky?"

"I agree. But the Boss doesn't think so. Remember, if we don't do what he wants, we'll have bigger problems to worry about. I'll pick you up at eleven thirty tomorrow night. Be ready."

The phone went dead.

Farther down North Avenue Road, Luke and Claire were watching Martin's house.

"This is one of the best ideas you've actually come up with, sweetheart. Having Champ's and Martin's home phone's bugged while we interrogated them. The department actually went along with it and also supplying these devices so we can hear the conversations. Gotta love technology."

"Yes," replied Luke. "It sure helps in our investigation. Now since they're not going to do anything until tomorrow night, let's go home and strategize.

The next day, the Boss backed his old, beat-up black pickup truck to the open garage door. Getting out, he inspected the back of the truck. Deciding that it needed to be clean, he walked into the garage looking for a broom. Finding one, he came out and jumped in the bed of the truck.

After he finished sweeping, he stepped down and went back into the garage.

He pulled out the garden hose so he could rinse out the animal smells and the blood.

After all, he thought, *it needs to be kept clean for tonight*. Tonight at midnight, his underlings will be put to the test. In the woods, where he will have lots of fun. With, or without his help.

He wishes it could last forever. But it won't.

Nothing ever does. Oh well.

After rinsing the truck, he stood back to admire his job. Perfect.

Putting the hose away, he went back into the driver's seat and started up the truck.

Already past ten, he would just have time for breakfast and make an appearance at work. Hoping to be back home for six o'clock, he would have time for a power snooze and still get ready for midnight.

Phil Blake wasn't getting better. He was still in a coma, no sign of waking at all. The doctors were starting to lose faith. They didn't think there was any more hope. A next of kin should be notified and prepared, they said.

The nurse on watch in his room was in a chair, beside his bed, reading a book. But she looked very tired and was fighting sleep.

Her eyelids were heavy, and soon sleep was the victor.

Her fingers that held the book loosened their grip, and soon the book fell from her grasp. When the book hit the tiled floor, it sounded like a gunshot, in the all too quiet room.

The noise from the book hitting the floor was like an open airwave in Phil Blake's mind.

His eyes were fluttering as if they were trying to open. His face was starting to sweat, and his hair was sticking to his skin.

He started to shift his body from side to side, until, at last, he remained still.

Phil Blake began to dream. He dreamed about the victims' brutal deaths. He saw each of them getting killed.

He saw how the figure dressed in black was lying in wait for each prey. He saw the knife each and every time, the way it was held before each kill.

He saw how the killer dressed in black, plunged it in the victim's back. He also saw the figure that was dressed in black.

The features. The face. It was horrible. Something was wrong with the face.

Would have been better off if there was no face? Too horrible too describe.

The head was covered. Covered by a hood. A black hood.

In his dream, the figure dressed in black took off his hood. In his dream, Phil Blake screamed.

19

Later that night, Luke and Claire were getting ready for Champ and Martin.

"What if they're not up to anything?" Claire was asking. "This'll be all for nothing."

"They're up to something all right," Luke was saying. "I'm going to find out what. Besides, if they're not up to anything, we're just protecting them from the killer anyway."

"Okay," Claire answered. "Like hitting two birds with one stone."

"Exactly."

It was just past eleven when Luke shouted, "Let's get cracking, Claire, before we're late."

"I'm coming, I'm coming. Take it easy."

They were pulling out of the driveway at eleven ten.

"We'll have enough time and five minutes to spare," Luke was saying. "Perfect."

Driving by Martin's place, Luke said, "Champ's already here. That's good. We shouldn't have to wait long at all."

Just as he was finished saying that, the front door to Martin's place opened. Champ and Martin were getting in the car.

It seemed like it was only them two. Margo was nowhere in sight.

"Maybe Margo Henderson isn't involved," Luke remarked.

"I hardly doubt that. Maybe she doesn't go with them, but she knows what they're up to. Probably gets a cut in there somewhere also."

Following behind them on this cool spring night, Claire said, "Looks like they're headed back to Champ's place. I wonder why."

Luke shook his head. "No. Probably going past it. Let's wait and see.

True to his word, Champ went right by his house. He finally came to a stop sign about two miles later. Then he turned right and went down an old dirt road.

When Luke approached the stop sign, he turned off his lights. He said, "The dirt road he took doesn't have an exit. He'll have to come back out this way. But I still want to see what he's up to. Let's go."

They turned right and followed the dirt path. Eventually the road veered to the left, and they took that when he came to a sudden stop.

"What's wrong?" Claire asked.

"His car is parked up ahead, and it's idling. There's also a black pickup parked there. Damn, I should have brought the night camera. Didn't think about it."

"So, what do we do now?" was the question.

"We wait and see what happens." He moved his car out of sight.

Champ was out of his car and went to talk to whoever was behind the wheel of the black pickup. After a few minutes, Champ went back to his vehicle and drove around the pickup. He made his way deeper into the bushes, and when he stopped, the pickup turned so that it would be facing the car diagonally.

Out of nowhere, another pickup truck came from behind Luke and aimed for the spot that would be between the other two. All three vehicles were about fifteen feet apart, and they formed a semicircle, facing east. There were no houses in that direction, and no one would be able to see.

All three vehicles shut off their engines and waited.

Luke and Claire watched the whole scene take place.

Luke asked Claire, "Are you able to get a good look at the driver in the black pickup truck?"

"No," she responded. "It's too dark to tell."

"I was afraid of that. Another reason for my camera. That guy in the black pickup seems to be the Boss. Champ must be getting instructions for whatever they're up to."

Claire whispered, "What are they waiting for?"

"I'm not sure, but I don't think I'm going to like it."

Just then, three heavy generators hummed to life. About fifty yards of the east part of the woods flooded with extremely immense light and froze the aging buck with a tremendous rack, deer, and her two fawns.

While the animals remained paralyzed, the three drivers slid out and met at the beat-up, black truck. The driver of that truck gave the other two rifles, and off they went into the woods.

When they reached the still-frozen animals, they shot them point-blank with tranquilizer guns to keep the noise down. Then the three men took out their knives and went to work.

When Martin joined them, the man with the black pickup truck gave him his knife and said to him, "Start cleaning."

Blood squirted everywhere.

The men worked silently, and the only noise was knife cutting bone.

Luke and Claire were disgusted with what they've seen.

Luke started up their car and backed up. Slowly he turned around. Making his way back toward the highway, Claire looked out back the way they just came and saw darkness.

"Wow," she said. "All that light in the woods, but well hidden from the trees. What are we going to do now?"

"What we're going to do is go home. Tomorrow we'll talk to Willard and plan our next move. At least we know who's killing those animals, and we finally know what our little friends are up to. But we're going to have to find out who's behind the black pickup truck. I think he's the Boss."

Claire waited until he finished talking before she said, "We're going to have to go see Champ and Martin again. Make them tell us."

"That'll be difficult considering we had problems with them before."

"Then what do you suggest?"

"We keep listening on their phone conversations. When they plan another one like tonight, we'll be prepared, and we'll bust the whole crew."

"That's if they do it again."

"They will. They must be getting paid big time for poaching. They're not going to stop. They have it good now."

"I hope you're right."

"I do too."

The next day in Willard's office, the three of them went over the previous night's events. Willard looked at Luke and said, "You actually saw them poaching. Why didn't you do something?"

"I wasn't prepared for that. Our better course of action would be to listen in on their conversations through the bug. When they plan another attack, and they will, we'll have you there behind us and take them all down. That would be our best move."

Willard thought about it and said, "I'll go along with that because you guys are my best detectives and never let me down. But let's just hope it's soon. That damn phone never stops ringing."

When the phone rang again, all three people jumped from the silence it broke.

Willard growled into it, thinking it was from the community about the animals.

But it wasn't from them at all.

When Willard's voice and facial appearance softened, Luke and Claire wondered who it could be. When Willard hung up the phone, he looked down for a moment before saying, "That was the Havenburg Hospital Emergency Center. They want me to go there. Talk to me about Phil."

"We'll go with you," Luke assured him.

"No, I'll go alone. No need for all three of us to be there. I'll come by and see you with any news. Besides, the autopsy report came in this morning, and apparently what killed Jim Parent was poisoning."

"Poisoning?" Luke was baffled.

"Yes, he was punctured with something sharp, which resulted in the poisoning."

"That explains the blood on his leg. But I wonder what was used," Claire was saying.

"I can't figure it out now, have to get to the hospital. I'll come by your place to let you know about Phil's condition."

They all got up to leave.

Arriving at the emergency center, Willard spoke to the receptionist.

"I believe I was told to wait here. I'm Captain Willard of the police department, and this is about a patient named Phil Blake."

"Oh yes, Captain. I was told about you. The doctor will be with you shortly. Please have a seat."

Twenty minutes later, a doctor walked into the reception area and went directly toward Willard. "Captain Willard, glad you could make it on such short notice. I'm Dr. Brent Logan. Won't you please step into my office?"

Willard got up from his chair and followed the doctor to his office. Entering the room, Willard noticed all sorts of diplomas hanging on the wall to his left. Small room with plush carpeting, a brown mahogany desk, which was tidy.

On the desk had a photograph of a woman and little boy of about ten years old. Must be wife and son, he thought. The walls were light beige in color with a small window to his right side. Behind the desk was a closed door, which Willard presumed was a bathroom.

"Where are my manners?" Dr. Logan said. "Please, have a seat."

"Thank you, Doctor. Now tell me, how is my friend Phil Blake? You sounded like it was extremely important."

"I'm sorry if I gave you that impression, Captain. To tell the truth, I don't know if it's an emergency at all. I know something happened, but I don't know how to say it."

"Just say it, Doc. What happened? What's wrong?"

"Well, it happened late last night. So we had to run some tests, which is why I only called you now."

"Okay, Doc. Just tell me what happened."

"Captain Willard. I believe Phil Blake had a dream last night!"

"What? What did you just say?"

"You heard correctly, Captain. Phil Blake had a dream last night, so hopefully that will speed up his comatose state."

"Wait a minute. Are you saying he had a dream last night, but he's still in a coma?"

"That's exactly what I'm saying. Of course, we're keeping a closer eye on him, but it's still up to him to pull through his coma."

"Do you know what his dream was about, Doctor?"

"At this time, it's not known what the dream was about. Apparently, he did speak in the dream, but we have no idea what he said."

"No idea at all?"

"No, Captain. But we hooked up a recorder on him so that if he dreams again and talks, the recorder will be able to pick it up. I hope."

"Is there anything else you have for me?"

"None at this point. I wanted you to know about his dreaming. I will keep you informed of his progress and any other developments that may come along."

"Thank you, Doctor. I appreciate everything you've done."

"Don't mention it, Captain. Always a pleasure to help."

When Captain Willard left the hospital, he couldn't believe what he just heard.

Is it possible? Comatose patients dreaming? Are they even aware? Would they remember what they dreamed when they awakened. If they awaken.

All of a sudden, Captain Bruce Willard felt a chill through his whole body.

20

Willard was sitting around Luke's table with a coffee in front of him. He didn't seem to notice until Luke cleared his throat.

That seemed to clear the cap's mind as he looked up and finally saw his surroundings.

"Earth calling, Cap, are you there, Cap?" Luke teased.

Willard looked at the two and motioned for them to have a seat. "What I have to tell you may sound out of this world, but you need to listen to everything I say."

Claire sat closer to him and said, "What's the matter with Phil?"

"It's hard to explain, but here goes." He took a drink of coffee before continuing. "Dr. Logan told me that late last night Phil seemed to have . . ."

"Go on," encouraged Claire.

Willard looked at them and said, "He might have had a dream. In his sleep, Phil Blake was having a dream."

Luke cut in. "A dream? You mean he's having a normal dream, and he's out of his coma?"

"No, Luke. You don't understand. He had a dream late last night, but he's still in a coma. The doctor says that he still has to pull through on his own, and he hope's that the dreaming will help him to do so."

"How does he know that Phil was dreaming?"

"The nurse that was sitting with him last night, saw tears in his eyes, so the doctor ran some tests on him. He believes that was from his dream."

"Does he know what the dream was about?"

"No, but they figure he was trying to speak in his dream."

"How can they tell?"

"Just the way his face looked I suppose. I'm not entirely sure, but they set up a recording so if he dreams again, he hopes the tape will pick up any talking."

"Wow," Claire spoke. "That's hard to imagine. A comatose patient able to dream. That almost sounds frightening." She got up to pour herself a coffee.

"The only thing we can do now is wait. Wait and pray for poor Phil." Luke added.

The next night at Dan's Cooler, it was hopping mad. Every table was used, and the orders were still coming.

Fred Dwyer couldn't keep up. If this kept going the way it was, he would have to hire a couple of waitresses. But for now, he was all they had.

He was never short of meat anymore.

Word of mouth made it a long way. Even people driving through would stop here.

Half the people here tonight, Fred never saw before.

As he was cleaning the countertop, a customer he hasn't seen in a long time came up to him and said, "I've never seen it this busy before. You must be doing something right."

"I must be. It's only been about a month that this started. I wonder how much longer it'll last."

"Oh, I'm sure it'll last for a while. I have complete faith in you."

"Well, thank you, kindly sir."

The customer excused himself, and Fred Dwyer was left alone cleaning his counter.

That was strange, he thought. *I guess there's all kinds everywhere. Oh well.*

XXXXX

The black pickup truck made its way down the road with the music blaring. What a great night this turned out to be.

The food was great; the place was packed. He couldn't wait to make that next call to go back in the woods.

But they had time for that later. Next few days or so. They were still good. Nobody suspected a thing. That was even better.

The money was great. Which reminded him. He had to check his account. See if everything was in order.

He turned into his driveway. He shut off the engine but remained in the truck for a few minutes longer. Just sat there and looked at everything.

Finally getting out and going inside, he thought a couple more beers, then bedtime.

Yes, life is good.

The next morning when Luke and Claire were getting ready for work, Willard called Luke and Claire to meet him at the emergency center in the reception room.

When they parked their car, the rest of the lot was filled also.

Getting out they made their way to the reception area, where they met Willard.

"Dr. Logan will be with us in a few minutes. Checking on a couple of things that were brought to his attention."

"Okay," Luke answered. "But why are we here?"

"I'm not sure, but I'm sure it has to do with Phil."

"I hope he's not deteriorating. Not more than before."

Willard was about to say something, when Dr. Logan entered the room. "Captain Willard, I'm glad you could make it. I see you brought along a couple of friends."

"Yes, Doctor. Two of my best detectives. This is Claire Davis." He indicated toward her. and they shook hands. "While this is Luke Myers."

As they all stood, the two men shook hands before Willard continued, "This is Dr. Logan."

"Pleased to meet you, Doc. I hope Phil didn't turn for the worse."

"Well, that's up to him I'm afraid. He has to snap out of his coma soon otherwise . . ." He let the sentence trail. "But it's not his condition I called you in for. Please, step into my office, all of you. Much more comfortable and private."

They all followed him, and Willard was remembering this exact walk only yesterday. When they reached the office, Dr. Logan made sure they were all comfortable before he began.

"Apparently, Phil Blake had another dream last night. We took the opportunity to listen to the tape."

"Well?" Willard asked him. "Did you hear anything?"

"That's just it, Captain, we don't know. I mean, it sounds like there is, but we can't understand any of it."

"You keep saying we, Doctor. Who else is listening to this?"

Dr. Logan answered, "My team, Captain. It consists of the nurse in charge of that floor and the two nurses that are watching over him."

"Is there a lot of talking?" Luke asked.

The doctor looked at him and asked, "A lot of talking?"

"Yes, Doctor. On the tape, is there a lot of talking?"

"Oh, I'm sorry. My mind must have been somewhere else. No, not a lot. A name maybe, but it's gargled, not clear at all. I was hoping your team could try to listen and make sense of it."

Willard cut in and said, "We'll try, Doc. That's all I can promise."

"That's all I ask, Captain. Thank you." He pulled a drawer open and extracted from it a tape, also produced the player with it and popped it in.

He pressed the On switch and leaned back in his chair and listened.

At first there was a lot of static and some squeaking noises. This went on for about ten minutes before getting quiet.

Then out from nowhere, a high-pitched-sounding like scream filled the room. Both Luke and Claire were taken aback. They looked at each other but remained silent.

When the screaminglike noise stopped, it got quiet again.

Then some shuffling, like someone was walking, on uneven steps. Like one foot being dragged.

Then the moment they were waiting for. Phil Blake muttered a name.

But nobody could understand what he was saying.

They rewound just that part of the tape to hear over about four times, but each time, it sounded more disturbed than the last.

Willard asked him. "May we borrow this, Doc? We have a technician that we want to pass it to."

"Not a problem, Captain. I was hoping you would."

"In the meantime, Doc, will you continue to tape his dreams?"

"Of course. I hope your technician can figure it out."

"I hope so too, Doc. I hope so too."

As they were walking toward their car, Luke couldn't get that scream out of his head. "Assuming that was Phil screaming in his dream, it's hard to imagine what could have scared him. He doesn't scare so easily."

"I agree," Claire said. "I've never once saw him react when he's at a crime scene. It's like he's already seen everything."

"Exactly," Luke answered. Looking at Willard, he asked, "What do you think, Cap? Do you have any ideas?"

"Not really. A dream could be anything. There are no boundaries, no rules. Whatever happens in a dream happens."

Unlocking their car door, Luke got in behind the wheel and started toward the precinct.

"The sooner we get this tape to the technician, the sooner we get an answer."

21

Later that day, Champ received a phone call from the Boss. While he was listening, Margo was slumped over the couch, not quite over her hangover from the night before.

Champ was still on the phone, when finally the conversation was over and he hung up. He walked over to Margo and put his hand on her cheek. When she didn't open her eyes, he left her alone and went back to the phone. He picked it up and dialed a number.

When he hung up, the man with the black pickup truck smiled. Things were going to plan. Soon he wouldn't need anyone at all.

Those hirelings were doing all the dirty work at half the cost. Two or three more times would be enough. After that, he could stop for good. He'll have enough money to blow this joint.

Go somewhere hot. New Mexico maybe. But for now, he has work to do.

At the end of this week will be one step closer to finishing for good. Such good times to come.

He picked up the phone to make another call.

XXXXX

Angelo Martin was surprised to hear from Champ so soon.

"Again?" he couldn't believe what he was hearing. "Why so soon?" he asked.

"I don't know why so soon, Martin. We're not supposed to ask questions. Remember? It's not good for our health."

"I remember. So when's the meet?" he asked through gritted teeth.

"This Friday night behind my place."

"Behind your place? Why there?"

"He said it was because we've never touched this end of the woods. He wants to know if it's just as good as the other places."

"How will we find that out?"

There was a pause on the other end.

Martin asked, "Champ, you still there?"

Champ said, "Yes, I'm here. He wants me to go out in the woods the next couple of days to scope it out."

"Really? By yourself?"

"That's the plan."

"That's a pretty stupid plan. Do you know how dangerous the woods are? It's almost suicide."

"The woods aren't dangerous in the daytime. Only at night."

"You don't believe that any more than I do. So what about Margo? Is she going to be joining us?"

"She sure is."

"About time she gets her hands dirty."

"Don't talk about her like that. You two are going to have to get along."

"Anyway," Martin was saying, "I'll hear from you on Friday then." He hung up.

XXXXX

When Luke and Claire were sitting in Willard's office, Willard's cell went off.

"Ya," he growled. "What is it?"

Listening for a few minutes, he disconnected the line.

"That was the undercover technicians monitoring the calls between Champ and Martin. They just talked about fifteen minutes ago. There's going to be another poaching party this Friday night. It's going to take place behind Champ's place."

Willard took a sip of water. "Apparently everyone involved will be there."

"Everyone?" Luke asked.

"Yes. Everyone including"—Willard looked at Claire with a big smile—"your friend Margo. How does that grab you, Claire?"

Claire smiled back. "It grabs me pretty good, Cap. I better make sure that I have plenty of lipstick. I'll have to look my best for her."

They all started laughing.

Later that day, Champ went into the woods behind his house. He was looking for any kind of tracks to show that the beasts were roaming in his territory as well as other parts of the woods.

He went one direction, knelt down to study the earth. He couldn't pick anything up, so he kept going. He was still having bad luck, so he changed direction.

When he headed due east, he was hearing tree branches and leaves rustle.

So he kept going. He crouched down to study the earth, but again he couldn't find any tracks.

What the hell was going on?

If there were no tracks, why were the branches and leaves rustling?

Was it the wind? No! The wind was not a factor. It was barely blowing. Then what?

He thought he heard a low growl. *Was that some kind of growl?*

He listened for it again. Nothing.

Should he continue? Maybe he should call Martin.

Call Martin. I don't think so.

He was scared of his own shadow. He'll have to do this on his own. He looked up and saw the path he would have to take. He took a deep breath. He continued forward.

Through the trees and onto the path he went. The rustling continued farther east. Like it was calling him. Like pointing a finger toward him and beckoning for him to follow.

Follow, he did.

When the dark figure saw the sheep go into the woods behind his house, it was almost too good to be true.

Watching look for tracks made it easy.

All the dark figure had to do was make little noises with the branches and leaves, and the rest was child's play.

The sheep followed, but it almost didn't work.

When he stopped following, deciding what to do, the dark figure thought all was lost. But then the sheep continued once more, and the plan was taking shape.

A little deeper into the woods and it would be game over.

When Champ came to a fork in the path, he had to make a choice.

But to his astonishment, the fork to the left was where he saw a slight movement. Not knowing if he actually saw anything, he decided to go that way.

The dark figure watched the sheep with the tattoo get closer.

Watching and waiting until the time was right, the dark figure had the knife ready. Raising it up high, the knife was flung forward toward its target.

The knife was flying at horrific speed.

Champ thought he heard a swishing sound coming toward him. But he couldn't see where.

Until it hit him square in the shoulder. The force of the knife practically lifted him off his feet and pinned him to the tree behind him.

The knife protruded through the back of his shoulder and stuck into the tree.

Champ felt no pain, for he was in shock. The blood from his shoulder was flowing like sap coming out of a tree.

Trickling freely from his shoulder, the blood drenched his shirt and pants, and onto the ground.

At the sight of his blood, he fainted.

22

When Luke was driving home with Claire sitting beside him, he said to her, "You know, I'm a little puzzled right now."

"A little puzzled?" asked Claire. "What are you talking about?"

"Well," he said. "All of a sudden we're right in the middle of the poachers and maybe wrapping it up soon. But the killer we're looking for hasn't killed anyone of late. Not that I want that to happen, but it's like he's waiting for us to finish with the poacher's so that we can concentrate on him. Only him. It just doesn't make sense."

"You are right about him not killing lately, but I'm sure he's still out there waiting to kill more. In the end, everything will justify itself. I wouldn't worry too much. He won't disappoint us. Have faith."

"I guess you're right. How sick does it sound that we hope he strikes again. We're just as bad as he is."

After that, they drove the rest of the way in silence, each to their own thoughts. It's going to be a long few days.

XXXXX

Martin felt bad that he got off on the wrong foot with Champ. He wanted to call and apologize, but he didn't want to take the chance that Margo would answer the phone.

He didn't want to talk to her, just yet. He didn't trust her. Martin was sure she was playing Champ, but he couldn't prove it.

Not yet.

So he would have to keep his thoughts to himself. For now. Until the time was right.

When the phone rang at the other end, the man in the black pickup truck lit a cigarette while waiting for the line to connect.

When someone did answer, the man in the black pickup laid out all the instructions for what he expected to happen this Friday night.

He disconnected the call with a grin that would have driven any mother insane.

Yes, he thought.

Things were finally going his way.

XXXXX

When the dark figure approached him—slumped over and head hung low, blood caked on the left side of his body—the dark figure felt a satisfaction.

The one who started it all finally down. A smile would have been seen if the dark figure had lips and not wearing a facial hood.

Grabbing the knife, pulling it from Champ's shoulder, he fell to the ground. The body was at an odd angle; to look at it, you'd think he was dead.

The dark figure just looked at him for a few moments before bending down to grab a foot.

Dragging Champ through the woods, over branches, leaves, and mud, he kept walking deeper into the woods.

Bumping his head over the rough path, Champ's eyelids fluttered open. Getting a moment to clear his head and gather his thoughts, he was watching the sky move.

That was odd.

Why was the sky moving? Even the trees were moving. Why?

He couldn't figure it out. Then he realized, it wasn't the sky or the trees moving.

It was him! He was moving. But how can that be possible? He was on his back. Then he knew.

Someone had his foot and was dragging him to God knows where. He looked up to see his would-be captor.

All he could see was the back of his head. Even that was covered with a hood. But there was also the walk. What was wrong with the walk?

That's it.

His captor was walking with a noticeable limp. Like he was dragging a foot.

But who the hell was this guy? Why was the face and head covered? What was that smell? Smelled like what? Blood maybe?

Then he remembered. A knife came hurling through the air. Right at him. Got him in the shoulder. There was blood. Lots of blood. That's when he passed out. Now he was awake. Being dragged deeper and deeper into the woods.

His back was killing him. Being scraped as he continued to be dragged along.

He felt raw. Like all his skin being stripped off him. He was so sore.

His foot in that lunatic's grip was very strong. So scared his foot would get ripped off his ankle.

Suddenly the dark figure stopped. Turning around and stared at Champ. Champ felt a shiver crawl down his spine.

The eyes. The eyes were the scariest of all. They were two red holes. Just staring.

Kill me now. I can't take that stare.

Then just like that, the lunatic continued on. The sudden jerk made his ankle even worse.

Ten minutes later, Champ was thrown roughly into the side of the shack wall.

XXXXX

Marcus Quint nodded at Luke and Claire as they walked into his lab.

"Glad you came over so quickly. I went over this tape five times and finally figured out what Phil Blake was saying in his dream."

"That's what I needed to hear," Luke answered. "What have you got?"

Marcus pushed the Play button since the tape was already set. As he sat down he said, "Remember all that static in the background? Well, I took it out and everything is clear. Listen."

A pause before the screaming started. When the screaming ended, there was a shuffling noise.

Someone walking like they were dragging a foot. But when Phil Blake spoke a name, the shuffling noise was all but forgotten.

Earnest.

Luke and Claire looked at each other. "Earnest?" Luke echoed. "Who the hell is Earnest?"

Claire said, "I haven't the foggiest. Phil may be the only one who can answer that."

They listened to more of the dream, but no more names were mentioned.

XXXXX

When the dark figure entered the shack with Champ and threw him roughly against the far wall, it got all of Mother's attention.

Waiting to see what would happen next, she remained quiet. It seemed to her that the human that was just thrown across the room was next to dead.

The dark figure advanced toward the human with a big, thick chain in hand.

Roughly grabbing the human by the feet, the dark figure wrapped the chain around the ankles about four or five times. When that was done, with the same chain, he grabbed the human and held his wrists, proceeding with the same process at the ankles.

After the wrists were tied, he used the rest of the chain to wrap it around the whole body and tie the other end of the chain to a hook that was on the wall behind the human.

Finally finished with the captive, Mother stayed quiet no more.

"Why did you bring that piece of nothing here? Don't you know all the trouble you'll bring? Do you want the humans to know where we are?"

Then the dark figure looked at Mother and walked toward the human.

He grabbed the human's wrist and turned it around, breaking it. Showing the tattoo so Mother could see, she finally understood.

The tattoo. The one who began the whole nightmare. Now that nightmare is here. Good. Very good. If the human was awake when the wrist was broken, he isn't anymore.

23

Earnest was running down the hallway, trying to avoid Laurel Champ. But no matter where Earnest went, Champ was close behind.

"You'll never get away from me, you little freak. I'll find you wherever you go, then beat you to a pulp!"

Earnest started crying as he rounded the corner and ran straight into the janitor, who had a bucket of water and mop.

When the collision was made, most of the water spilled against the wall and down the hallway. The mop tipped out of the bucket and fell to the floor a few feet behind the janitor.

"Hey, watch where you're going, you little brat," yelled the janitor.

At that moment, Champ caught up and put his hand on his shirt collar, picking him clean off the floor. Holding him up until they made it to the boy's room, he stuck Earnest's head down the toilet.

When Champ pulled Earnest out of the john, he gasped for air.

Then Champ threw Earnest roughly into the wall where he remained motionless. Champ kicked him in the ribs a few times when Phil Blake screamed.

He sat up in a sitting position and spoke gibberish. Then he lay down again. In his coma.

XXXXX

Luke and Claire were back at Willard's office, going over the tape. "The name Earnest probably doesn't mean anything," Willard was saying. "Any names can be mentioned. I really don't think there's anything there."

"I'm wondering maybe if Phil knows someone named Earnest. That would explain a lot. But as long as he's in a coma, we'll never know," Luke went on to say.

Claire added, "I don't know, guys. Phil doesn't have family here. He said so. He keeps to himself when he's not at work. I bet he doesn't even know an Earnest. If that's the case, I'll go out on a limb here and say that name means something."

Luke and Willard were quiet for the moment. Then Willard said, "That may be true, but for now, we have no way of knowing. We're still at square one with this."

Luke and Claire left the office and went out for coffee.

Maybe the captain is right," Claire was saying. "We have no clue as to who Earnest is. Unless this Earnest falls out of the sky and onto our lap, we probably will never know."

They got their coffee and brought it back to the precinct.

"Let's get to work," Luke advised.

When Martin answered the phone, he was surprised to hear Margo at the other end. "Yes, Margo, what can I do for you?"

Margo was in a panic. Worried. Martin never heard her this way before.

"Is Laurel with you? Did you hear from him?" she asked. "When I woke up, he wasn't here. Gone for hours and I'm worried about him!"

"Don't worry about Laurel. He can take care of himself. He's not here, but I did hear from him."

"You did? When?"

"Earlier this morning. He said the Boss called him today, for us to go out at our meet Friday night."

"Friday night? That's two nights from now. Where's it going to be?"

"The Boss wants it behind Champ's place. Lots of woods back there."

"Behind our place? But we don't even know if it's safe!"

"Yes, well, there's another thing."

"Another thing? Like what?"

"The Boss wanted Laurel to go out there to look for tracks. In fact, I bet that's where he is right now."

"He's out there by himself? It's too dangerous to be out there alone. Maybe something happened to him. He should have been back by now."

"Maybe he lost track of the time."

"But can't he see it's almost getting dark. I'm worried sick."

"I'm sure he'll turn up. In the meantime, get some rest."

"I've rested enough. I have to be up when he gets here."

"Okay. See you Friday night."

Toward the end of his day, Willard was at his desk alone. Peaceful. He could breathe. Thinking about Phil took away all his strength.

Phil was always there for Willard, through thick and thin. No matter what.

Now that Phil needs him, what the hell did he do for him?

Nothing! Nothing at all!

Willard felt helpless. He didn't know what he could do for poor Phil.

Now there's these dreams that he's having. What's that about?

He's never heard of that before. It was a long day. Time to go home.

Then his phone rang.

XXXXX

When Champ still hadn't come home, Margo grabbed a flashlight, along with her coat and shoes. Leaving the house at a dead run, not bothering to close the back door, she made her way toward the back of the yard where it met the woods.

Turning on the flashlight, she took a moment to try to figure out which way Champ may have gone.

After a few minutes still wondering which way to go, she started yelling his name. Her voice started to get hoarse, so she gave that up.

But she couldn't give up. Not yet.

She bent down on the ground with the flashlight to study the landscape the way she seen Champ do.

She got up and faced east. Deciding to go that way, she followed the path for twenty minutes until she came to a fork.

Stopping for a moment, she wondered if Champ even came this way. Drinking some water from a bottle she brought from home, she chose the fork on the left.

XXXXX

After Luke finished showering and shaving, he began to feel better. But that didn't save the fact he just couldn't get Earnest out of his head.

Was he real? If he wasn't, why would Blake say his name? Why would he even dream of him?

So back to the original question. Was he real?

If he is, how does he fit in all this?

That was why Luke was stuck. He couldn't figure this part of the puzzle.

That's exactly what Earnest is. A puzzle.

Was he a corner piece that held an important part of the investigation? Or was he just a middle piece? A small part that wasn't important.

Claire was still in the shower, but it didn't matter. She wouldn't know the answer either.

Maybe he's thinking too hard in this and should let it go for now. If it does have meaning, it'll come to him.

If it doesn't, have a nice day.

XXXXX

When Margo chose the left path, she wasn't sure if she made the right choice. For all she knew, he might not even have come into the woods at all.

He's home right now wondering where I am. Leaving the back door open and all.

But she was this far. Might as well continue while she's here. But it was getting dark out. Her flashlight might not last another hour.

Thinking over her options, she tripped over a log that she hadn't seen. She scraped her elbows, and where her pant leg tore just below the knee, she saw a scrape there also.

There was blood on her new injuries.

Moaning, sore, and tired, with her hair a tangled mess, fingernails full of dirt, she slowly made her way up.

What she saw made all her troubles and injuries seem like a pot of gold.

XXXXX

Willard calmly said, "Hello," into his phone. When the caller identified himself as Dr. Brent Logan, he straightened up in his chair.

"Captain," Logan was saying. "Phil Blake had another dream, and it seems like he's talking more than he did before. I don't know if it's important or not, but I thought you'd want to know."

"Yes, of course. You did the right thing, Doc. I'll get my team and meet you there."

Luke and Claire were preparing dinner when his cell rang. Putting down the wooden ladle that he was using to stir the pot, he answered.

"Cap, what's up?"

"Not sure yet, but the two of you better meet me at the hospital. Phil had another dream, and apparently, he talked more than before."

"All right, Cap. We're on the way."

Reaching the emergency waiting room, Luke and Claire were about ten feet behind Willard who just got there himself.

Taking a seat, the three of them waited. Luke was starting to get restless, and Claire was playing locks with her hair.

Willard seemed to be the only one taking the waiting calmly.

Fifteen minutes later, Dr. Logan finally made an appearance, apologizing for the wait. Greetings were made all around before heading for Logan's office.

When they were all seated, Logan said, "Thank you all for coming at such short notice."

Reaching into his desk drawer and pulling out the tape, he continued.

"We went over this tape, maybe three times, and it's still difficult to make out what he's saying. But it does sound like the same thing, whatever it is."

Luke spoke up and said, "If I were a betting man, I'd have to say Earnest."

"Excuse me?" Logan asked.

"Earnest. The name he's saying would probably be Earnest. That's what he said in his last dream."

"Well, that's progress then," the doctor said. "I hope that name means something for your investigation," he added.

"I'm afraid not, Doctor," Luke shot back. "I've never heard of an Earnest before. It probably doesn't mean anything."

"Sorry to hear that," the doctor commented. "But let's get on why we're here." He picked up the tape and put it in the machine.

On a tree about seven yards away, Margo spotted a piece of cloth stuck on the rough part of a bark. Getting completely on her feet, slowly, she made her way to the tree.

Reaching about shoulder height, she tore the cloth off the bark and examined it.

It was partially blood, which freaked her out. Dropping it, she wiped the blood from her fingers on her pants.

Taking deep breaths, she managed to calm down. Then her mind focused on the cloth she dropped. She knelt down to examine it more closely.

She saw this cloth before.

Laurel.

It was Laurel's. His shirt that he was wearing earlier today.

So Laurel was here.

The blood that she wiped on her pants must have been his. She looked at the tree again. There was some more blood on the tree around the spot where the cloth was.

She looked down. More blood. There was more blood on the ground.

My God! What happened here? Something terrible. Laurel is hurt. Needed help.

She flashed her light to see if the blood left a trail.

Not this way.

Changing direction, still she didn't see any. She went back to the original sighting and started again.

Walking farther this time, she spotted what looked to be blood. Bending down to touch it gently on her fingertips, she realized it was blood.

What the hell is going on? This leads deeper into the woods. I have to call for help.

Crying, she turned and ran all the way home.

XXXXX

They listened to the tape a few times, but his speech was slurred, as though he was drunk. But like before, they still couldn't make heads or tails of what was being said.

Luke said, "It's not crystal clear, but it still sounds like Earnest is the key here."

"The key to what?" Willard wanted to know. "We never even heard of that name. For all we know, it could be a childhood dream." Willard looked at Luke and said, "No pun intended, that has nothing to do with anything."

"None taken, Cap, but getting back to Phil's dream, I'm sure it does have something of importance. I'm just not sure how."

Claire waited for all the talking to be done before she said, "Guys. Don't worry about Earnest. We'll just keep it on the backburner for now. If something shows up, then we'll act on it."

XXXXX

Shaking uncontrollably, Margo picked up the phone. She kept misdialing, so she finally slammed it down. Getting a grip, she tried again and managed to dial correctly.

When Martin answered, she blurted out everything. Martin had to slow her down.

"Whoa. Slow down. Tell me exactly what happened."

Calming down some, she told him everything up to where she found the cloth of Laurel's shirt and blood around it.

"You saw blood with the cloth?"

"Yes. Haven't you been listening? It's his shirt and blood. He's hurt and needs help. Our help."

"Maybe it isn't his shirt. You could be wrong about that."

"NO!" she screamed. "I know it's his shirt. We have to do something."

"Like what?" he wanted to know.

"I don't know. Call the police. They'll search for him."

"Sure. Tell the police. While you're at it, don't forget to tell them we're also poachers. Ask them what they're doing this Friday night. Why, they'll ask—oh, no reason, Officer, we're just going to poach Friday night, so I was wondering if you're busy or not."

Margo couldn't believe what she was hearing.

"He's your best friend, you son of a bitch. How dare you talk about him like that."

She hung up on him.

24

Once again Luke and Claire were in the lab with Marcus Quint.

"Back so soon? At this late hour?" Marcus was teasing. "Must be my good looks," he went on to say.

"Must be something," Claire pointed out. "But good looks wasn't what I was thinking."

"Ouch," Marcus responded. "That hurt." Then he started laughing. "How can I help you, like I don't know?" He spotted the tape Luke was holding.

"You guessed it, friend. Another dream. More talking than before, but I think same result," Luke added as he gave Marcus the tape.

"Not a problem. I'll get on it ASAP. I'll yell when I'm done."

When the two detectives entered Willard's office, the captain seemed anxious.

"Something bothering you, Cap?" Luke asked.

"You can say that," was the reply. "The technician team were getting ready to change shifts when Henderson called Martin. She was in a panic because she claims that Champ's missing."

"Wait a minute," Luke said. "Champ's missing? Since when?"

"Since sometime today. Something about the woods behind their house. Go home and get some sleep. Tomorrow go see Henderson and find out what's going on."

XXXXX

Margo Henderson was pacing in the living room not knowing what she should do. Even though she was pissed off at Martin at the way he spoke to her, she knew deep down that he was right.

Imagine her calling the police and they send that bitch she had trouble with. They'd have a field day. No way they'd care if they found Laurel or not.

Alive anyway.

They wouldn't shed any tears. No, she understood what she had to do. Find him herself.

First thing tomorrow when there would be light. Nothing she could do tonight. Except have a drink.

Just one.

The next morning when they were on the highway, Claire said, "I wonder what's going on. I suppose Champ could be missing, but it's hard to believe."

"We'll soon find out one way or another. We'll be there in about ten minutes."

When they did get there, the house looked dark.

"Before we go knocking, let's check the backyard," Luke suggested. Looking around the back, they made their way to the edge of the yard where it met the woods.

"It sure does look spooky," Claire remarked. "I wouldn't want to be lost in that."

"Agreed. Now we'll go knocking."

As they turned to face the house, Claire caught movement. Looking back toward the woods, she saw it again.

"Luke," she said a little too loud. "Look over there and tell me if I'm seeing things."

He looked where she indicated and drew his gun. "No, I see it too. But what is Margo Henderson doing out in the woods this early in the morning?"

"It must be true. She's looking for Champ."

Luke holstered his gun, and they went into the woods after Henderson.

Margo Henderson went into the woods behind her house to continue the search. She approached the tree where she found the cloth.

She was trying to find the blood that would lead her deeper in the woods when she froze.

What was that sound? Like someone or something crunching branches.

Trying to be quiet. But it wouldn't work. She was too smart for that.

Nobody was going to sneak up on her. Nobody.

She hid behind a big tree and waited.

Luke was able to see Henderson up ahead, but when he accidently stepped on a branch and cracked it, she heard the noise and was able to slip away. Now he lost sight of her. She could be hiding anywhere.

Being careful not to make any more noise, he made for the tree he saw Henderson approaching. When he was a few feet away, he stopped dead in his tracks.

Margo Henderson watched Luke Myers approach the tree and stop.

She couldn't believe it. What were the cops doing here? How did they know?

Did Martin break down and call them himself? Did they find out about the poaching and arrest Martin?

Are they here to arrest her also? Martin must have broke.

The cops know about the poaching. They're here to arrest her also.

When she gets her hands on Martin, she'll kill him. But now she was getting a headache.

Very sore. Blacking out.

Claire was coming the opposite direction that Luke took but was coming up empty. No sign of Henderson, but maybe Luke caught up with her.

As she went to join him, she wondered what he was doing at that tree and what he was looking at on the ground. She still couldn't tell as she approached him, and when she put her hand on his shoulder, he jumped.

"My God, you scared the crap out of me! I just saw ten years of my life," Luke said.

Claire was holding back the giggle that was trying to form but said, "Sorry. I didn't know you were preoccupied. What's up anyway?"

"I'm not sure but there definitely is a substance that could well be blood. Also, if you look closely on the bark of that tree, you'll see a tiny piece of what could be cloth or material of some kind. We need to bring these to the lab right away."

Not realizing her nails were raking the bark to which she was leaning on, Margo Henderson began to regain her composure.

When she came to her wits and her headache disappeared, she noticed the bitch along with that other cop.

Her anger was returning at the sight of Claire. Just when she thought nothing else could happen, a voice appeared in her head.

So faint at first. But it built up power. The words were becoming clearer.

"Soon, child. Very soon. Hahahahaha!"

No! The laughing. She couldn't take the laughing. She stormed out of her hiding spot and charged Claire.

XXXXX

Willard couldn't believe what he was told.

"Tell me again what you said. I must be getting old, so I know I must have misunderstood what you just said. Maybe I'm the one who's dreaming."

"I assure you, sir, that you are not dreaming or misunderstood what I said," Marcus Quint was saying. He called Willard instead of Luke because of what he found out from the tapes. "I managed to decipher almost everything that Phil Blake said in his dream. Luke told me earlier tonight that he thought the name Earnest was what it would be. He was right, but what he didn't know was this time there was another name."

"Yes, so you said. How can I tell my best detective that the other name mentioned was Luke. How the heck does that fit in? He's having problems with his own dreams. This is going to tear him apart."

"Listen, Captain. Luke is a friend of mine. All of you are. I don't want anything to ever happen to any of you guys. But my job was to figure out what Phil said in his dreams. I don't know why he mentioned Luke, but he did. I don't know what that means."

"It's all right, Marcus. Of course it's not your fault. I'm just shocked about it, that's all. I'm sure it doesn't mean anything. Thank you for taking care of this quickly."

"Anytime, Captain."

XXXXX

By the time Claire realized that a crazy madwoman was charging her, it was too late for anything. She was bowled over like a bowling pin.

She tripped over a log she hadn't noticed and banged her head on the ground. Moaning with displeasure, Claire was scrambling to her feet.

Henderson was screaming like a banshee and charged again. This time Claire managed to just get out of the way. Even at that, Henderson managed to clip her shoulder.

Shrieking at the miss, Henderson turned and started for Claire again. This time she connected to the forehead of Claire.

When Henderson came toward her, Claire blocked the punch and gave one of her own. Making contact with Margo's chin gave Claire some satisfaction.

While Margo Henderson was rubbing her chin, Claire advanced and punched her square in the face.

Now the two women were standing in front of each other. Claire asked her, "Why are you attacking me, Margo? What have I done?'

"You lying bitch! You know why I attacked you. You're here to bring me back. Well, I won't go back! Not with you!" Just then Henderson held her head and screamed. "I CAN'T TAKE THE VOICE ANY MORE. IT'S DRIVING ME MAD!"

"What voice, Margo? What are you talking about?

"What do you care? You hope I go mad! So they put me away!"

"That's not true, Margo. I do care. I just don't know why you have so much anger against me. I only fought you because you attacked me."

"You're a liar. You hate me, and you want to see me go down."

Before Claire could answer, Henderson held her head.

"Stop it! I won't do it! Get out of my head!"

Claire was at her side. Trying to get a grip, she asked Margo, "What is the voice saying?"

"The voice wants me to kill you."

Then she fainted.

Finally moving from his spot, Luke was beside Claire. "Are you all right. When you banged your head, I thought you were done."

Luke held her and kissed her lips. When he finished, Claire looked at him and said, "Maybe I should get beat up more often."

"No, I don't think so. But we better call for an ambulance."

While they were waiting for the ambulance, Willard buzzed Luke's cell.

"I need to see you in the office right away."

Luke looked at Claire and said, "Wonder what that's all about."

25

Couple of hours later, leaving the emergency room, they headed for the precinct. Willard was staring out his window overlooking the not-so-busy traffic, when Luke and Claire finally showed up.

Turning around, seeing Claire's face, all bruised and bandaged, softened him. He asked her, "How'd you make out at the emergency?"

She replied, "Not bad. Waiting was the long part. Didn't take them long once they got started."

"That's good," he said. "But I'd hate to be the other person."

It hurt Claire's face when she laughed. After they all settled down, the captain turned more serious. He said to them, "Please take a seat. I don't know how to say this, and you must remember, Phil's dream is only that. A dream. They might not mean anything."

Luke spoke up. "Cap, just tell us. What is it?"

"Okay, here goes. Marcus from the lab called me. He managed to figure out what was on the tape. He said the name that Phil was saying was Earnest."

"Yes," Luke answered. "But we already knew that. You didn't call us in for that."

"No," Willard agreed. "I didn't. The reason why I called you in was because there was another name mentioned."

Luke looked at Willard to continue.

Looking directly at Luke, he said, "The other name that he muttered was Luke. Yes, your name. He said the name Luke. Now remember, it might not mean anything. It's only a dream."

Luke was taken aback. "He said my name? But what can it mean? What do I have anything to do with Phil's dreams?"

"That's the point I'm trying to make. You have nothing to do with his dreams. But because he mentioned your name, I had to tell you."

"I appreciate it. I just don't know what to do about it."

"Do? There is nothing to do. Except wait and see what happens."

XXXXX

Luke and Claire were getting out of their vehicle at the emergency parking lot when Luke said, "I think you should talk to Margo alone."

"Alone? But why?"

"It seems she might talk to you. I think there's a connection with the two of you."

"Really? Is that what your psychic mind told you? Or do you know a secret that I don't?"

When they approached the emergency desk, they were informed Margo was released and gone home.

"Okay," Luke said. "She went home. We'll just have to go there and talk to her."

On the way to her place, Claire asked him, "What are you going to be doing?"

"Nothing," he said. "I'll just wait in the car until you're done. I don't think it will take too long."

Arriving at the house, Claire started toward the front door. When she rang the doorbell, she waited a minute to give it time.

Ringing it again, she was about to lose hope when the door opened.

Margo looked terrible. A black-and-blue bruised face. Her upper lip was cut, and her left cheek had a couple of scratches.

Seeing Claire standing in front of her, she threw up her arms in disbelief.

"Why, am I not surprised? You might as well come in."

Having a seat in the kitchen, Margo said, "To what do I owe this expected visit?"

Claire cleared her throat and said, "I just want to ask a few questions. First question would be where's Champ?"

Margo started laughing.

"Where's Champ you ask?" she said in her sarcastic tone. "Who knows where he is. Why do you think I was in the woods. I was looking for him. For all I know, he's probably dead."

"Did you report him missing?" Claire asked.

"Why would I do that? Would you personally go searching for him?"

"Maybe. But some of us would be."

"Where's your partner?" she asked, changing the subject.

"Outside in the car."

"Why didn't he come in?"

"He wanted me to talk to you alone. Since you and I have a history."

"Some history."

"It didn't have to be this way. But you gave us a hard time from the start. Anyway," Claire was saying. "I want to ask you a question about our fight."

"I was waiting for that."

"Well, I was wondering if you remember about that voice you said was in your head."

"I remember vaguely. What about it?"

"You said your head hurt, and it was because of that voice."

"So?"

"What did that voice say to you?"

"I shouldn't be saying anything to you. We're not exactly friends."

"No, but I could take you to the precinct and discuss your part of the poaching gang, along with Champ and Martin. I could arrest you right now and be done with it."

"You know? But how? We were secretive. We were never followed." Her eyes were so big, almost like the deer they poached.

"Never mind how I know. Now, answer the question. What did the voice say to you?"

After a minute or two of silence, Margo finally said, "The voice wanted me to kill you. She also wants your partner dead."

"She?" Claire asked. "It was a she?"

"It sure sounded like that. Also very strong."

"Do you have any idea who it might be?"

"Nope. Not a single clue."

Claire was getting up before saying, "You've been almost helpful. Don't leave town. I probably will be back to ask you questions. Give us a hard time, I won't be so nice the next time."

"Well, don't think this was fun. I'm almost positive it wasn't."

Claire saw herself out.

When Claire sat in the car and they were well under way, she said to Luke, "I managed to get her to say a couple of things that I didn't think I would."

"Really?" Luke replied. "Like what?"

"Champ really is missing. She knows nothing of his whereabouts. She thinks he's dead somewhere."

"I believe that too. I think our friend got him."

Claire looked at him. "That's just awful."

"Yes, it is," Luke agreed with a distaste in his voice. "What else you got?"

"I asked her about the voice in her head."

"You did? She told you anything?"

"Not at first. She said she didn't have to tell me anything because of how well we get along."

Luke smiled at that remark.

"Anyway, I let her know we're onto her about her involvement with the poaching and her goons that she calls friends."

Luke pulled the car on the shoulder and said, "You told her what?"

"You heard me."

"But why would you do that? Now she'll warn everyone, and we'll never catch them in the act."

"Relax, handsome. She doesn't realize we know about Friday. So it's still going to happen. But getting back to the voice, she said it wanted her to kill me."

"The voice told her that?" he asked as he pulled the car back into traffic.

"Yes, but that's not all. She also mentioned that the voice is a woman."

"A woman?" Luke was taken aback. "You're sure?"

"Pretty sure. But she has no idea who it might be. She never heard that voice before. Also, she also said that the voice wants you dead too."

"Wants me dead? Boy, do I feel special."

"It's not funny, Luke. Until we know more about this voice, we should take precaution."

"Precaution? How more cautious can we be?"

"I don't know. Just watch things more closely. Be extra careful."

"Hey," Luke shouted. "Wouldn't it be a blast if that voice and Phil's dream with my name mentioned be connected. That'd be something."

"Don't even joke like that that. I told you already, it's not funny." Claire had a thought herself. "Speaking of dreams, isn't it time you went for yours?"

"Yes, but I'm going to wait."

"Wait for what?"

"After Friday night. If that bust works out, I'll go first thing next week."

XXXXX

Late that night, the hospital was very quiet. Except for monitors making beeping noises in most patient rooms, nothing could be heard.

When Earnest woke up, lying down in the hallway, he slowly tried to get up. So painful, some ribs must have been broken. When he did get up, he had to hold on to the wall for support.

There was no janitor in sight. Also no pails or mops were anywhere to be seen.

As though he imagined it. But he hadn't.

His sore ribs. He could taste blood. His lip must be cut.

Just then Champ and his buddies were walking down the hallway.

As they got closer, he braced himself for the attack he knew would come.

But as they approached, not only did they not attack, but they also actually did not look at him either.

They just walked past with no acknowledgment. That was strange. That never happens.

Wonder what's going on?

Maybe they got tired of beating him up.

As he turned the corner and neared the office, he knew why.

They were in the principal's office getting a tongue lashing. Now he's in greater danger than he's been before.

Phil Blake's eyelids were fluttering but remained closed.

XXXXX

The man with the black pickup truck was anxious. He couldn't wait for Friday night to happen. He was wondering about Champ and if he made any progress with the wooded area.

Deciding to find out, he picked up the phone and dialed the number. Letting it ring many times, he wondered why no one was answering.

That no good for nothing girlfriend of his should be home. Why wasn't she picking up? Was something wrong?

No, he didn't believe that. She was probably out there, helping him. It was a big area.

Maybe they both got attacked by a bear and came to their demise. That was funny. He couldn't stop chuckling about that.

Giving up, he hung up the phone. He would try later. When he got home from work.

XXXXX

Luke and Claire were in Willard's office, telling him what happened with Margo.

"You should have went to see Martin also," the captain was saying.

"We would have," Luke said. "But we didn't want to scare him for Friday night. As long as Margo doesn't say anything, we should be okay still."

Claire said, "Which doesn't leave us with much time. Tomorrow night is it."

Willard answered, "Yes, and the team will be made up tonight. By lunchtime tomorrow, everyone involved will be brought up to speed."

Claire remarked, "That's good, and on that note, maybe we should be heading home and getting a good-night's sleep. Be ready for tomorrow."

Willard added, "I'm all for that. If all goes well, Saturday morning we'll start looking for Champ. That is, if he's not dead by now."

XXXXX

When Champ opened his eyes, he was still groggy. He was chained up from neck to ankles. He couldn't move too much. Even his fingers didn't respond. His wrist was welting from where it was broken.

So tired and sore.

When he looked up, he noticed the dark figure on a chair by the table across the room. His beady red eyes—not bloodshot red but actually red—were staring right at him from underneath that black hood.

Didn't move a muscle. Just stared.

Champ looked over to his left and saw a sight just as disturbing.

An old skeleton, looked badly burned from top to bottom with long, dark hair, sat on a rocking chair. It looked like it was grinning.

Like it was alive or something. But everyone knows skeletons aren't alive.

Then the rocking chair moved. But how?

He looked back at the dark figure. Still there.

Looked back at the skeleton. Chair was rocking like crazy.

Who was making it move? This was impossible.

Then just as the sudden movement began, it stopped. Had he imagined it? No, he didn't think so.

Something weird is going on here.

To top it off, the dark figure rose from the chair. Very slowly, advancing toward Champ. Stopping two feet in front of Champ, the dark figure stared down at him. Through those hateful red eyes.

Then raising both hands, putting them behind the hood, he pulled it off. What Champ saw was enough to almost swallow his tongue.

What the hell was he looking at? He was looking at a face from hell. Burnt to a crisp. He couldn't be human.

Nobody could be alive looking like that. Those red eyes again. Bore into him. But he could make out something else also.

This creature thing, or whatever it was, had a scar on the side of the face. Even though the face was badly burned, he clearly noticed the scar on the face. The fire wasn't enough to rid that mark.

The soul was too deep. But he saw that scar before. Where had he seen it? He knows he saw it.

But from where?

It hit him all of a sudden. High school. That kid from high school. What was his name?

Champ tormented him all the years they were there. What the hell was his name? It was a wimpy name.

Like Herman. No, not Herman. Eugene maybe. Not that either.

When that detective asked him if anyone was after him, he replied no. He thought of that person immediately. Didn't believe it was a threat.

But there he was. Standing in front of him.

Earnest. That's it. The name was Earnest. He's the one standing right here. I'm sorry, Champ thought. *Sorry for everything I've done to you. Please don't kill me.*

Too bad his tongue wasn't working for him to say those words out loud. Not that it would have mattered.

How ironic Champ's death would come at the hands of the one he hated the most.

The dark figure put back on the hood. Then proceeded to move the area rug. Underneath the rug was what looked to be a door.

A door in the floor.

That rhymes. He started laughing in his delusional mind.

A trap door. That's what it was.

His captor opened it up. The stench.

Please don't put me down there.

That's when the dark figure grabbed the chain from behind Champ and dragged him down the trap door.

26

Principal Kim Lacy was at her desk going over some paperwork when suddenly the pen fell from her hands.

She held her head in her hands for a minute, hoping the feeling she just got would recede. When she couldn't take the pressure any longer, she buzzed her receptionist.

"Yes, ma'am, how may I help you?" the receptionist replied.

"Could you come in my office for a moment?"

"Yes, ma'am."

Upon entering the office, the principal said, "I'm not feeling well. Would you be so kind to get me some aspirin, please?"

"Certainly, ma'am," she answered and went quickly to the health care office.

Principal Lacy was having a hard time breathing, trying to will the headache away. She was afraid she was going to have a stroke when suddenly a voice whispered to her.

You know what must be done, child. You will do it now.

And suddenly the voice disappeared.

When the receptionist returned, Principal Kim Lacy was reaching in her drawer.

"Here's some aspirin along with some water. Will there be anything else before I leave for the night?"

Principal Lacy was standing in front of her desk at this point, thanking her and said, "There is one last thing before you go."

By now she was standing next to her receptionist and said, "You could die."

Lacy raised her hand with the scissors she took from her drawer and thrust it deep in the receptionist's heart. The victim didn't see it coming whatsoever, no time for her to scream.

When it was all over, Kim Lacy pulled the scissors out of the body and realized what she had done. Not able to look at her receptionist, she made for the bathroom just off her office.

She was sick for a good twenty minutes before she went to use the phone on her desk.

Willard's team met at the precinct, crowding in his office. They consisted of Luke and Claire, with two other detectives who had to be taken off their own case.

Forty-year-old Dennis Hanely, five feet ten inches. He weighed in about two hundred and thirty-five pounds. Slightly heavy, with thick black hair was leaning against the far wall.

Thirty-seven-year-old James Atkins, junior partner with Dennis Hanely, was six feet two inches tall. Slender, weighing one hundred and eighty-five pounds, sported short blonde hair with thicker eyebrows than his partner.

He would be the better choice to run down a fugitive than Hanely. He was sitting on one of the chairs provided by Willard.

"Just remember, people. No heroics. You work as a team. Now, Dennis and James, you will be in one undercover vehicle. Luke and Claire, you'll be in another vehicle."

Willard took a moment to see the reaction from the detectives. Then he continued, "We need to park at both ends of the street, seeing as how wide open that road is. It doesn't matter who's on what end. You'll be in constant communication with one another."

Watching for more reactions and getting none, he continued once again. "No one, I repeat, no one acts alone. If there's action to be taken, you guys will act together. We want the leader, whoever he is. Do I make myself clear."

He looked at all four detectives to emphasize his point before adding, "The department will provide with everything you'll need. Any questions?"

When none of the detectives said anything, Willard added, "Good. We meet back here at ten thirty sharp tonight. So go home and get some rest. Adjourned."

When they were getting ready to leave, he held Luke back.

He told Luke to have a seat. "I know you and Hanely don't get along at all, but I'm asking you to take the high road. I know he's an idiot, and he always will be, but you're my top man, and I need you to be cool and collective. Just for one night. Think you could manage?"

"I'll try, Cap, but he makes it very hard to be calm. I'll get Claire to pull my ear if I get out of hand."

The captain smiled just as the phone rang.

In the early evening, Martin called Margo and asked her, "Did you hear from Champ yet?"

"Of course I didn't hear from him. I told you he's missing. He's probably dead. That maniac that's killing everyone is sure to get him. He was from the same class, wasn't he? I don't expect to see him anymore."

"Don't talk like that. He'll show up, just in time for tonight. You'll see." Then he hung up.

When Willard answered the phone to a hysterical woman who asked for Luke Myers, the captain held the phone for Luke.

"It's for you, and it sounds important."

"Hello," Luke answered. "This is Luke Myers. How may I help you?

A hysterical lady on the other end trying to control her emotions and blurted out, "I'm sorry to disturb you, Detective Myers, but you see, there's been a murder in my office earlier today, and I was wondering if you and your partner might come right over?"

"A murder in your office, ma'am? May I ask your name first of all?"

"Detective Myers, I thought you would have recognized my voice. After all, I did lend you those photos from the year book in my library."

"Principal Kim Lacy? I'm sorry, ma'am, but I never expected a phone call from you. Tell me what happened?"

"Not over the phone, my office. I'll be waiting." The phone went dead.

Luke handed Willard the phone, saying, "Strange. That was Principal Kim Lacy. She said there was a murder in her office, and she wants me and Claire there right away."

"Do you believe any of her story?"

"I don't know why she would call to lie. We'd better check it out. So much for my rest tonight."

XXXXX

Margo was staring at the receiver thinking what Martin said. "Just in time for tonight." She doubted that very much, but now she didn't feel like going.

Not worth it anymore.

The phone rang again.

What did Martin want this time?

Picking it up, she snarled, "Now what?"

"Hello to you too, dear. Are you ready for tonight?"

"I don't know."

"What does that mean?"

"Laurel's been missing a couple of days. I'm not sure I want to go without him."

Now the Boss understood. Champ was missing. That's why the phone was never answered. She was out looking for him.

Out loud he said, "Yes. Well, he showed up here a little while ago."

"He did?" Margo was shocked.

"Yes, but I sent him on a mission. He'll be back later in time for tonight. We'll be coming in together. I just called to see if you were ready."

"I'll be ready if Laurel is here." And she ended the conversation.

Luke and Claire were entering the high school parking lot when Luke said, "I told you I didn't like going to the principal's office."

Claire responded, "Yes. You sure did. A little birdie must have told you something was going to happen here." And she chuckled.

Walking up the stairs, Kim Lacy was waiting for them at the door to let them in. As they passed her in the hallway, she relocked the door.

"I'm sorry to take you away from your detective work, but I'm afraid I need your assistance. You'll see what I mean when you enter my office."

True to her word, as they opened the door to her office, they could see blood on the floor. As they opened the door wider, they also saw the body.

"Wow," Luke commented. "You weren't kidding about the murder. Would you happen to know who did this?"

"Yes, Detective. I killed her."

Both Luke and Claire stared at the principal in disbelief.

"You did this?" Luke's weak voice blurted.

"Yes," replied Lacy, her face ashen. "Something overcame me, and the next thing I knew, I plunged my scissors into her heart."

"Something overcame you? Was somebody else here with you?" Luke asked.

"No. Nothing like that. I experienced a headache all of a sudden. I never get headaches. But this one was a woozy. Anyway, while I'm dealing with my headache, a voice spoke to me."

"A voice spoke to you?" Luke and Claire were looking at each other. "What did the voice tell you?"

"The voice wanted me to kill my receptionist. I couldn't help myself. As soon as it was over, my headache disappeared."

Claire spoke for the first time. "Tell me something, was the voice that of a woman?"

"Why yes, it was. Do you know something about this?" she asked.

"Not enough I'm afraid. Anyway, we're going to call for the ambulance, and then we'll take you to the precinct. You're going to be asked questions, and they'll want you to tell everything you told us."

While they waited for the ambulance, Luke took a minute to call Willard and explain what happened.

A short time later, the ambulance arrived and took the body away. Luke and Claire brought in Kim Lacy, Willard waiting for them at the doors.

"It's very nice to meet you, Principal Lacy. My two detectives here told me so much about you. I'm Captain Bruce Willard."

They shook hands while Lacy said, "They told you about me. Not good things I would imagine."

"Of course good things. If it wasn't for you, we would never know who to try to protect while these murders are taking place."

"Which reminds me, Captain, how is the investigation going?"

"It's going okay. These things take time, but we have our very best working hard around the clock. Now, if you'll excuse me, I have some matters to attend."

As they watched him leave, Kim Lacy said, "He's such a nice man. A gentleman."

"Aaahh yes, he is. Now, not trying to rush you, but we'll have to bring you through the proper channels. I'm afraid it'll have to be someone else. We're busy tonight and lots to do."

"Of course. I don't want to delay you any more than I already did."

"Nonsense. But we do have to be going."

XXXXX

Hanging up the phone, the Boss was in deep thought.

Champ is missing? How is that possible?

He had to think. How could he make it seem like Champ's with him so she'll come out in the field?

He'll think of something. He always did.

If worse comes to worse, he'll just have to kill her. No problem.

Luke, Claire, and the others were in Willard's office at exactly ten thirty sharp getting last-minute instructions.

Dennis Hanely was standing just inside the door, staring down Luke who was sitting in his normal chair. He must have had the impression, because he turned and smiled at him. Hanely's face reddened and looked away.

Willard saw the transaction and had to smile. "So remember, guys. Teamwork from everybody. I can't emphasize enough, we need to nab the big fish. If we get him, we stop the whole poaching. Period. If you don't work together, we won't get him. That's a guarantee."

Willard stopped a moment to take a sip of water.

"Now people, here on my desk are the radio equipment and walkie-talkies. Make sure your guns are loaded and ready to go. Help yourself."

He watched them all get their gear and set up. Made sure all guns were loaded and all radio, earpieces fit in place, and walkies talked.

As they were leaving, Willard yelled after them, "Good luck, everyone."

When they were in the basement garage parking lot, Luke said, "Listen, guys. We need to be careful around that house. They're nervous people, and if we do one thing wrong, it'll blow up in our face."

He looked at the other two detectives, who remained silent.

"Dennis, you and James take the west end of the street. Claire and I will take the east end of the street."

He looked at them again, and they still gave no expression.

"Any questions?"

Nothing was said.

"Okay. Let's get moving before we're late."

XXXXX

The Boss was pacing in his living room. How to deal with Champ missing.

Whatever could have happened to him? No time to figure that out. He had to deal with the problem at hand.

Coming with an idea, he stopped pacing. Looking at the time, he knew it was time to leave.

Taking his keys off the hook from the kitchen wall, he left the house.

Getting into his black pickup truck, he started the engine and backed up.

XXXXX

Luke, being in the lead with the other detectives following, said to Claire, "The reason I took the east end is because we'll be coming in from the west, and we could check out the house as we pass by it."

"That's a good idea," Claire answered. "We also know the house."

"Exactly," Luke said. "Also, if we get there early enough, we'll see all the vehicles come right by us. We'll have an idea of what we're dealing with."

Claire was beaming. "You're always thinking."

At the other end of the street, Hanely was drinking coffee out of a Styrofoam cup. He turned to look at Atkins and said, "That Mr. Know-It-All, too good for everyone else, is going to get his one day. In fact, when the time comes for action, I'll act. You can join me or stick to the original plan. I'll show him one way or another."

Atkins said, "I don't know if you should; Willard's in charge. You would have to answer to him."

"Who cares about Willard? They stick up for each other. If one's against me, then both are against me."

James was quiet. He didn't know how to calm his partner down when he got like this. He drank his coffee.

Luke and Claire were waiting for any sign to indicate something's going down tonight. While they were waiting, Claire said, "You know, dear, at one point we're going to have to make heads or tails about that voice. That's two people that we know of that acted on the dark side because of it."

"I know," Luke said. "I was thinking—" Just then two pickup trucks drove by. Not only that, but the second pickup was carrying Angelo Martin.

The game was on.

The Boss in the black pickup truck drove into Champ's driveway as the second pickup parked right next to it.

The Boss said to the other driver, "Marc. You take your pick up and drive around the block. There's an opening from that side; we'll be able to drive right in. I'll meet you in a few minutes. Oh, make sure Martin here doesn't try anything funny. If he does, shoot him."

Martin was sweating, knowing nothing good will come of this night.

Watching him leave, the Boss went to ring the doorbell to the front door.

When Margo answered, he asked, "Are you ready?"

"Where's Laurel?" she demanded.

"He went with Marc and Martin to show us the way in. You'll come with me to meet them there."

"All right. I'll go with you, only because Laurel's there."

"Good. Let's get going."

All four detectives saw what was going on, and Luke radioed Hanely.

"He's just leaving. We'll wait a few minutes. Then I'll go around from this end; you go around the opposite way. We'll try to block them in."

The Boss took Margo in his pickup and went around the block. He saw the opening where Marc went through and aimed his truck to the same spot.

He parked beside Marc's truck and slid out the door.

He said to Margo, "You wait here until I come back for you."

Margo watched him go talk with Marc, wondering where Laurel is. She could just make out Martin's head between the two men.

Not being able to see Laurel, she was frantic with worry. Deciding what she should do, the Boss came back for her.

"You can get out now," he told her. "Come around to this side with me."

"What about Laurel? Where is he?" She wanted to know.

"He's in the bush setting up so we know where to go."

"He's in the woods all alone? In the dark? You were supposed to already know where in the woods to go. You don't have Laurel at all, do you? It was all lies so I'd come out tonight!"

In that instant, before Margo could make a move, the Boss grabbed her by the hair and pulled her to him.

She was about to scream when he pulled out his gun and shoved it roughly into her ribs. "You stay quiet and do what I say, you little bitch. Any sudden moves and I'll put a few holes in you. *Got it?*"

Luke and Claire arrived at the same spot that the Boss used, thirty seconds before Hanely and Atkins got there.

The detectives rechecked their handguns to make sure they were loaded.

When they met outside, Luke said, "We'll split up in two teams. We'll stay east. Hanely, you and Atkins keep to the west side—" But before he could finish, Hanely darted toward the black pickup truck.

"Where are you going?" Luke shouted. "Get back here!"

But Hanely paid no heed. He continued on his way, never looking back.

Luke followed Hanely and said to the other detectives, "Let's go!"

Margo was shoved ahead with a gun at her back when the Boss said, "Stop. This is a good spot. Marc, take fat boy with you back for the truck. We'll put the generator here. Then I'll go back for mine and do the same."

So Marc pointed his gun at Martin and made him march back through from which they came.

As they were trampling in the bush, Marc said, "Be quiet, fat boy. You're scaring all the meat away. You don't want me to waste you, do you?"

So Martin walked more quietly, shaking in his skin.

He's going to die tonight, he thought.

How did I ever get into this mess? How will I ever get out of it? What about Margo? What will happen to her? I don't like her, but I don't want her to die.

As he turned slightly, he thought he heard something.

Hanely instantly heard a ruckus up ahead somewhere but couldn't tell how far away. But his mind was elsewhere. How dare Myers boss him around. Giving him orders like he was a big man.

Who does he think he is anyway?

Hearing that noise again brought him back to reality. He hid among the trees. Getting his gun ready, he waited.

"Can't you be quieter? How are we supposed to get deer tonight if you're scaring them away?" Marc complained.

Martin said, "I'm sorry. Trying to be quiet is hard when there's loose twigs everywhere."

"I don't want to hear excuses. Just keep going."

Marc was thinking how quiet it got all of a sudden. He wished they'd get this over with. Being out here in the woods this time of night was not his idea of fun. He only did this because the Boss promised he'd share a big part of the profit with him.

At last, the truck was in sight. Fifteen more steps and he would be at the driver's door.

He nudged Martin so hard with the barrel of the gun that he lost his balance and fell roughly on his hands and knees.

Hanely heard their footsteps for a while now, but now they were close enough that from his hiding spot, he could touch Marc if he chose to.

That's exactly what he did when Martin fell on the ground.

Hanely attacked, knocking Marc off balance. With Marc still holding the gun, Hanely was quickly upon him. Grabbing each other, both men were wrestling, trying to get the upper hand.

Hanely held Marc's wrist that held the gun. He was banging that hand against the ground, but Marc still wouldn't let go. The two men continued to roll around on each other, but neither would give in.

Hanely managed to get his hand over Marc's trigger hand but still couldn't make him let go. Struggling to get possession of the gun, Hanely squeezed harder.

Everything was suddenly quiet as two shots were fired.

Martin froze when the shots rang; Hanely and Marc just stared at each other. But Hanely managed to get up with splotches of Marc's blood dripping from him.

When he stood erect, he noticed that Marc was dead. Hanely turned around to see Luke Myers glaring at him.

27

When the two shots were fired, the Boss grabbed Margo's wrists tightly. They were held so firmly that you could see red welts starting to form.

She was about to scream when the Boss punched her square between the eyes with the gun hand. She dropped to the ground instantly.

He looked at her for a moment before giving her one last kick. Bored with her, he turned his attention toward his truck.

What happened? Why did Marc fire? Did fat boy try to make a break for it?

He was about to go that way, when he heard shouting. He decided to stay back and out of view.

When Luke and Claire arrived at the scene, Hanely and Marc were wrestling on the ground.

Claire quickly went to Martin to steer him out of harm's way.

When all three were safely behind Marc's truck, the two shots were fired. Everything was quiet after that. Luke had already left the safety of the truck and was standing behind Hanely.

Now, when Hanely turned around, he was point-blank face-to-face with Luke.

"Why did you do it, Hanely?" Luke was not impressed. "Why did you go against our plan to work together?"

"Work together?" Hanely repeated. "With you? Are you crazy? You think I'm actually going to work with you?" Hanely laughed like he was insane. "I've been on the force years before you, boy. I'm more than a decade older. Now I'm going to take orders from a kid? I don't think so!"

"No, you'd rather just go ahead and kill someone instead. Nice move. Now we'll never get whoever their leader is, thanks to you. Hanely, you can go now. You're off the case."

With that said, Luke turned and walked away. Meanwhile, Claire was busy with Martin. "You hang in right here. I'll be back for you. Stay put. Understand?"

"Like where am I going to go? It's all woods that way."

Claire left to see Luke.

"We're not finished yet, partner. We still have the Boss in the woods. He's also got a gun on Margo."

"I almost forgot. Let's go."

The Boss heard enough. He left Margo where she lay out cold. A vicious punch and kick will do that to a person.

Fat kid ratted him out. Marc was dead. It was time to go. Can't go south. It's blocked. Turn around and head north, deeper into the woods.

He started north and kept to the trees. He could still get out of this.

When Luke was ready to look for the Boss and Margo, he forgot Martin was there.

"Martin," Luke said. "You'll have to come with us. Don't want to have to worry about you later."

"But I don't want to go in the woods. It's scary at night," he complained.

"No arguing. You're coming with us, and that's final. Besides, Margo may need you. She's in danger, and we need your help to find her."

So they trudged on. Luke was first, followed by Claire and Martin, who walked side by side.

Just as Luke's flashlight beam began to get weak, he thought the light found something, or someone.

Lying in a heap, Margo was still unconscious. Luke was at her side feeling for a pulse. "Still alive, but barely," he yelled. "Call the ambulance, Claire; I'm going ahead to investigate."

So he continued his futile search. There was no hope.

Whoever the ringmaster is, he's long gone.

Exhausted, he turned around and made his way toward Claire. When Claire saw him coming back, she met him halfway, knowing it was bad news.

"He could be anywhere in the woods. If he knows his way, we'll never find him."

Claire held his hand. It was no use to say anything.

Reaching Margo, he could see there was no change.

"Actually," he said looking at his partner. "He did make a mistake. Thinking no one knew about his poaching, he parked out in the open. Be right back."

He made his way to the black pickup truck.

The Boss knew that if he kept still long enough, they wouldn't find him.

He was right. They retreated. He'll have to circle around from the east, in about an hour or two, get his truck and get the hell out of here.

Oh no, my truck. They'll be able to find out who I am. Of all the crummy luck. Well, what's done is done.

He'll think of something later. He always did. In the meantime, he continued north. No way would he use light now.

Those damn detectives are a nuisance. They see everything. Especially Luke Myers. He's sneaky. His partner isn't bad either, but Myers is the more dangerous one of the two.

The Boss continued north, stopping beside a boulder.

Staying low, he looked back the way he came, to see if he was being followed.

Nothing.

They must have given up for good. He stood up and slowly made his way. Until he thought he heard something.

After Luke got off the phone with Willard, he walked to Claire and said, "I just spoke with the cap. He's checking with the Ministry of Transportation, about the black pickup. In the meantime, he wants us back in the office."

Looking at Martin, he said, "You'll be coming with us also."

"Me?" Martin was acting so surprised. "What did I do?"

"Oh nothing," Luke replied. "We just like your company. We're also going to ask you questions, and you better have some answers."

Martin began to shake. His hands were trembling, so he put them in his pockets. But he couldn't stop the sweating from his forehead.

"Martin," Claire said. "You look really worried. Something we should know?"

"N-noo," he was stuttering badly. But it was plain to see that he was hiding something.

Shortly thereafter, the ambulance crew arrived, and they rushed to Margo with a gurney and medical supplies.

After checking with the attendants, Luke approached Claire and said, "Time to go. We're done here."

The noise came from somewhere up ahead. It sounded like a low growl but didn't know for sure.

Not knowing what to do, the Boss stood still and waited. Not hearing it any longer, he decided to continue north.

Taking a break, he sat on a boulder when he heard the noise again. Now he was starting to panic.

Something close by. Something dangerous. Need to keep moving. Continuing north, he realized he didn't hear any crickets or frogs. As a matter of fact, he didn't hear any insects. Checking his watch, already two thirty.

He was walking in the woods for two hours. But now he doesn't know where he is. Lost. That growl.

He was spooked because of that damn growl. Now he doesn't know which direction he going. Then he saw it.

When they arrived at the office, Claire was exhausted. Looking up from what he was doing, Willard noticed how dead-beat tired Claire was. That's when he noticed Martin in his office.

"I take it Martin has something to say?" he asked.

"I hope," Luke responded. "He may have some information as to who the leader is."

Putting Martin on the spot, he became fidgety.

"So what about it, Martin? Who's the captain on your team?" Luke asked him. Now Martin was sweating in his shoes.

"I don't know who the Boss is. Names are never mentioned. We only hear from him a couple of days before the hunt."

Martin was drenched in sweat from head to toe. "Honest, guys. He always goes by the name Boss. That's all I know."

Luke studied Martin before he said, "I believe you, Martin, which is why I'm letting you go home."

"You are?" he exclaimed. "Thank you!"

"Leave now, before I change my mind!"

"Don't have to tell me twice." And he left.

Watching Martin leave, Willard said to Luke, "I have a team keeping an eye on that black pickup truck. They'll stay the whole night if they have to. Meanwhile, I sent that license plate you gave me to MTO, and we should hear something tomorrow. Which brings me to another question. What the hell happened out there? It was supposed to go smooth. We should have caught everyone involved. What went wrong?"

"Hanely went wrong. He refuses to take orders from me because he's much older. Anyway, I kicked him off the rest of the case."

"That doesn't matter," Willard went on to say. "He'll have more than that to worry about. I'm going to put an end to this once and for all."

"Great," Luke said. "But now, I'm taking Claire home. She's half-asleep."

A cabin. The Boss was looking at a cabin or shack in the middle of the damn woods.

Who the hell lives way out here?

Being cautious, he started toward the shack. Reaching it, he stopped. Looking around, there was no one to be seen. Spotting a window on this side of the shack, he peered in.

Too dark. Couldn't see a thing.

He used his sleeve to clean the window, when suddenly he saw a black hood with what looked to be red eyes, reflected in the glass. Turning around very slowly, he was face-to-face with *the dark figure.*

28

When Hanely and Atkins were taken off the case, they didn't entirely leave. Driving down the street in a different spot than before, they parked their car and waited.

Blowing smoke from a cigarette he just lit, Hanely said, "That young detective thinks he got the best of me, but he doesn't know who he's messing with."

"What are you going to do?" asked Atkins. He didn't think he was going to like the answer.

"Do? What am I going to do, you ask?" He took another drag of his cigarette. "I'm going to solve this case on my own. I'm going to catch whoever it was that escaped into the woods; then I'll catch that serial killer also. We'll see how long it'll take to wipe that smile off his damn face."

Hanely glanced at Atkins and said, "Are you with me?"

Atkins was as nervous as can be, replying, "I don't think you should be doing that. Lots of trouble will come out of this."

"I should have known you'd chicken out. Always doing what you're told. Don't forget to kiss Willard's shoes when you get back. Now get out. Our partnership is over."

"Come on, Hanely. That's not what I meant. It's just that you're going to retire soon, and you shouldn't jeopardize that."

Drawing his gun, Hanely pointed it at Atkins square in the face and said, "If you don't leave now, I'll blow your brains all over the front seat." He was cocking his gun when he said, "Leave now!"

Slowly Atkins opened the door and got out. Walking down the road, he turned to see Hanely watching him every step of the way.

The black hood with the red eyes was a hell of a lot more sadistic looking up close than just a reflection from a window. Frozen, the Boss remained a statue when the dark figure grabbed him in a flash, holding him by his throat. Lifting him up a good eight inches off the ground, the dark figure was pressing him up against the glass.

The Boss thought for sure he would get thrown clean through the window, when suddenly he flew ten feet away. When he stopped rolling, he looked up to see the dark figure watching him. The Boss scrambled on to his feet, all bruised and sore.

Seeing his chance, he started to run away from his attacker. But because of his injuries and the fact that he was lost and scared, he didn't know where he was heading.

Any place, other than where that beast is, would be good. But how can anyone or anything have eyes like that. Unless that actually is the devil. What am I dealing with? How did it survive? How long did it exist? Is anyone or anything in that shack?

A lot of questions arose when suddenly he stumbled and rolled down a little hill. When he got his composure and took in his bearings, he noticed he was near water.

In all the times he's been in the woods, not once had he encountered water. Where the hell was he?

The low growl. No doubt it came from his attacker.

Leaning against a tree so he wouldn't fall, something brushed his leg. Looking down, he saw an arrow.

An arrow nicked his leg. A small scratch. Didn't even hurt. But who would be throwing arrows? That beast thing?

Who else is out here?

He forced himself to drag his feet, until he got to the next big tree. Stopping to catch his breath, he noticed his vision blurring. Falling to his knees, he felt sick to his stomach, heaving. Breaking into a sweat, he tried to make it to the water. About two feet from the water, he dropped to his knees. With a sweat he's never known before, he fell on the ground face-first.

Reaching with an outstretched hand, his index finger touched the edge of the swamp. That was the last thing he knew.

XXXX

Hanely waited until everyone was gone, then got out of the car, and made his way to the black pickup. Starting his way into the woods, he made sure his flashlight was strong. Heading north, he made his way through brushes and trees. Finding a path, he followed it until it turned to bush.

Taking a break, he wondered which way to go. Deciding to stay north, he continued slowly and stayed close to the trees.

Never being in the woods this late at night was a little frightening; maybe it wasn't such a bright idea. But he couldn't back down now. Not after his performance with his former partner. He has to see this to the end.

As he continued north, he heard a twig snap, which made him stop. He listened for a couple of minutes but couldn't hear anything else.

He continued once again.

XXXXX

When the sheep made a break for it, after he was thrown about ten feet, the dark figure held the arrow using it only once before. The dark figure loved the arrow. Doesn't know why it didn't get used more often. Maybe it wasn't practical.

Anyway, following the enemy until the sheep got tired, the dark figure attacked with the arrow. Watching the puny human thrash around in pain was amusement enough. Getting tired of this game, the dark figure left.

Knowing the sheep will die soon, other matters are more important. Mother, for instance. She hasn't been too upset lately. Which was good.

A quiet Mother is a happy Mother.

Returning to the shack, the dark figure entered and took his seat in the far corner. Everything settled down and became quiet.

The rocking chair moved.

XXXXX

Hanely made his way up a hill and around a bend when he believed to come to some kind of clearing. He noticed a small building, maybe a shack or cabin, so he killed the light and hid behind a tree.

Waiting a good thirty minutes, nothing of the ordinary happened, so slowly he stepped out into the clearing and made his way to the shack.

As he approached the window, he peered inside but couldn't make anything out. It was black inside so it must have been empty.

Leaving the shack and continuing north, he wondered if anyone lived there. Turning his flashlight back on, he pushed forward, but one tree looked the same as all the other trees, and made very difficult to remember the way back.

Twenty minutes later, very tired, hungry and thirsty, he thought he came across water.

Lots of it.

Licking his lips, he started toward it. When he stumbled upon the body.

29

THE NEXT MORNING, WILLARD couldn't believe what he was reading. He just got the report from MTO about who that black pickup truck belonged to.

While he dialed Luke's number, there was a soft knock, and then his door opened quietly; a clerk stuck her head inside to inform Willard he had company, and it was important.

Waving them in, Luke answered the phone, and Willard put him on hold. Looking at the intruder, Willard said, "Mrs. Haswell, it's nice to see you again. How may I help you?"

Diana Haswell made her way to Willard's desk, putting a box on it, saying, "I'm sorry to barge in on you like this but would Claire Davis be in?"

"She's not in yet, but will be shortly. I've got them on the phone now, so it won't be long."

"Thank you very much. I hope it's not a bother."

"None at all. Please, have a seat."

Getting back on the phone, he said to Luke, "Better get in quick with your partner. Diana Haswell is here, and she's asking for Claire."

"Wow, wonder what's up. We're leaving now," Luke answered.

Entering Willard's office, Luke and Claire noticed a box on the captain's desk. Sitting in a chair where Luke normally sat, was Diana Haswell.

Claire instinctively went to her friend's side before asking, "Diana, it's good to see you again. But are you here on bad news? What's wrong?"

"It's good to see you also, Claire. I don't know if it's bad news or not. I'm hoping it'll help you solve your case."

Both Luke and Claire were puzzled. "I don't understand," Claire went on to say. "What'll help solve our case?"

Diana put her hand on the box and said, "This box. I went through Larry's office in the den. Getting rid of some of his things, I came across this photo album when he was in high school. You did say the killer is believed to be one of his classmates. Is that still true?" she asked.

"Yes," replied Claire. "We still believe that."

"Have you gotten any closer to who it may be," she asked.

"No, not yet. But progress is being made."

"Well, maybe you can go over these photos, see if it'll help. Who knows, maybe there's pictures that you haven't seen yet.

Anyway, I'll leave you to your investigation. Sorry to have bothered you."

With that, Diana got up from her seat and started for the door.

Claire said, "I'll see you out."

Watching them leave, Luke turned to Willard, asking, "What did you make of that? Is it possible we're missing some photos?"

"Maybe. You won't know until you check that box out. Anything is better than nothing."

"I suppose you're right. But I'll have to get Claire to check that box. I have to be going home and get ready for my appointment."

"Appointment?" Willard asked.

"For my dreams. At the clinic. It's time I get my dreams looked at again."

"Right. I hope everything goes well for you."

"Thanks, Cap."

"Send Claire back in before you do leave."

Walking Diana to her car outside, she said to her friend, "Diana. You're never a bother. You come down here anytime you want. Thank you for those photos. We definitely will go through them."

"I know you will, Claire. That's why I like you so much. You never let me down. But I do have to get going. Please, come visit me with Luke some time. It'll be nice."

"Yes, we will. Thank you again."

As Diana was leaving, Luke stepped outside and was beside Claire. Watching her go, Luke said, "Did you girls have a nice chat?"

"As a matter of fact, we did. She invited us to go visit her someday. What about you? What are you up to?"

"I'm going home to get ready for my appointment."

"That's right. Today's the day. Am I coming with you?"

"No, you're not. As a matter of fact, I need you to stay here and go over that box. Check for any new photos. We could have missed some."

"All right. I promised Diana I would anyway. If I find out anything interesting, I'll let you know. In the meantime, get out of here."

"Besides," Luke continued, "the cap wants to see you."

"He does? Did he say why?" she asked.

"No. Nothing at all. Probably to check the box, just like I told you. Anyway, I have to run along. Hope you find something."

Stopping at Mary's Coffee and Doughnut Shop, James Atkins was considering his next option. Should he just forget about his former partner, or should he tell Willard?

Maybe forget the department and leave altogether. There wasn't anything for him here otherwise.

It was probably the toughest choice he's had to make. Somebody's life could be at stake. If it was, it was his duty to report it. Or act on it.

Finishing his coffee, he knew what he had to do. Leaving the coffee shop, he got in his vehicle that he stopped at home to get and headed down the highway.

XXXXX

With no watch since he lost it in all the ruckus that happened to him during the night, and the sun that was beading directly in his face, Hanely had no idea what time it was—except that it was no longer night; the sun was hurting his eyes.

Shielding his face, he took in his surroundings and noticed the body. Remembering the night's events, everything came to place. Checking for a pulse, he found none.

Looking at the face, he realized he never saw him before. Maybe he was in the police records, but in the meantime, he checked the deceased's pockets for a wallet but found no identification.

That'll have to wait.

Then he remembered the shack. He made his way slowly toward it, very slowly. As he approached it, he wondered if somebody lived there and how many if they did.

Making his way toward the window on the door side of the shack, he peered inside but couldn't see anything. Cleaning the window with the sleeve of his jacket, it made for a better view.

He saw a small room, with a table in the near corner and a couple of chairs. Empty in the middle, he noticed an old rocking chair in the far corner.

But what was that sitting in it? A skeleton? No, it couldn't be. Why would there be a skeleton, in an old rocking chair, in plain view?

Maybe he should have a closer look. Going to the door, he gave a little tap. Knowing nobody would answer, he slowly turned the knob. When he pushed the door in, it creaked.

Taking two steps in, he yelled, "Hello, is anybody here?"

Expecting no answer, he closed the door behind him and took two more steps in. Now standing in the middle of the room, he took everything in.

Looking at the rocking chair more closely, there indeed was a skeleton sitting in it. A female it appeared, judging by the long dark hair. Still as can be, it didn't look threatening, but it was creepy just the same.

Except for the furniture that he saw through the window, the rest of the room looked bare. Noticing something on the wall behind him, where the table and chairs were, he strolled to have a better look.

Wow. A whole row of chains. Why are they here? Who is using them? For what purpose?

At the far end of the chains, something else caught his attention. Taking a closer look, he noticed it was a bird cage. The door of the cage was ripped off, and on closer inspection, there seemed to be blood on the floor of the cage.

So, somebody does live here.

His skin was crawling. What had he stumbled into? Thinking he heard something, he turned around to see nothing there.

The skeleton. Did the skeleton have a grin on her face before? He didn't think so. But she did now. He must have imagined it.

Getting freaked out, he turned to leave. But the sight before him was enough to add twenty years to his life.

XXXXX

It would take about fifteen minutes to reach Champ's place. James Atkins would have plenty of time to figure out a plan of action.

Thinking about the way Hanely treated him, he didn't know if he should help or not, but he knew deep down he wouldn't betray him.

XXXXX

While Claire and Willard were sorting through the box of photos, Willard said, "I received the answer to who owns that black pickup truck. Here's his name and work address, there was no house address listing."

Looking at the information, Claire's eyes widened. "Are you sure about this? I never would have thought he'd be involved."

"We're positive. I had them check it three times. All three times, we got the same answer. But that's tomorrow. Today, we finish this job. Kapeesh?"

"I understand."

"If you get there before it's too late, go see Margo Henderson. Maybe she can add something that Angelo Martin couldn't."

"Will do, boss man. In the meantime, let's check these photos. There sure are plenty."

"One more thing," Willard went on to say. "I want Hanely in my office first thing in the morning."

"Yes, sir," Claire replied.

XXXXX

A few minutes before getting to Champ's place, James Atkins knew exactly what he was going to do.

Just before going home, Luke ended up at Mary's Coffee and Doughnut Shop. Had he gotten there ten minutes earlier, he would have ran smack into James Atkins.

He got his coffee and sat in the far corner, exactly the same table Atkins sat in earlier, and started sipping.

His mind was wandering into the past. He never saw eye to eye with Hanely, and everyone at the precinct knew it. Hanely was hot tempered and didn't like taking orders from anyone.

That was the main reason Luke was made into lead detective over Hanely. Mainly because Luke followed protocol, while Hanely did not.

Luke didn't ask to be lead detective. They gave it to him. Hanely was not a team player. Last night proved it. They would have had the Boss if Hanely followed their plans.

Back to the present, he noticed his coffee almost empty. He got up and left.

On his way home getting ready for the clinic, Luke couldn't understand why Hanely has so much hatred still. But Luke couldn't think about that now. He had to get ready for his appointment, and he didn't want to miss it.

Showering and shaving, he was ready. Getting his keys off the kitchen wall, he made for the car still thinking about Hanely.

XXXXX

"Boy, we've been at this for one hour and some change, and not even getting close, we still have half the box, but so far we recognize all the photos. I hope it's not a dead end," said Claire, wiping at her brows. It was getting warm in Willard's office, and her face was sweating.

"I hope it's not a dead end either, but we have to check all the photos. If there's just one that's different, it could mean finding the killer."

"I know you're right, but we need coffee and something to eat. Otherwise, I'm not going to make it much longer."

"I suppose you're right. Okay, we'll take a break. I know a fast place around the corner; then we'll come right back. Let's go."

XXXXX

Reaching his destination, he parked right beside the pickup truck. For the truck and the police vehicle Hanely was driving to still be here, something must be wrong.

Getting out, he walked slowly the way they saw that henchman with Angelo Martin coming out from.

When he walked a few minutes, he noticed the ground all marked up, as though there was a battle. Bending down, he examined the footprints.

Most were scattered, confusing him, but he managed to keep track of one set that led north.

He was checking to see if his gun was loaded and his flashlight working, hoping he wouldn't need it. He still had a good two hours of daylight left and proceeded.

When Atkins got out of his car, the two detectives watching the pickup noticed. Both alert, they took in everything Atkins did.

"What the hell is Atkins doing here? We better warn Willard," the detective behind the wheel said.

After confirming with the captain, he turned to his partner and said, "We're to stay put and continue to watch the pickup until further notice."

XXXXX

"That was my two men watching the pickup. They say James Atkins just arrived at the scene and went into the woods."

Willard sipped more of his coffee before continuing, "Why in Sam hill is he there? Another two hours and it'll be dark. What's he up to? What does he expect to find?"

Claire waited until he was done. "I'm not sure I know the answer to that, Cap, but something seems to be up. In the meantime, I might have found something!"

XXXXX

When Atkins continued following footprints, he found it wasn't difficult. Broken branches and twigs matched the same path the footprints brought him.

He was moving at a quick pace, hoping the search will shortly come to an end.

About an hour later, daylight beginning to lose its edge, he rounded a path that led up a hill, and below he was in a clearing.

A shack. Then he heard three gunshots.

XXXXX

Willard bent over Claire and asked, "What have you got?"

"Not sure exactly, but these three photos, we never saw them before. One of them could be the killer."

Willard picked up the book that had those three photos to examine them more closely.

Ben Mosely. Jack Barnard. Earnest Connelly.

XXXXX

Hanely turned around to see a dark figure looming over him with a hunting knife. Backing up to stay away from whatever that thing was, he ended up being cornered with that thing in front and the skeleton in the rocking chair behind him.

He took his gun out and at point-blank range fired three rounds. He made three hits, all in the chest, but that freak was still coming toward him.

He shot another three rounds in the chest and still couldn't drop that thing from hell. Turning around, he dashed for the window beside the rocking chair, but in that instant, he felt the blade of the knife enter his shoulder blade.

He fell hard on the floor, just in front of the window he was so desperately trying to jump through. He reached up to touch the window, but the dark figure had reached him and pulled Hanely up from his collar and threw him again hard on the floor.

The landing of the throw was not good. He fell on his bad shoulder, and it took him a few minutes to slowly get up in a sitting position.

At that same moment, the dark figure, grabbed him roughly by the hair and lifted Hanely up six inches off the floor.

Hanely screamed so loud, if he was surrounded by neighbors, everyone would be outside to see what was happening. But being in the woods, his loudest scream was like whispering in someone's ear.

With the blade of the knife, the dark figure finished the job and let the body drop to the floor. Walking slowly, the dark figure dragged the body by the hair, opened the trapdoor and pushed him down the stairs.

When the dark figure was satisfied the body hit bottom, the trapdoor was slammed shut.

30

Arriving at Havenburg General Clinic, Luke shut the engine off. Taking a minute before getting out, he looked at the building in front of him.

He wondered how many more weeks of therapy he'll have to endure. Sighing, he opened his door and slowly made his way to the front entrance of the building.

Pushing his way to the desk in the lobby, he greeted the registered nurse and announced his arrival. He never saw this receptionist before and wondered if there was anything wrong with the one he knew.

Waiting for Dr. Karen Lamford, he took a seat and picked up a magazine. Browsing through the pages, he really wasn't paying attention to the articles. He was more focused on Hanely, why he did something so stupid as to go in the woods at night all alone.

While he was contemplating this, he never noticed someone standing in front of him.

"I've heard of being stood up, but this is ridiculous."

Startled at the voice, Luke actually dropped the magazine. "I'm sorry," he said. "I was preoccupied and didn't hear you come in."

"I suppose I can forgive you this time, provided it doesn't happen again," she needled. "Now, why don't we get you to your room and get ready. Would that be okay?"

"Sure, not a problem. Lead the way, lady. I'm right behind you."

XXXXX

"Earnest Connelly? I wonder if that's the same Earnest that Phil kept saying in his dreams. How the plot thickens. Okay, you could rule out Ben Mosely. He looks strong and muscular, doesn't fit the pattern. However, Jack Barnard and Earnest Connelly both look small and fragile. They even wear glasses, like nerds. Have those two checked out first. If one of these three is our killer, I'll bet on the latter two. But make sure you check on Earnest, in case it is connected to Phil's dream."

"Not a problem, Cap. It'll all get looked into."

Claire picked up the book and ripped the out the page with the photos and then put the book back in the box.

Looking at the three photos again, she noticed the two nerdy-looking boys lived two blocks from each other. The third one lived much farther away.

Claire said to Willard, "I should have time to check up on these two addresses. But if anything comes out of this, will have to wait until tomorrow. I'm really bushed. It was a long day."

"Actually, wait until tomorrow; that way you'll have Luke's help. It'll go faster."

"Boss, you're the greatest."

"I know."

When Luke finished undressing and putting the ever oh so familiar gown on, Karen Lamford stepped into the room.

"Are you all settled in?" she asked.

"As ready as I'll ever be I suppose. I just don't like coming to these places. I wish it would be over soon. That would be a big weight off my shoulders."

"I wouldn't worry too much about that, Luke. As I told you the first time you came here, we get results on a very high percentage of patients. I'm sure we'll get to the bottom of your dreams in the very near future."

"I hope you're right, Karen. Anyway, I'm ready anytime you are."

Karen smiled. "Okay. Let's get started."

XXXXX

When Atkins heard the three shots, he was stunned.

Who shot those rounds?

Getting closer to the window, he heard three more shots; they definitely came from that shack. As he got to the window, he heard his former partner scream.

Rooted to the spot, he gazed in the window and saw what was unfolding. Hanely was dangling from his feet, being stabbed to death.

Atkins's eyes wandered to the rocking chair and noticed a skeleton. A skeleton with a grin. As though the skeleton was alive.

A thump took him away from the skeleton.

He saw Hanely's body being dragged to what seemed to be a trapdoor and was then roughly thrown down the steps.

After that, he caved in, bent down on his knees, and vomited.

When he was finished, he got up and ran. He ran and didn't stop until he got to his car, got in, and with squealing tires, sped away.

XXXXX

As before, the two assistants came in the room to prep him. They strapped him to the bed so he wouldn't thrash his hands in case the dreams got intense.

Next, they attached wires to his brain to get the appropriate readings. When this was all completed and the two assistants departed, Karen Lamford slipped into the room to check on her patient.

"How are you doing? I had my helpers putting more wires on your brain, hoping more of your dream will be revealed. I hope you're not too uncomfortable," she said.

"I'm not too bad right now, but it's difficult when you can't move. I hope the night goes quickly on a positive note. It'll be nice to get this over with."

"I agree with you on that remark. Now, I'll give you a sedative to relax you and to get this show on the road. Good luck."

On her way home from the precinct, Claire stopped at the emergency center to see Margo. Given directions to her room, Claire slowly made her way.

Tapping on the door and getting no response, she slowly turned the knob and peeked in. Margo was sound asleep, but that didn't stop Claire from entering.

Looking down at the sleeping girl, Claire could make out some bruising on her face. Whatever else she couldn't see was covered in bandages.

The nurse warned her that Margo was heavily sedated and that she probably would not wake up to answer questions. Claire stayed another minute before deciding to leave. With the police knowing the identity of the Boss, it wasn't an emergency to talk to Margo.

It could wait.

Around ten o'clock that night Willard received a phone call from the two detectives watching the pickup truck.

"What have you got?" he said.

"James Atkins took off like a bat out of hell. He hasn't returned, and that was an hour and a half ago. What should we do?"

"I take it the pickup is still there?"

"Yes, sir."

"Go home. We know who it belongs to, so don't worry about it anymore. Get a good sleep and we'll see you tomorrow."

31

Leaving Luke in his room, Karen Lamford went to the monitor room to get ready for the night. She had a coffee and was settling in her chair.

Turning on a switch, she picked up a microphone and said, "Okay, Luke. Almost ready, it'll take a couple of minutes."

No response. Karen took that as a sign Luke was sleeping. Good.

XXXXX

When his phone call concluded, Willard decided to go to Dan's Cooler to wind down. Not understanding what James Atkins was doing in the woods all alone at night or why he was there in the first place was unsettling.

As he arrived, he noticed the parking lot was about half-full. Taking his time, he noticed one of the precinct's vehicles parked to one side.

What the hell was one of their cars doing here? Then he remembered, the car that Hanely and Atkins drove for the raid that went south.

Atkins. Atkins must be here. Interesting. Wonder what he has to say. Soon find out.

He took one last look around, then headed for the front entrance.

XXXXX

Karen was watching the monitors, but nothing out of the ordinary was registering. Luke's brain waves were normal.

Sipping her coffee, she began to rub her temples. Must be getting tired. But it was still early in her shift and she did sleep before coming in.

Keeping her eyes on the monitor, she began to develop a headache. Just like the last time when Luke was here. But it must be a coincidence. It never returned again after that.

Yet here we are again, and I have that same old feeling again. Stop it! It's just a headache. Nothing more. It'll go away soon. It has to.

XXXXX

As Willard entered the bar, he gazed around the room, and lo and behold, there he was. With his back to the wall, Atkins was downing his beer like it was the last one.

Going to the bar and ordering his beer, he made his way to the far end and said, "Mind if I join you?"

Looking through glazing eyes, Atkins was having trouble focusing. Realizing it was the captain, he said, "Go ahead. I don't think anyone will mind. At least not Dennis Hanely."

"Dennis Hanely? What about him?"

"I k-k-know that he w-w-on't be both-thering anyone else anytime s-s-sooon. Especially Luke." He was hiccupping and stuttering so badly, Willard had a hard time understanding.

"You've had enough to drink. Go home and sleep it off." He got up to help Atkins to his feet, but Akins didn't appear to be ready to go just yet.

"No!" he yelled.

Everyone stopped what they were doing and stared at the duo.

"Calm down, Atkins. You're drawing a crowd."

Atkins didn't seem to notice.

"You want me to calm down?" he asked sarcastically.

"Yes, I do. Please."

"I just saw my partner getting killed from who knows what the hell that thing is, and you want me to calm down."

Willard took a deserving drink; then he asked, "What did you say?"

"I said I *saw my partner getting killed. That's what I said. Would you like me to repeat it again?*"

Again, everyone stopped what they were doing, and stared at the two.

Fred the bartender approached them and said, "Listen, Captain. My customers are complaining about the noise. Tone it down; otherwise, I'll have to ask you to leave."

"Sorry, Fred. It won't happen again."

After Fred left, Willard glanced at Atkins and said, "Tell me again, exactly what happened. But keep your voice down."

XXXXX

As the black cat jumped the fence at the same precise time thunder and lightning struck, the apparition that appeared to be a man pointed toward the little boy.

He managed to scamper away from the two buildings and continued running down the sidewalk. Looking over his shoulder, he couldn't see anyone following him. Slowing down to catch his breath, he heard a voice from behind him that sounded like it came from the grave.

Trying to block out the voice, he ran harder than he's ever ran before. But no matter how hard, or how hard, it was no use. That voice kept following him, under every rock, in every hole, around the next bend.

It was everywhere. The voice that he's been trying to block forever. Never wanting to know what it was going to say.

But he was tired. Very tired. Couldn't run anymore. He fell on his knees on the sidewalk. Rain was pouring down on him. But no matter what he did, the apparition and voice were always there.

With the finger pointed at him, the booming voice right behind it was saying, "Earnest. Earnest will be a threat in your life, Luke. You best beware, your destiny awaits."

With that, the voice began to fade until it dissipated completely.

Luke Myers woke up.

XXXXX

When Willard arrived home, he couldn't get out of his head what Atkins told him.

Is it possible Hanely was dead? What about that thing that killed Hanely? How could such a creature exist? It couldn't be human.

Atkins was drunk out of his mind. Didn't know what he was saying. He probably wouldn't remember talking to Willard the next day.

So what should he do? Ignore it? But if there was a little truth to what he heard. He was confused. Believe, or not to believe.

He went in the kitchen to retrieve a glass.

He poured himself a drink.

XXXXX

As Luke was dreaming, the monitors jumped like crazy. Something definitely was going on. Karen checked them more closely, then looked at Luke.

He was drenched. If the straps weren't on, Luke would have fallen on the floor; he was squirming so much.

Then just like that, Luke stopped. The monitors returned to normal, and Luke's eyelids opened. He was awake.

Finishing her cold coffee, Karen watched him from the monitor room. Her headache was returning. Clutching her head, she massaged her temple to soothe them. Taking a minute to compose herself, she left the monitor room.

XXXXX

At Havenburg Emergency Center, all was quiet as it usually is after midnight. Not all the beds were occupied. About a third of them were empty, which made it seem all the more quiet.

Phil Blake's nurse, who was sitting in a chair beside his bed, went to the nurse's desk for a small break, knowing nothing unusual would happen. At least, not in the next ten minutes.

She couldn't have been more wrong, because two minutes after she left, Phil Blake's eyelids began to flutter.

As Earnest left the school grounds at the end of the day, he looked over his shoulder to see if he was being followed. Seeing that he wasn't, he began to relax. Going at a more comfortable pace, he made it home, but just before he went up his walk and to the door, he couldn't help but have a strong feeling of being watched. But when he turned to see, there was nobody there. Still, the feeling of being watched was still nagging at him.

Who could it be?

Laurel Champ?

No!

He wouldn't hide.

He would have attacked already.

Trying to figure it out, he went in the house and straight to his room.

The lurker watched the house from behind a tree across the street.

Knowing he could never reveal himself, he'd been following Earnest for two weeks now.

Couldn't understand how such a nerdy boy could be so destructive. So now all he could do was wait. Wait and hope all this madness would come to an end.

Earnest.

Phil Blake returned to his mind, and there the dream ended.

When the nurse returned to Phil Blake's room, she took her spot on the chair beside the bed. Only when everything became quiet did she realize that she had a flat line.

32

Entering Luke's room, she saw that he was watching her, waiting to be unstrapped. As she approached him, she saw his eyes.

Never had she seen his eyes like that. It was as though he had gone insane. Maybe she shouldn't unstrap him just yet. Maybe she should wait until she knew it was safe.

When he spoke, it was like a gunshot from a barrel at close range. It snapped her out of her trance.

She reached him and took the wires out of his skull, then continued to take off the straps. As she finished, he got up off the table and said, "That was strange." As he was about to continue, he noticed her clutching her temples.

"Karen, what's the matter?"

As Karen looked up, her eyes were clouded, and her will was gone. Seeing Luke before her, she raised her arms toward him and charged.

"die," she screamed. "you must die, for the voice commands it."

Luke took a couple of steps back and said, "Karen, fight the voice. You're in control, not her. Fight the voice. Damn it, fight."

With her migraine headache, Karen had no choice to attack Luke. It's the only way it would go away. Screaming like a banshee, Karen continued to advance toward Luke.

XXXXX

Unable to sleep, Claire found herself heading to the clinic to see how Luke was making out. Pulling her car into the parking lot of the clinic, she took the keys out and made her way to the front entrance.

XXXXX

Deciding to wait for Luke and Claire in the morning to decide how to handle the Hanely information, Willard took his last gulp of his glass, then tried to get some sleep.

XXXXX

Karen lunged at Luke, and all she got for her trouble was some air. Luke vacated the spot Karen attacked seconds earlier.

Now they were facing each other once again when the voice intervened, *Time is now, child. Strike him now, before it's too late.*

She rushed him and kneed him in the midsection. He yelled in pain as he went down. "Listen to me, Karen, it's me—Luke, fight the voice. It's evil. You're not."

"NO. YOU'RE LYING. YOU JUST WANT TO KILL ME. LET MY GUARD DOWN. BUT I WON'T. I HATE YOU, AND I'M GOING TO KILL YOU!"

All Luke could do was stay out of her way. He didn't want to hurt her. She became a friend over the sessions. Now the voice that took hold over Margo and Kim Lacy had a hold on Karen.

He didn't want to harm her, but he didn't know what else to do.

When Claire entered the building, she noticed how unusually quiet it was. There wasn't even anybody at the desk.

Why wasn't there anybody at the desk? It was also dark. You'd figure the waiting area would be lit. Even the corridor behind the desk that led to some of the rooms weren't lit.

Why? Slowly, she took out her gun and checked to make sure it was loaded. She held it in front, with the barrel pointing up.

In a bit of a crouch, she stepped into the corridor behind the desk.

Karen sprang at Luke, but he managed to grab both of her wrists. Hanging on to them was a whole different story.

She was very strong. The voice in her head must be giving her the strength. She bared her teeth, and with an extra ounce of power, she broke free of his grip.

Looking at her more clearly, he saw the insanity in her eyes. She was like a wild animal, cornered, trying to break out.

Saliva was dripping down one side of her chin, and she actually had sharp claws. One slice with those and Luke's had it.

"Karen, please." Luke was pleading now.

"STOP IT! STOP CALLING ME THAT NAME! I'M NOT HER!" With that last thought, she jumped on the table that he finished his dreams in, and catapulted on Luke, sending him sprawling on the floor.

He bumped his head against the floor. He needed to catch his breath, put some distance between himself and her, but Karen wouldn't let him.

The farther down the hall Claire went, the noisier it became. There seemed to be some kind scuffle towards that middle door to the right.

Is that where Luke is? Why does it sound like someone's trashing the place? Who is that screaming? What the hell is going on here?

She made it to the door and, with a gentle nudge, pushed it in.

When Karen landed on Luke, it took his breath away. Holding him down, her face inches away from his, he saw the pure evil in her eyes.

The saliva he saw on her chin earlier was now dripping on his face. He tried to squirm free, but no matter which way he moved his face, saliva still managed to find it.

"Karen, for the love of all humanity, fight the voice. You can win. Please!" When he spoke of love, her grip weakened, and her eyes started to mellow.

"NO. DON'T LISTEN TO HIM! HE'S LYING TO YOU! THEY'RE ALL LYING TO YOU! KILL HIM! KILL HIM NOW!"

With that, the hatred returned, and she raised her claw. Striking downward, Luke managed to use his knee to push her forward, which forced her to puncture the floor ahead of him.

With her off balance, he shoved her the rest of the way off him. She rolled a couple of feet, but that was enough for him to get up.

Still a little wobbly, he had to lean by his table to keep from falling. Karen was already on her feet, ready for another strike.

Claire couldn't believe what she was witnessing. That must be Dr. Karen Lamford. Her description fit from what Luke told her.

It sure did look like her, but she also looked like a wild animal. A closer look, she saw Karen's hands.

Were those claws?

My God! What's going on?

She looked like she was ready to attack. Luke was unsteady on his feet. Why wasn't his gun drawn?

Slowly, Karen was advancing. Luke was backing up. As Karen was getting ready to jump, a tremendous weight knocked Karen clean on the floor. Taking the fight out of her, Karen lay sprawled on the floor.

Luke took a moment to sort everything out. Then he noticed Claire slowly getting to her feet. He rushed to her side to help her the rest of the way up.

"Claire, what are you doing here?"

"You're welcome, sweetheart. I love you too."

"I'm sorry. Thank you very much. But how did you know?"

"I didn't. Just couldn't sleep, so I decided to come see how you were doing. Good thing too. Didn't know you had a fight on your hands."

"Oh no! I almost forgot. Have to see how she is."

Going to her side, Luke checked to see if she was okay. Karen was moaning softly, so he knew she would be okay.

Looking at her eyes, the wildness was gone. Even her hands were back to normal, the claws gone.

"Did anybody get license plate of the truck that ran me down?" Karen asked.

Luke laughed. "I see there's nothing wrong with you. Let me help you up."

As Karen got to her feet, she realized what just came down.

"Luke, are you okay?"

"Yes, I'm fine. Just a little sore from where you pinned me down. Other than that, just dandy."

"I'm sorry. But that voice in my head was going batty. I couldn't stop it."

"I know. By any chance, was the voice female?"

Karen looked at him in astonishment. "Yes, how did you know?"

"We came across some innocent people who were influenced throughout our investigation. Speaking of which, Karen Lamford, this is my partner, Claire Davis."

Claire walked to shake Karen's hand, "Yes. We've met, I was that truck which ran you down."

Karen was laughing. "Thank goodness, I believe that was what broke the spell on me. I'm Karen Lamford. Luke's doctor."

"I kind of figured that, which reminds me why I came here in the first place." Turning to Luke, she asked, "How did that go?"

"Very unsettling. I have to sort out what it means."

Claire pressed. "But did the man talk? What did he say?"

Luke looked at both ladies and took a deep breath before he said, "The man in my dream said, 'Luke, beware Earnest. He's going to be a threat in your life. Your destiny awaits.'"

33

Luke and Claire were pulling into Wayne's Garage parking lot. Getting out of the car, Claire said, "I couldn't believe it when Cap gave me this address. I never would have thought he'd be involved."

"I know. Just check it out and see what happens. Things should start to get interesting now."

As they approached the garage doors, they drew their weapons. Luke went in first, then gave the okay signal, and Claire followed.

As they advanced, it got a little darker, but not so dark that they couldn't see. Luke stopped, listening for something, and when it didn't come, he edged forward.

Up ahead, a door was looming, and Luke pointed toward it. When they got there, Luke very slowly turned the knob.

Pushing it wide open, Luke and Claire rushed in with their guns ahead of them. There was a man sitting at the desk and yelled in surprise at the sight of them.

"Don't move," Luke said. "Where's your boss. I want Bob Gerald."

"He's not here," the man answered. "He hasn't been here for the last three days. Honest."

Claire nudged Luke. "He's telling the truth. He's too scared to lie."

"So, when will he be back?" Luke asked him.

"I-I-don't know," he stuttered.

"Okay. But don't get any ideas about telling anyone we were here. Otherwise, I'll be back for you! Got it?"

"Y-yes, sir. I got it"

Luke and Claire were gone.

Halfway back to the precinct, Claire called Willard to update him. When she got off her phone, she said to her partner, "He wants us in his office ASAP."

"I wonder what's up."

"He wouldn't say. But now we have to figure out that dream of yours. It's funny that Ernest was mentioned to you also."

"Yes. I was thinking the same thing. I wonder if it's the same Earnest mentioned in Phil's dream."

Claire added, "I wonder if it's the same Earnest in the photos we found in Larry Haswell's box."

Luke looked at Claire. "What did you say?"

"You heard correctly. I wonder if there's a connection with the three times we heard that name. It's been coming up too many times for it to be coincidental."

"I agree. There must be a way to figure it out."

"I'm sure there is. It's right in front of us. But let's go see Willard first. Maybe he can shed some light on all this."

Sitting in his office, Willard was quiet. He didn't know where to begin. Finally he looked at his two detectives and said, "I don't know how to say it, so I'll just come to the point. I received a call from the hospital this morning, and I'm afraid to say, we lost Phil."

He looked at Luke and Claire to see their reaction. They were shocked. When it hit them, Claire broke down.

Luke hugged her while she cried on his shoulder. They both knew this day would come but had hoped not this soon.

Finally Luke asked, "When?"

"Early this morning. You were at the clinic when he passed. They called me an hour ago."

It was quiet in the office, each in their own thoughts.

Finally, Claire composed herself and said, "I'm beginning to understand. Phil was in a coma for a very long time. He even had dreams and actually gave us a name. Earnest. Now I'm more sure than ever that he hung on long enough for Luke to get his dream unravelled. Earnest was in both dreams. I'm sure it's the same one. I know this is going to sound far-fetched, but this Earnest

Connelly, whoever he is, will help finally solve this investigation. We need to find Earnest Connelly right away."

Luke just looked at her stunned. "Wow, I have to admit that this Earnest's name does come up a lot, but there's no proof of anything."

Claire looked at him and said, "I think that him just being in your dream, and in Phil's dream at the same time, and Phil hanging on just long enough for you to figure your dream out, with Earnest in it, is proof enough. I say we find him and bring him in for questioning or have a surveillance team on him."

Now it was Willard's turn. "That's fine, but before we decide, there is something the two of you ought to know."

Both Luke and Claire looked at the captain puzzled. "What should we know?" asked Claire.

Willard looked at both of them before replying. "Last night when you were at the clinic"—he was pointing at Luke—"I decided to go to Dan's Cooler for a drink. I ran into James Atkins."

When Willard stopped talking to sip on his coffee, Luke blurted out, "James Atkins? What about him?"

Willard said, "Atkins believes Dennis Hanely is dead!"

"What? Dead? Why would Atkins say such a thing?"

"I don't know, Luke. Don't know what to make of it. He was pretty drunk at the time. Maybe he saw something so terrible that his mind is playing games. He told me the killer was huge, not even human, and that he wore a black hood."

Luke stood from his chair and said. "Not human? Now I agree his mind is playing games. Maybe he did see something, because he hardly drinks. But I can't imagine what."

"Well," Willard added, "whatever it is, I don't buy it. Hanely knows he screwed up and went into hiding. We'll worry about him if we don't hear anything for a few days. Imagine Atkins trying to convince me there's a cabin deep in the woods where the killer's living. But I think this Earnest Connelly should be investigated. The sooner we find him, the sooner we can investigate other options."

On their way to the high school, Luke looked at Claire and said, "If nothing comes of this Earnest character, we may have to talk to Atkins and find out everything he thinks he knows. We may have to go in the woods to do some investigating."

"I was thinking the same thing. But let's try to find Earnest. If he exists. Maybe he'll lead us to the killer's hideout."

They were pulling into the parking lot of the high school. Looking at the building, Luke remarked, "It sure looks spooky now. I guess a little killing does that."

Claire agreed as she got out of the car. She took a moment, and taking a deep breath, she started toward the front door.

Captain Willard was given a set of skeleton keys for the school, since it involved the investigation, and they were using them now to get in.

As they entered, Luke had a shiver going down his spine. "It looks just as unnerving in here as it does out there. Let's get this over with."

Passing the reception area that led to the principal's office, Luke and Claire glanced toward the office, but continued on down the hall.

As they reached the door at the end of the hall, they used another key to open it. As it swung open, it reminded Luke of a mystery and suspense movie that he watched once, when a door swung open in a dark basement and squeaked on hinges. He jumped ten feet, expecting something to jump out.

Now as the door swung open, he waited for the squeak that never came. After a minute Claire nudged him and asked, "What's wrong?"

When she nudged him, he did jump as he had not expected that. "Don't do that," he cried. "This place reminds me of a movie that I once saw, and it freaked me out. Then when you touched me, I jumped out of my skin."

"Oops, sorry. Did not know that. But I think now I know why you never liked the school. Okay. Let's get to the archives."

When Willard was all alone in his office, he stared out the window not seeing anything. His thoughts went back to the Atkins conversation.

Is it possible some deranged murderer is living in the woods? Wearing a black hood? No! Can't be true. It just isn't possible. Is it? What did Atkins really see? It must have been some imagination to see what he said he saw. But what? What was it that scared him?

He had no solution for any of this. He would have to figure something out. He just had to.

Luke and Claire entered the library that led to the archive at the back. Going on instinct from their last visit, Luke went to the correct row where the files for the class of ninety-seven were located.

Reaching it, Luke put his hands on the file and said to Claire, "Hopefully we'll find what we're looking for in these files. We better get started."

At the Havenburg Emergency Center, Margo Henderson was half-conscious; she was whispering a name. As soon as the nurse could understand what Margo was saying, she rushed to the nurse's station and picked up the phone.

Once they got started, Luke and Claire were whizzing through the pictures. "It helps that we already saw these photos. But we better start slowing down. We need to see the ones we missed, and if Earnest is here, I don't want to overlook it," Luke was saying.

They continued looking, working in silence.

XXXXX

Willard slammed the phone down, then left his office in a hurry. Reaching his car, he got in behind the wheel and turned the ignition. He made a U-turn and sped down the street, fishtailing around the corner. He needed ten minutes to reach his destination.

XXXXX

"Wait a minute," shouted Claire. "I think I may have found something. Take a look."

Luke moved over to Claire and took a peek over her shoulder. He looked at the photo and, after a long minute, managed a smile.

"That sure looks like him. But this picture doesn't do him any justice. I never realized how frail and nerdy he looks. That would certainly fit the profile."

Claire said, "All we need is an address. I wonder if we'll get lucky and find that too."

"That shouldn't be hard to find. They must have addresses to go along with each photo. We just have to find it."

"Wait. Take a look at this." Claire pointed to a marking on Earnest's photo. "What does that look like to you?"

Luke took a closer look at Earnest's cheek and said, "I'm not sure. Maybe some kind of scar, but I'm not positive."

XXXXX

Willard was entering the emergency center when he asked a nurse at the information desk, "I'm here to see Margo Henderson. She asked to see one of my detectives, but she's out on assignment."

"May I have your name?" she asked.

"Yes. My name is Captain Bruce Willard."

"One moment please. You can have a seat. The nurse in charge will be here momentarily."

"Thank you very much."

"Captain Willard, I'm Nurse Faye Barris. I'll take you to see Ms. Henderson now. Don't be alarmed, but her ribs are bandaged, and she's just waking up. She's still tired and weak, so try to keep it to a minimum."

"Thank you, nurse, and I shouldn't be long."

They walked to the end of the corridor and opened a door at the end of the hall. As he was quietly entering, he once more thanked the nurse.

XXXXX

Luke scanned the files until he found what he was looking for. "I think I found it. According to this, he lives on 207 Caster Avenue."

Claire was looking over Luke's shoulder, but a look of concern spread over her face. After a full minute, it hit her,

"Luke, I'm not sure, but I think that address doesn't exist anymore."

"What do you mean it doesn't exist? It says right here that it does."

"I'm not saying it doesn't, but there seemed to be some kind of accident. It was all over the news. Don't you remember?"

"I'm sorry, but I don't. What happened?"

"I think a fire burned the house. Don't remember if anyone got hurt. But from that point on, it was condemned."

"That was the same house?"

"I don't know. But I'm pretty sure it was that street."

"Okay. Then we're going to have to go in the news of the archive. Go back fifteen years and see what exactly did happen."

Once again they went to work, to check what happened fifteen years before.

XXXXX

Willard was at the foot of the bed when he called to Margo Henderson. "I'm sorry to bother you, Ms. Henderson. Claire couldn't make it; she's busy on police work."

Slowly Margo Henderson turned her head at the sound of Willard's voice and asked, "Who are you?"

"My apologies. I'm Captain Bruce Willard. Claire Davis's boss. I was informed you were asking for her, so I came instead. Hope you don't mind."

After a long pause, Willard thought she fell back asleep, but then Margo said, "Of course not. I was just hoping she would be here herself. I wanted to thank her for trying to help me, even though I was such a bitch with her."

She was trying to reach for her glass of water, Willard reached over to help her with it.

"Thank you," she said. "The nurse told me that Claire was here earlier while I was sleeping, which made me realize she was actually trying to help me."

"How was that?"

"When we were fighting in the woods, she told me she was trying to help me. I didn't believe her, and I tried to kill her."

"Well ya, about that. It wasn't your fault. That voice controlled you. It made you do what you did. We had problems with other people around town that did worse controlled by that voice."

"What? You had other people that were controlled by that voice?"

"Yes, and some not so fortunate. Anyway, about your involvement with the poaching, if you cooperate, I'm sure the DA will go easy on you.

"Thank you. Considering what I've put all of you through, you're being so nice. I don't know if saying sorry is enough."

"Believe me, Ms. Henderson. It is enough, but I'd like you to answer a question for me. If you're not too tired."

"I'll answer your next question, if you call me Margo."

"All right. We have a deal. Margo, I was just wondering if you've heard from Champ. We figured he went into hiding, but Claire mentioned that you thought he was dead. Is there any truth to that?"

Margo sighed. Not because she was tired, but because she was waiting for this day to arrive—the day when the police would come asking her about Champ.

She looked at Willard and replied, "I don't know anymore if it's true or not. All I know is two days before we had that last poaching exhibition, he went behind our place to scout. He never returned. I went looking for him and found part of his shirt ripped. He should never have went by himself."

"I'm sorry to have to ask you this next question, Margo, but is there any reason why you didn't go with him?"

"I was on the sofa, still hung over. I didn't even know he went in the woods until Martin called me and told me."

"Yes, we'll have to pick Martin up for questioning also, but in the meantime, there are two people we have to search for in the woods."

"Two people?" Margo asked.

"Yes. The man that you worked for, he calls himself Boss, the one who beat you? He continued on into the woods later and never returned. His black pickup is still parked by your place. He never came back for it."

At the mention of the Boss, Margo's stomach churned. "I never want to hear that name ever again. I can't believe we fell for his phony promises."

"You can't blame yourself. He had everyone fooled. Sometimes people just turn out like that. Margo, I've asked you enough questions; I'll let you get some rest."

As he was getting up to leave, Margo grabbed his hand and held it for a moment. "Again, please tell Claire and her partner I'm terribly sorry for what I put them through."

"Rest assured, Margo, I will tell them. They will both be pleased. Thank you for seeing me." He exited the room.

XXXXX

In the archive room, Luke and Claire seemed to find what they were looking for. A newspaper clipping dating back fifteen years stated that a house caught fire and burned completely to the ground. There were never any bodies found, according to the article, and no traces of how the fire started was ever found. The fire chief in charge commented that an investigation was under way.

Claire said, "What about the address. They have to mention an address."

"Let's see. The address noted here is 207 Caster Avenue. It states here Margaret Connelly lived there with her sixteen-year-old son, Earnest Connelly, both of whom were never seen again. If that doesn't sound fishy, I don't know what does."

"That would make Earnest thirty-one years old. The right age. It's gotta be him, and that has to be the right house also," Claire finished.

"Hang on," Luke said. "It says here that the fire was believed to have started between midnight and one o'clock."

He turned to look at Claire and said, "That doesn't make sense."

It was Claire's turn to look puzzled.

"Why not?" she asked.

"Where would you be at one in the morning?" Luke challenged.

"Probably in bed sleeping."

"Exactly. I would be also. Where was the family if they weren't home?"

"I don't know. Maybe they were out of town."

"Or maybe Earnest was busy burning the house down," Luke added. "Killing his mother in the process."

"Okay, hotshot. If you're right, where's her body?"

"Wherever Earnest buried her."

34

When Willard picked up his coffee on his way back to the office, he couldn't help but think about his conversation with Margo Henderson.

Why is she so friendly all of a sudden? She was so vicious all their other encounters. Is she manipulating the police department? To avoid jail time? Who knows?

Willard could never figure women. He would let Claire handle this one. He had other problems. Such as where Champ disappeared to.

Was Margo Henderson telling the truth about his disappearance? What about the Boss? Was he missing also? Or just hiding?

Then there was that wild story about Dennis Hanely.

James Atkins was convinced his partner was dead, and that he witnessed it. A monster seven feet tall, to boot. How do you believe something like that? Lots of things to sort through.

He'd need to talk to Luke and Claire to see what their best course of action should be.

Speaking of which, I wonder how they're making out.

XXXXX

Pending our investigation, the fire seemed to originate on the second floor, possibly the mother's bedroom, toward the hall outside her room, down the carpeted stairs, and finally finishing in the kitchen. A couple of kerosene lanterns were found on the kitchen floor, where possibly the perpetrator just threw them on the floor and ran.

That article was dated October 17, 1997.

"Another thing that doesn't make sense," Luke said to Claire. "If there was nobody home, why would they start from a bedroom, second floor, and make a path toward the kitchen where he possibly used the back door from the kitchen to get out?"

"What's the difference?"

"If you just burn a house with no intention of killing, and you think the house is empty, you would just burn from the main floor. You soak it enough so everything catches; then you leave. I think he killed his mother, then took the body."

Claire was silent for a minute, taking in Luke's assumption. Finally she said, "If you're right, we have to find the body; otherwise, there's no proof."

"Unless, when we catch him, he confesses where he buried her. Either way, I'm convinced that is who we're looking for anyway. For all the other murders."

"So where do we go from here?" Claire asked.

"Go tell Willard what we suspect, then go take a look at the scene of the crime."

"You want to go to the house that's not a house anymore?"

"Yes. Poke around a bit, see if we can find something that'll help us with our investigation. Maybe something was missed. In the meantime, let's check for more articles."

"Okay. We keep looking. Hopefully, we'll get lucky."

"Speaking of lucky, there's an article right here dated October 20, three days later. It states here that arson was the cause of the fire, but no suspects were brought in for questioning. It also reveals that with no bodies found in the fire, they too were wondering where the family is. Nobody ever did show up, and as time went by, the story was eventually forgotten."

"Wow," exclaimed Claire. "With none of the family returning, I'd say they would probably be prime suspect."

"Now you're seeing. But I still say Earnest killed his mother, covered it up by burning the house down, and also removed the body. It's imperative now that we do our best to find Earnest. The only question remains is, why did he kill his mother? Maybe we'll find the answer when we find him."

"I agree. Now let's go tell the cap what we suspect then decide what to do."

XXXXX

They opened the captain's door to see Willard lost in thought at his desk. They went to sit in their regular chairs, and only then did the captain notice them.

"You're back!" the captain half-shouted, not realizing how loud he sounded. "Did you find anything out at the archive?"

"We did," Luke replied. "Apparently, the address that this Earnest supposedly lives in has been burned to the ground for the past fifteen years."

"I don't understand."

Claire cut in, "We suspect that Earnest burned his house down fifteen years ago. Also, we think he killed his mother and burned the house to cover his tracks."

Willard asked, "Was the body recovered?"

"Never. We think Earnest removed it, but we have no proof." Luke was pacing the room.

Willard was thinking; then he asked his detectives, "What's your next move?"

Luke said, "We'd like to go to that address now to see if we can find anything that may have been missed. It's a long shot, but I'd like to try."

"All right. Do that, but keep me posted. If you come up empty, you might have to strike up a chat with Atkins. Maybe you can figure out what's going on with him. I can't make sense about anything he's told me."

"Fine. But only as a last resort. Imagine, a hooded monster that lives in the woods. I've heard it all now."

"Great. Now scram. "I've work to do."

On the way to 207 Caster Avenue, Claire was looking out her window. When she faced front, she said, "I know you're hoping to find something that may have been missed, and I hope you do, but you have to realize fifteen years is a long time. With weather being a factor over time, it probably took away any chance we may have found."

"I realize all that, but I still want to poke around a little. Just to see. After that, we don't have to worry about that place any more. Be able to checkmark it off our list and continue other possibilities in our investigation."

"Deal."

As they turned onto Caster Avenue from the north end, they drove slowly down the street.

"This street looks quiet enough," Claire mentioned. "You have to go to the other end. It's the corner on the right."

"Yes. I see an empty lot farther down. That must be it."

As they got closer, they could indeed see that it was an empty lot. Average-size lot. They could also see parts of a police line that is used to keep the crowds back. After all these years, it was withered and decayed.

The empty lot, on which the Connelly house once stood, seemed to loom over the town. Anybody who knew about the

Connellys avoided this corner of town. They would simply stay on the other side of the road, scurrying as they did so.

Others would just not be at this end of town whatsoever. It was believed that anyone cutting through that particular yard would be cursed and turn evil, just as they believed the mother and her boy were. Of course there was never any proof, and nothing was done.

Even stray cats and raccoons seemed to stay clear, as though they understood everything happening around that lot. The police stopped investigating shortly after the fire incident, wanting to just wash their hands of that place.

Once when this story was hot, all the news reporters were flocked on this corner, but soon, even that diminished. Then it stopped completely.

Even the city refused to come and clean it altogether so they could rebuild, but it was not meant to be. Even the bums stayed away.

From that point on, that lot stood on its own.

Stepping out of the vehicle, they stood in front of their car and looked around. After a couple of minutes, Luke asked, "Are you ready?"

"Anytime you are, love," Claire answered as they started walking forward.

When they reached where the house used to stand, Luke said, "It looks like when the house burned, the city was afraid to come here and clean up the mess. Parts of cement blocks that used to be part of the foundation are still visible. Other parts crumbled over time. It almost looks like they turned to dust."

Claire agreed as she bent down to have a closer look. Other than the area not being cleaned up, nothing looked out of place. "It does seem like this is a dead end after all."

Something was nagging at the back of her mind. When she realized what was bothering her, she took a step backward.

"What?" Luke noticed her reaction. "What's the matter?"

"You really don't remember about this place, do you?"

"No. Not at all."

"Well, it was such an eye grabber; everyone was talking about it. Every news channel had it. Or they did for a while; then just like that, it stopped. All the channels stopped running the story. As though something happened to them."

"Did it?" Luke asked,

"Not sure. But a couple of months later, I remember at our dinner table, my mom and dad started talking about it."

"What did they say?"

"Something about the place being haunted or cursed. Something along those lines. I remember because I got scared. When they saw how I felt, they never mentioned it again."

"Do you believe them?"

"You mean if it's haunted or cursed?"

"That's what I mean."

"I-I don't know," she stuttered. "I heard around town later, a high percentage of people living here believe it. I don't know if I do or not."

"Would you feel safer if you waited in the car?" Luke suggested.

"No. I'll stay here with you. We'll be done quicker this way."

"That's my girl."

XXXXX

The dark figure was agitated. Indoors for the last couple of days listening to Mother was maddening. Outside, armed with the hunting knife, the dark figure was hunting.

It was quiet everywhere. No chirping of the birds. No insects. No mice or rodent. Like they feared coming out, to avoid certain death. Like they knew what was in store.

They're smarter than the sheep. They know when to hide. Like now.

The knife was swinging wildly. Taking out branches and leaves. His frustration was satisfying.

Feeling much better, hunting was all that mattered. Nothing in particular. Anything.

Mother was soon forgotten.

XXXXX

When Luke and Claire finished their poking around, Luke looked dejected. One last look, then he faced Claire and said, "I'm sorry I brought you here. What a waste of time. Not even close to finding anything. I know it's been fifteen years, but I was hoping something would show up. Let's just get a coffee, then go home."

"I wouldn't feel to upset if I were you, sweetie. We both knew what we were up against. Fifteen years is a long time, and with all the weather conditions to boot, it was a long shot. Now you promised me a coffee?"

Luke was laughing despite himself. Putting his arm around her, lead her to the car. When he stopped in his tracks Claire turned to him and asked, "What's wrong?"

"I don't know," Luke answered. "Something just caught my eye."

He walked back the way he came, then bent down.

Claire, right behind him, stopped. He stopped so suddenly, she had to dig her toes in the dirt to keep from falling over him. She bent down beside him to look at what he was doing.

Something stuck in the ground, and he was having a hard time forcing it loose. After a couple of minutes he yelled, "Finally. I got it."

Upon further examination, he couldn't believe his luck. He turned his palm over toward Claire so she would see.

The ace of spades.

35

"The ace of spades?" exploded Claire. "How did you know?"

"Just as we reached the car, I saw something protruding from the ground. Didn't know it was anything, but it appeared weird. So I thought I'd better take a look."

"Good thing you did," she said. "You do know this may be the break we need. It practically puts Earnest Connelly as primary suspect."

"Yes, I realize that. In fact, I think the captain will make this priority one. Drop everything, and concentrate on finding Connelly."

"Oh, I'm so excited about our breakthrough; let's get that coffee on our way to the office."

"Whoa, relax. We can get that coffee, but it's late so we're going to wait until the morning to tell Willard. Understood?"

"I understand. You're lucky, boy."

"Lucky about what?"

"That I let you be the leader of this team. That's all I got to say about that."

"Oh, thank you, Royal Highness."

"You found the ace of spades on that burned lot?" Willard couldn't believe what he was hearing. "What are the odds of that? Fifteen years later, and you still find a clue."

Luke pulled the card from his pocket and placed it on the desk. Half the card was missing diagonally, but there was no question.

It definitely was the ace of spades. Willard picked it up and looked at it more carefully. When he put it back down, he said to Luke, "Last night while you were snatching up clues, I had another visit from our friend Atkins."

"Atkins?" Luke asked. "What did he want this time?"

"Oh, nothing much. Just demanding that we do our job and go check out the woods where he still believes Hanely was murdered."

"Was he drunk again?"

"No, not really. Not as bad as before. This time I was able to look him in the eyes and see they were clear. Whatever really happened in the woods, and that's a big *if*, he honestly believes what he saw. If this is true, you may also find our killer."

Luke went to the machine beside the desk to pour himself a coffee before stating, "It sounds like you're starting to believe his story."

"It's not that I believe it or not, but Atkins really does. Think about it, Luke, Atkins never gave you or the department any problems. All your problems were with Hanely. Atkins stayed in the background. That's why I find it difficult not to at least consider this story."

"You do have a point, Cap." Luke took a sip of his coffee before asking, "What do you propose we do?"

This time Willard took a sip of coffee before he answered, "I think it's getting to the point where we will have no choice but to check it out. It's not like you're going in blind. Atkins gave coordinates as best he remembers them. There's supposedly a shack, or cabin, that you will be looking for specifically. According to him, the killer is dressed in black with a hood over his head. But everything happened so fast, he's not entirely sure."

"When will this take place?" Claire asked.

Turning his attention toward her, he said, "I'm not sure yet. I don't want you to go in alone, in case there's truth to this story, and you run into problems. I'm going to see if I could send in a SWAT team to tag along."

"A SWAT team?" Luke was puzzled. "They'll just go blow everything up."

"No. The two of you will still be in charge. They'll be taking direct orders from you. They'll blow everything up, only if you say so."

"Really?" beamed Luke. "Can I introduce myself as Captain Luke Myers the Great?"

"Get out of my office. Get out of my office *now*."

XXXXX

Mother was agitated. She sensed danger coming her way. So riled, her chair was rocking back and forth to beat the band.

Those humans that she detested figured a way toward her. But how did they know? Somehow, she knew deep down, this day would come.

That meddlesome son of hers slipped. Somewhere, somehow, they discovered his comings and goings. It was bound to happen.

He hunted them so frequently, they were bound to get wise eventually.

Soon. It would be over soon. One way or another. It would finally be over.

Then she could sleep.

XXXXX

Claire was deep in thought as Luke skillfully manoeuvred his vehicle in and out of traffic. Finally, he noticed how quiet it was and said, "I know you hate my driving, but giving me the silent treatment isn't the answer."

"What. Oh, I'm sorry. I was just wondering how Margo was making out with her injuries. Wonder if she'll get better."

He turned to look at her and said, "All of a sudden, you feel sorry for her? After everything she put you through?"

"Well, she's starting to come around and was disappointed when I didn't show to visit her. Makes me feel like I actually was getting through to her. Do you understand?"

Taking a glance at her, he was saying, "Of course I do. That's why since it's on our way, I'm headed that way now so you can visit her for a few minutes."

"Oh, thank you." She moved closer to him and gave him a big kiss on the side of his face.

"Okay, okay. That's enough. Do you want me to get into an accident? Maybe that's your plan so you could have the bed next to her."

They both laughed as they pulled into the parking lot.

XXXXX

For the rest of the day, Willard was trying to contact Colonel Russ Fraser, the SWAT team leader. After the third phone call, he gave up and left a message. If we ever get in a life-threatening situation, it would have to go to voice mail, thought Willard sarcastically.

Leaving his office, he ended up at Mary's Coffee and Doughnut Shop. Getting a coffee to go, he decided his day was done and headed home.

XXXXX

Later that night, Luke and Claire were watching the news channel. As they kept surfing the tube, Luke said, "I keep thinking about the woods."

"What about them?" asked Claire.

"Now Cap has me thinking about that far-fetched story Atkins was spreading. I really wonder how much truth there is to that."

"I was kind of wondering myself. Even if half is true, we may be in up to our necks. Not that we aren't already."

"Yes, I agree. I believe Hanely is probably dead. I also believe that of Champ. Oh, speaking of him, how did your visit with Margo go?"

"It went fine. I really believe she's trying. She asked if we were looking for him, even though it's probably of no use. Margo just wants to know for peace of mind."

"What did you tell her?"

"I told her we're doing our best, considering the killer is still loose. But now I believe we'll get that chance when Willard gets hold of SWAT."

"We'll have time to look for both Champ and Hanely. I hope we're wrong, but I'd be very surprised if we saw either one of them alive."

Claire became quiet. What else was there to say?

XXXXX

She watched the two detectives when they went to visit Margo at the hospital. She watched them leave. She followed them as they went home but stayed back far enough so as not to be recognized.

She parked farther down the road, until she was certain they were not going anywhere. Between the two detectives, they had the answers she so desperately craved.

She finally left, but would return.

Soon.

36

Bright and early the next morning, Willard arrived to his office. Whistling a tune he hadn't heard in a long time, he wondered how he got it stuck in his head.

Sitting down at his desk, he checked forms that lay in a neat pile in front of him. Sipping his coffee, the phone rang.

The noise startled him, but he quickly recovered. Picking up the receiver, answering quite politely, he said, "Captain Willard, how may I help you?"

"Captain Willard?" the voice asked.

"Yes. Who might this be?"

"I'm sorry. This is Colonel Russ Fraser. SWAT force. I received your message. How may I be of service?"

"Colonel, thank you for getting back to me so soon. I was wondering if we could meet in person, at your convenience. Wherever it would suit you?"

"Captain, it sounds from your tone of voice, it's an urgent matter? Not to be discussed over the phone?"

"Correct on both counts, Colonel."

"Fine. I'm checking my calendar. How about later this afternoon, say around two o'clock?"

"That's perfect. Where?"

"Well, since it's confidential, how about your office?"

"Great. I'll see you then."

The conversation was over.

Colonel Russ Fraser was seated in front of Captain Willard's desk. While sipping on the coffee provided to him, he took a moment to gather what was being told to him.

"So, you want me to assemble a team ASAP to head into the woods. We're to look for a cabin or shack and also check if someone is actually living in it?"

"That's right, Colonel. It's come to my attention that there is indeed someone living there and that the person living there is very dangerous. I can't express how dangerous. We believe he's the Trump Killer."

"If you're right, Captain, how am I to proceed toward this . . . Trump Killer as you call it?"

"Let me make this clear, my two detectives are in complete charge. They will direct you as to what must be done you will answer to them. We really would appreciate your help on this."

Colonel Fraser drank some more coffee before he said, "Captain, I'm in. How long do I have?"

Willard thought a minute before saying, "How long will it take you to prepare your team?"

"We're midafternoon now, so I would say by the end of the day."

"Perfect. Tomorrow you can go over it with them. Please answer any questions they may have. They need to be at their best. First thing, day after tomorrow. Nine o'clock sharp at the meeting place."

"Where would that be?"

Willard jotted down the address and handed him the paper. "Remember. Day after tomorrow."

XXXXX

Luke and Claire were in Willard's office going over the case. "Anyway, I spoke to the SWAT leader, and he'll have his team ready later today. Tomorrow he'll clue in his guys so they're prepared. First thing Thursday morning, we're all to meet by Champ's house."

"Since that's where it began," Luke finished.

"That's right." Willard stood at his desk and added, "You guys need to familiarize yourselves with that part of the woods. You have the rest of today and all of tomorrow."

Willard reached inside his desk to give Luke a piece of paper. These are the coordinates as best as Atkins remembers. Just do your best."

Luke reached for the paper and glanced at it. When he was done, he handed it to Claire and said, "We practically have a head start. We were already in those woods, so I remember a bit of it."

"Great, because you're going to need it. Now, I suggest you go and I'll see you at your house Thursday morning before the meet."

XXXXX

She watched them enter the police station. She was already parked there before they showed up. She waited awhile before they got there. She would wait as long as it took for them to come out. She had nowhere to be anymore. She had all day.

XXXXX

When Luke and Claire left the precinct Claire asked him, "Why are you so quiet all of a sudden?"

"I don't know. Just a feeling something seems wrong, but I have no idea what."

"Really?" Claire turned in her seat and looked around, but all she saw was a light-brown sedan parked farther down the road. Nothing else.

Facing Luke again she said, "Nothing out of the ordinary. Maybe you'll think of it later."

"I hope so. Let's get going." And he sped off.

XXXXX

She was lucky the woman detective hadn't recognized her. They practically made eye contact, but the detective didn't know what to look for. That was to her advantage. But she needs to be more careful. The next time she won't be so lucky. She kept pace with them but kept well back.

XXXXX

The next morning Luke and Claire were having breakfast when Claire asked him, "So, Detective, what's our next move?"

"Well, Detective, first I was going to finish my breakfast in peace. Then I will place the dishes in the sink so that you can wash them. After that—"

"I can punch your lights out," she finished for him.

"I'm shaking like a leaf. I felt your punches before. I better start washing the dishes myself."

They both laughed at that remark. When they settled down, Claire said, "I think we should go to Champ's place and start checking out the woods. We should try to find that shack right now, by ourselves."

Luke just looked at her and finally said, "We never went against Cap's orders before. Besides, if Atkins story holds any truth, it may be dangerous. I agree with the captain that we will need help."

"Fine. I promise I won't mention it again. But we should still go there and look around."

"I agree. We will go there, and I have just the thing to bring with us." He walked past her and headed for the basement.

"What could you possibly have down there that will help us?"

"Follow me woman and find out. See, if you lived here, you wouldn't have had to ask that question. You would already know."

Luke turned the light on as he went down the stairs. The whole basement, except the very far corner, illuminated.

"Now let's see. Where did I see them?" He scrimmaged around a shoe-size box, when he found what he was looking for.

"Ah, always the last place you look." He pulled out some orange-type flags and put them on the table so Claire could see.

"What are those?" she asked.

"These helped me a long time ago so I wouldn't get lost in the bush. I put them on trees, so I can find my way back."

"Really, Luke. We have the SWAT team with us. We're going to be just fine. Now put them away; we won't be needing them."

"Okay, okay. I was just trying to be helpful."

"I know. But we don't need them. Let's get going."

XXXXX

She put the newspaper down, when they came out of the house. Waiting for them to pass her, she slowly made her way down the street.

She had no idea where they were going, but she knew it wasn't the police station. It didn't matter. She would follow them for as long as it took. She wasn't worried. She had all the time in the world.

Eventually, they would make a mistake. Then she would pounce.

37

The next morning, Willard was knocking on Luke's door. It was eight o'clock, but they had a long day ahead of them.

"Open up, you two." He banged again when Claire finally opened the door. "What the devil took you so long?" Willard complained.

"We're just getting up. Luke's getting dressed. I just made some coffee; would you like a cup?"

"Gladly. Thank you." He took the steaming cup of hot coffee and took a sip. "This really hits the spot."

At that moment, Luke appeared in the doorway and gave a stifling yawn. "Morning, Cap. How goes it?"

"I'm glad you could join us. I hope you're ready. It's going to be a long day."

"We're ready. We scouted the place for a while yesterday, and we could only do so much."

"That's all I ask. Before we get started, do any of you have anything on your mind? Something you'd like to say?"

Luke cleared his throat. "Yes, Cap, when you leave, there will be a light-brown sedan parked down the road. I believe you passed it on the way in. It's been following us for a couple of days or so. Can you take care of it?"

"Yes. I did see that sedan but gave no thought to it. Don't worry. I'll take care of it. Anything else?"

"No, that's it."

Claire said to Luke, "Now I remember, that's the sedan I saw parked out of the precinct the other day. When you thought there was something wrong."

Willard said, "I will take care of it. Not to worry. Now, you guys will meet the SWAT team in about thirty minutes at Champ's place. I told them to get it off Gore Buff road, so they should be okay."

"Perfect," Luke answered.

"They will cooperate with you. They won't give you any problems, so don't be scared to take charge. Do I make myself clear?"

When neither responded, Willard barked, "Do I make myself clear?"

Luke quickly answered, "Yes, sir. Crystal."

Willard then turned to Claire, glaring at her.

She quickly responded. "Yes, sir! Quite!"

Willard finished off his coffee and muttered, "Smart-asses."

XXXXX

They set out for Champ's place, arriving ten minutes early. They parked beside the black pickup and waited for the SWAT team.

While they waited, they took the opportunity to check their nine mm handgun. They were fully loaded, and they also carried two extra clips, just in case. They holstered their guns and were checking the walkie-talkies and binocular when two black vans screeched around the corner.

They braked on the curb in front of Champ's place, and some men were getting out of the vehicle, even before it came to complete stop.

SWAT!

Both vans seated seven men, and they all came swarming out. But one man seemed to stand out as he was barking orders—the leader of SWAT.

All equipped with M16 assault rifles and twelve-gauge shotguns, all the men had black helmets with visors. They all had tight, black leather jackets with black slacks and black boots to complete the look. When he was done giving direction to his men, Colonel Russ Fraser approached Captain Willard.

Extending his hand, Willard said, "Thank you for putting your team together on such short notice, Colonel."

Shaking his hand, Colonel Fraser replied, "Not a problem, Captain Willard. All my men know they can be called at a moment's notice. It comes with the training."

Colonel Fraser was a tall man registering at six feet and six inches. He weighs approximately two hundred and thirty-five pounds with military-crop hair and brown eyes.

He has high cheekbones with two freckles on his forehead. His skin being white, he would burn in the sun, rather than tan.

"Colonel Russ Fraser, I would like you to meet my two best detectives. Luke Myers and Claire Davis." All three gave greetings and shook hands. Then they noticed a swat member hanging behind.

Colonel Fraser said, "Please forgive me. This is my second in command, Giovanni Marzolli."

All the greetings were repeated. When the men composed themselves and became quiet, Willard continued.

"Okay, everyone. I gave directions as best as Atkins remembers them. We're going to find out once and for all if there's truth to this story. Good luck to all of you."

Luke and Claire started walking toward the back of the yard until they met the entrance to the woods.

He stopped and said to the colonel, "We go in here and start north. Just ahead of us, we battled with the owner of this house, so this is where we begin."

"Okay. But before we go any farther, Giovanni, take your group east and work your way in. We'll meet when we come close to our destination. Keep radio contact. No heroes. Something happens, call. Understood?"

"Yes, sir," Giovanni replied. "Come on, men, you heard the Colonel. Move out."

XXXXX

She watched as Luke, Claire, and all those other men whom she'd never seen made their way into the woods. Why they would go in there was beyond her. Not knowing if she should follow or wait them out, she had to decide soon.

XXXXX

The dark figure sat in cabin. Headache since the sun came up. The headache was getting stronger, with each passing hour. It was because the sheep were coming.

It had to be. The only way to get rid of the headache, the sheep had to die.

Mother was in her rocking chair. It seemed she was laughing. But she remained quiet.

Good.

The dark figure didn't need Mother to make matters worse. The sheep were enough of a problem. But they were dumb. They walk over one another like one's better than the other.

When the dark figure will be finished with them, it wouldn't matter whose better. They all look the same dead.

XXXXX

Luke and Claire kept to the trail, staying alert. Keeping low, they jumped when a family of partridge scampered across.

Claire said, "It's pretty spooky in the woods."

Colonel Fraser was behind them, laughing. "It's not so bad. Once you get your surroundings, and you know where you're going, it's a lot better."

Luke said, "According to those directions, if we keep to this trail, we'll have an easier go of reaching the clearing. As long as nothing jumps us."

Colonel Fraser asked, "Are there any other routes we could take?"

"What's wrong with this one?" Luke wanted to know.

"Nothing. But if I could bring a couple of my men into the thicker foliage, we could arrive at our destination at another point. We would have better access of attacking, if we need to."

"You can if you want. We're coming to a fork just up ahead; we'll split up then."

"Fine. Three of you, come with me. The rest of you, stick with Luke." He turned to Luke and said, "Thank you, Luke. Be careful and good luck."

"You too."

XXXXX

The dark figure was out hunting. Four sheep went a different direction all together.

Interesting.

Better to keep up with them. Knowing the woods, hiding behind trees and boulders, they will never reach their destination.

XXXXX

It was slow going for Colonel Fraser. On more than one occasion, he held his hand high for his team to stop. He could have sworn he heard some kind of low growl.

He waited an extra minute, but it never repeated itself. Nothing ever came of it anymore. He would continue on, but then would hear another noise. Maybe this wasn't such a hot idea. It was too late to go back now.

Luke and Claire were still on the trail and were walking at a decent pace. The other men were behind them, muttering to each other.

Luke and Claire ignored them for now. But for the moment, they needed to concentrate because they believed they were getting closer.

Giovanni Marzolli's team headed east like they were instructed to do. But as the trail they were on was twisting and turning, they were now heading east.

But they seemed to be on the right trail. Every now and then, they would stop to catch their breath. Each taking a drink of water, they resumed their walk.

XXXXX

Mother was alone. That son of hers stormed out to keep those trespassers away.

He'll fail. He always does. Never learns. But that doesn't matter. She doesn't need him. She never did.

Ever since the fire, she never needed him. She grew stronger ever since.

When he fails again, she'll be there to pick up the pieces. But she's tired now. She needed to rest. To be at her strongest when the trespassers arrive.

38

Colonel Fraser and his men were starting to make decent progress. He never heard that low growl again, which made him feel a whole lot better.

He turned to his men and yelled, "Okay, men. Take five, but then we have to get going." He leaned back on the boulder and watched his men take big gulps of water.

Opening his canister, he took a big swig also. When he was done, he looked at his men before yelling, "Let's move out. We have to gain ground."

Luke and Claire were leading the troops when the man trailing yelled to Luke, "Hold on a minute, sir."

Luke turned around to face the man who just shouted voiced his concern. "What seems to be the problem?"

The young man to whom Luke was referring said "I'm sorry for the disruption, but I could have sworn I just heard a noise behind me."

Luke walked toward the man and looked beyond him. Then he turned his attention to the young man and said, "You heard a noise?"

"Yes, sir."

"What kind of noise?"

"I'm not sure, but it sounded like a crunch or maybe twigs snapping."

"Maybe a raccoon? Or a rabbit?"

"I don't know, sir. Possibly."

Luke thought for a moment before replying. "We're going to keep moving, but I want everyone to keep an ear open."

Everyone nodded.

"Okay. Let's go."

Giovanni Marzolli's group were sticking to their route when he thought he heard a noise coming from his right. He couldn't see anything, but it sounded like a low growl.

Keeping his stance still, the other men followed suit. Frozen for a full minute, the noise did not reappear. He looked at his men and shouted, "Okay, men. Let's go but stay alerted."

They continued their quest.

XXXXX

Something woke up Mother. That made her very angry. Bad things happen, when she's angry.

Her eye sockets were black as coal, her clawed fingers seemed to get sharper, and her jaw shut.

She closed her mind to everything. She concentrated.

Out of the blue sunny skies, came black clouds. Heavy winds appeared out of nowhere, knocking off loose branches from close by trees. Sand was blown as effortlessly as flipping a switch. Winds were creating havoc with whatever they touched. Even the strength of trees couldn't help but be uprooted.

A tropical storm came with the winds, with the aid of lightning. Anything that wasn't glued on the ground was given a new home. Even things that were stable were knocked around.

Mother was very happy at the moment. Things were going her way.

XXXXX

When the storm hit, Colonel Fraser and his men took cover. But not expecting this storm all of a sudden, a couple of his men never had a chance.

One tree that was uplifted fell on him, crushing his back. From that same tree, as it was falling, had two thick branches impale his face and throat.

The one thick branch that stuck his throat went right through the other side, staking him to the ground, killing him instantly.

For the time it took Fraser to try to help those two poor souls, it was much too late.

When Giovanni experienced the storm, instinct clicked in. Turning around, he grabbed his closest man to him and shoved him behind the boulder two feet beside him.

He yelled at his other men, "Hurry, men. Behind boulders and trees. Please keep your head down at all times. HURRY," he yelled.

Maybe it was his quick thinking, or maybe his men were just as quick witted as he was, but all his men were safe for the time being.

All of the men wondered how such a storm at that level could be created as quickly as snapping fingers. But none would dare to voice it.

Luke and Claire saw a nest of twigs and brush just off the path and escorted the men under their wing to that location. One man was hit by flying twigs, but nothing came of it. Luke was scratched by another twig on the side of his head but shook it off.

Claire was at his side to see if he was all right.

"I'm fine," he assured her. "Nothing serious."

Just as quickly as it started, it ended. The day returned with the bright sun and blue sky. Just like before.

Except for the damage, you would never know a storm even came through. Luke felt the side of his head, a reminder of what just happened. He said, "This storm we had makes me wonder."

"About what?" she asked.

"Remember a little while back in town we had that similar storm?"

"Yes. I remember. You're wondering if that storm and this storm are connected."

"Well, isn't it possible?"

Claire said, "I suppose it is. But how can that be? It's not that someone is actually controlling the weather, is it?"

Luke just shrugged his shoulder. "I just never experienced two bad storms in a row, ending in less than five minutes. Never."

Claire remained quiet. Her partner had a point. Instead, she turned toward the men to see if they were okay.

XXXXX

As Mother calmed down and relaxed, the weather returned to normal. She didn't know why the storms stopped when she relaxed.

They just do. She had no trouble starting them. She wished she control them longer. Maybe when she has more practice.

But for now, it'll have to do.

39

Getting the walkie-talkie out, Luke tried to get a hold of Colonel Fraser, but he wasn't responding. He turned to Claire and said, "I don't like this. He should have answered."

"Maybe he had problems with the storm and is busy," Claire answered.

"I don't know. Let's try Marzolli." But just as he was about to make that call, his walkie-talkie came to life. "Luke, are you there?"

"Yes, Colonel. I was just trying to get hold of you. How are you making out?"

"Sorry about that. I lost two good men in that storm. We just got started again. What about you?"

"Nothing serious. One of the men, along with myself, got hit by twigs. But we're okay. We're also back on track. Maybe ten fifteen minutes away."

"Good. I figure the same. By the way, have you heard a growling like sound?"

"A growling sound? None that I'm aware of."

"Maybe it's nothing. Safe journey. Out."

Claire asked him, "I wonder what he meant by that growling sound?"

"I don't know. Maybe a dog is loose somewhere. Let's get moving."

Just as they rounded the corner, Luke's walkie-talkie came to life again.

XXXXX

The dark figure watched the sheep go by. Lingering behind, it was more amusing letting them think they're so brave.

When they were so sure that nothing would happen to them, that's when the attack would come. Hardly making a sound, keeping pace with them was so easy.

The hunt would be more fun and challenging if it was a more formidable opponent. The sheep were so predictable. Very easy to figure them out.

Oh well. Sometimes, you can't be choosy.

The dark figure continued to watch.

XXXXX

"Go ahead," Luke said into the walkie.

"Sir," replied Giovanni Marzolli. "I'm just calling to make sure everyone's okay."

"Thank you, Giovanni. We're fine. A couple of scrapes, but nothing a Band-Aid can't cure."

"Very good, Luke. We're all fine ourselves. I'm also calling to warn you."

"Warn me? About what?"

"I'm not sure. But I thought I heard a noise. Sounded like a low growl."

"You heard a low growl?"

"Yes, sir."

"That's interesting. So did the colonel. He didn't know what it was either. Thank you for bringing it to my attention. Out."

When he put the walkie away, he turned to Claire. "I wonder. If the other two groups heard it, it must mean something. What can it mean? What are we up against?"

"I don't know, but may heaven help us," Claire answered.

With his high-powered binoculars, Colonel Fraser thought he could make out the clearing. They still had a few more minutes of hard walking, but with their training, it was manageable.

He turned to ensure that his remaining three men were very close. "But men," he said. "We need to keep this pace. I know it's tough, but you can do it. Let's go."

As the men followed, the last man in the group stumbled over a piece of wire that was hidden in the bush. As he was untangling himself, he felt something behind him.

As he turned to see, the last thing in his life he saw was a giant in a hood, holding a knife.

A very big knife. With a very sharp blade. His throat was slashed.

XXXXX

The dark figure was trailing the sheep, when one of them had trouble keeping up. It seemed his foot got caught on something.

When the rest of the flock continued, the dark figure held back, watching the fallen sheep who will soon be no more.

Finally, playing enough of this game, the dark figure, with knife in hand, attacked swiftly.

XXXXX

Colonel Fraser stopped. When he turned to address his men, he noticed he was one man short.

Only one was standing in front of him. There should have been two. "Where's Liam?"

The one remaining soldier facing the colonel said, "I don't know, sir. I thought he was behind me."

Colonel Fraser looked behind him and said, "I don't see him."

The soldier didn't know what to say, so he remained quiet.

The Colonel said, "We have to go back and look for him."

The two men started back the way they came.

Luke and Claire were up on a hill, shielded behind rocks and trees. Down the hill in front of them was the clearing.

Beyond the clearing stood an old building. Crooked, the wood that served as its frame, rotted, most of the shingles long gone, and a door, two of the three hinges gone that if one sneezed would probably knock it right over. A small window would be the only vantage point if you wanted to peek in.

The cabin!

Luke was staring at the cabin in disbelief. If he hadn't seen it with his own eyes, he never would have believed it.

He said to Claire, "Would you look at that? That cabin really does exist. Maybe the rest of the story is true also."

"It is hard to take in," Claire concluded. "But where are the rest of the men? Shouldn't they have been here by now?"

"You bring up a good point. I'll give them a shout, see what's taking them."

XXXXX

While the sheep were busy poking their heads where they didn't belong, the dark figure went around so as not to be seen.

Coming up from the swamp, he lumbered toward the far end of the cabin. Once reaching a particular spot, the dark figure pushed a huge boulder to one side.

A hidden entrance.

Taking a step or two, the dark figure was engulfed by the shadows. Reaching on one side of the wall, flipping a switch, the door closed.

XXXXX

Luke was just about to call Giovanni when he showed up with his men. "Sorry we took long, but it was a rough storm."

"Not a problem. Just glad you're here safe."

One of Luke's men suddenly yelled, "Look over there." He was pointing behind them, at the bottom of the hill.

Luke said to Claire, Giovanni, and the men, "Stay here, everyone." He started down the hill to meet with the colonel, but he could see something was wrong.

Luke caught up to him and asked him, "What is it? What's wrong?"

The colonel looked defeated as he shrugged his shoulders and said softly, "I don't know how it happened, but another one of my men got killed."

"What! How?"

Again shrugging his shoulders, he said, "Somebody cut his throat. Dead instantly."

"I'm sorry."

"Thanks. So how did you make out?"

"Why don't you walk to the top of the hill and see for yourself."

They climbed the hill, and when they reached the top, the colonel couldn't believe his eyes. "That's the shack we were supposed to find?"

"I believe so. The clearing is right ahead. Beyond that, the cabin. Well, there it is."

"It's so old, crooked, and it looks rotted right through. How could it survive all these years?"

"Your guess is as good as mine. Anyway, we need to act. We need to surround the cabin. But we need to invade it. Once we get into position, I'll peek into the window quickly. Depending what I see, I'll signal yourself and Claire. We need to break that door down and go in, guns drawn."

"Sounds okay to me," the colonel responded.

"Remember, if our killer is around, he's very dangerous. Don't hesitate to shoot."

"Copy that," the colonel answered.

Luke looked at his partner. "Claire?"

Claire looked at him and also replied, "Read you loud and clear."

"Good. Now I'm going in. Get your men to start surrounding the place."

XXXXX

The dark figure was standing beside Mother. His headache was back. Pounding.

It always hurt when Mother was in a foul mood. Mother's chair was rocking violently. It almost looked like it would fly through the wall.

Then, without warning, the chair stopped. Then Mother's voice entered his head.

It's time! Pick me up! Take me to my room!

The dark figure turned to look at Mother. Red eyes stared at eyeless socket eyes for more than a minute. Red eyes looked away. Too weak.

Bending down, putting arms around Mother, he scooped her up.

That's right, you weakling! Make yourself useful and bring me to my room! Son!

Then they were gone.

XXXXX

Luke couldn't see anything amiss through the window. Signaling to Claire and the colonel, he went to the door and drew his weapon.

The colonel reached him by then and said, "On the count of three."

Luke kicked the door in, and it went flying on weak hinges. "Wow, that was easy. I wish I could say the same for the rest of the job."

The colonel laughed. "I say that to myself every day."

Luke smiled. "Okay, let's get this over with. Look around, everybody, for any sign of life or clues."

Claire noticed a rocking chair in the corner, so she took a stroll toward it. Kneeling close to the chair, she noticed, very softly, the chair was still moving.

"Luke," she said.

He came at her and said, "Find something?"

"I believe so. This chair was still rocking. Someone was here, not that long ago."

"Good work, Claire." He continued to scan the area, which brought his attention on the floor, about four feet in front of the rocking chair.

"What's this?" he said to no one in particular.

"What's what?" Claire asked.

"This rug. It looks like someone tripped on it, upending it, not fixing it." He went to it and kicked at it.

Underneath the rug, the floor was a different colour than the rest of the floor.

"My, what have we here?" Luke said wide eyed.

A trapdoor.

40

A TRAPDOOR.

Claire was flabbergasted. What the hell was a trapdoor doing in the cabin? What was underneath? Where did it lead?

All questions Claire had, but no answers.

Luke said, "Colonel, are your men in position around the cabin, like I asked?"

"Yes, sir. Marzolli took care of that. Just the way you wanted."

"Excellent." Luke was deep in thought before saying, "Colonel, have your man guarding the south end of the cabin to be extremely cautious."

"May I ask why, sir?"

"Certainly. We came from the north side of the cabin. But there was nothing of interest on that side. Nothing that stood out. Able to see the west side, which is the entrance we came in, was of no interest on that side either," Luke explained.

Continuing on he said, "the east side was also visible from our vantage point, with nothing interesting. That leaves the south side. We don't know what's there. Could be the entrance from this trapdoor."

"Very well put, sir. I'll get on it."

Claire smiled. That was her man.

XXXXX

Paul Adams was bored. Very bored. He was told by the colonel to guard the south side of the cabin. It was way too quiet. He couldn't even see the other members anywhere. Including inside the cabin.

No windows anywhere. Only the west side. Even at that, it was so small that even a fly would have trouble looking in.

Oh well.

He knew this came with the job. So he better stop complaining. He was starting to get hungry. No food.

Hey, wait a minute.

He pulled something from his pocket. A candy bar. That put a smile on his lips. This was much better.

As he unwrapped it, he thought he heard a noise behind him.

XXXXX

The dark figure, watching the sheep get restless, knew this was going to be easy. Waiting until the prey was vulnerable and hidden from view, he attacked with the speed of a cheetah, the slither of a rattlesnake.

With the hunting knife deep in the victim's back and a violent twist of the blade, the soldier was dead before he hit the ground.

Pulling the knife out and wiping the blood off the blade, the dark figure looked at the body in disgust and knew without a doubt from that demented form they call a brain that it was right.

It was easy.

Suddenly the dark figure threw something on the body.

XXXXX

"God damn it!" cried Colonel Fraser. "He's not answering my call." Quickly, he pointed to two men standing at attention and said, "Go check on Adams. Find out why he's not answering."

"Yes, sir."

With just a handful of men left in the cabin, Luke was poised over the trapdoor. He said to everyone in the room, "I'm going to open it up."

Lifting up from the handle, the door creaked so loudly, it felt like a dozen hands scraping on a chalkboard at the same time.

"Whoa!" Claire said, making a sour face. "What a stench. What the hell's down there?"

"We don't know. I'm going down to find out."

"Not alone you're not. I'm coming too."

He looked at the colonel. "How about you?"

The colonel looked at his remaining men and said, "You men stay here. I'll call if I need you." Turning toward Luke, he said, "Let's go."

The two men made their way to the south corner. As they approached, they couldn't see Paul Adams. Checking where he should have been, nothing.

Then they walked farther into the woods and froze. Paul Adams was lying on his side, all covered in blood.

On his forehead, even though there was some blood, was also something else.

The ace of spades.

One man knelt beside him, to check for a pulse, but it was plain to see he was dead. The other man, who was standing by, was looking farther into the woods.

There was a swamp; it seemed to go forever, with seaweed on its edge. Tangled in the seaweed seemed to be something that didn't belong.

"I think I see something by the swamp. I'm going to check." Going slow and checking by trees so he won't get jumped, he finally managed to reach the swamp. "Oh my God!"

He hurried back to the kneeling man and said, "Quick. Call the colonel."

"What did you see?" asked the kneeling man.

"Another body."

Luke, Claire, and the colonel were making their way down the stairs. They had handkerchiefs covering their noses.

It stunk so badly, they had no idea what they would find. When finally reached the bottom, they all turned on their flashlights.

Soon the darkest corners flooded with light. Looking around to see which way would be best to proceed, they noticed a dead end toward the north.

There was no east or west. It was about ten feet in width that ended in cement walls. All that was left was the south path.

The south path was very long. The flashlights couldn't reach its end. It was wide enough so that all three could walk beside the other.

Where the corners met at the walls and ceiling were covered in cobwebs. Totally disgusting.

On their left side, it was just walls with nothing on them. Not worth paying any attention to it. On their right side, however, was a different story.

Three doors, spaced about four or five feet from each other, were all closed. The stench was at its strongest toward them.

When they reached the first door closest to them, Luke put his hand on the handle. It was locked. But that was no problem.

He kicked the door so hard, the inside handle banged noisily against the wall. Luke intercepted the feedback, so it wouldn't hit him.

He reached beside the wall for a light switch but found none. Shining his light, he noticed a small table with one chair and one rocking chair.

Both were empty, as was the room. Backing out of the room, he closed the door. After all, he was raised proper.

Advancing upon the second door, that too was locked. Again, kicking the door in, he practically knocked it off its hinges.

The stench came from this room. You could smell the stale blood. Lots of it. When he reached for a switch on the wall beside the door, he was almost beyond shock when the dim light worked.

Adjusting to the light, his gaze was on the wall to the left. "Am I seeing things?"

Claire looked at that same wall to see what had Luke's attention.

Taped to the wall, the ace of spades were plastered all over. Hundreds of them. "Well, at least we know where our killer gets his calling cards from."

Colonel Fraser said, "Now I know why your boss calls this the Trump Case."

Trump

"Cap told you that?" Luke asked.

"Yes. The day he asked me to assemble my men."

"That's the first I've heard of it. I'll have to have a talk with that man."

Moving back on the opposite side, the wall on the right was just as amazing. It was covered with different kind of knives.

Claire looked closer before saying, "There's one knife missing. Look at the outline on the wall. From the look of the shape, it's the biggest of the bunch. Probably a hunting knife."

It was true. Luke picked one knife up and saw an outline for it. It was the same for the rest of them. But when they came to the end, they froze.

On the very end, beside the knives, was an arrow. An arrow without the bow.

The colonel went to examine the point of the arrow and noticed a dark stain.

"Look here," he said. Luke went over and peered closer to the arrow. It was a rust kind of color, and he said, "Blood. This arrow was used also. But not too often."

Now turning focus to the rest of the room, there was a table in the center. No chairs there, but in the far corner was another rocking chair.

"That's the third rocking chair in this cabin that we saw," Luke commented. "Were they on sale at Sears or something?"

Running out of room, they stopped at the table and looked up.

Now he wished the light didn't work, for on the wall ahead facing them, what he and his two allies witnessed was enough to drive anyone insane.

41

Giovanni Marzolli heard shouting registering from the south corner of the cabin, so he rushed to see what the problem was.

"Men," he shouted when he reached them. "What's the problem?"

"Sir," the kneeling soldier said. "I was about to contact the colonel. We found Adams lying in among the trees and grass."

"Go on?" Giovanni said.

"He's dead, sir!"

"Dead? How?"

"He has a deep wound in his back, sir. Probably a knife."

"Okay. I'll tell the colonel. You two stay put and keep watch. Gentlemen, be very careful."

"Oh, sir?"

Marzolli turned around and said, "Yes?"

"I almost forgot to tell you, sir. He left something on Adam's forehead."

Marzolli waited for him to continue.

"The ace of spades."

"Oh my God!" Claire cried. "I think I'm going to be sick." She put her head on Luke's shoulder and closed her eyes. "I can't look any more."

Luke was paralyzed. *What the hell is going on this place? What have they stumbled into? Maybe he should have let Colonel Fraser blow everything up. This is maddening.*

On the wall ahead of them, hanging with meat hooks out of their eye sockets, were the remains of Laurel Champ and Dennis Hanely.

"C'mon, guys. Snap out of it. Move or we'll end up like that."

That was enough to get Luke motivated. He put his arm around Claire and told her, "Are you okay?"

"I-I've been better." Her voice was so weak, Luke thought she might faint.

"We have to keep moving, or we're in trouble."

"I'm better now. Let's go."

"Good." He steered her to the door and out.

Just then the colonel's walkie talkie came to life. All three jumped. Being in small quarters, the static on the walkie-talkie seemed very loud.

After barking orders to his men, he turned to Luke and said, "My attention is needed elsewhere. Apparently, the body counts are getting higher."

"What. Somebody else is dead?" asked Luke.

"Yes. But I don't know the details. I'll fill you in later. You gonna be okay?"

"We'll be fine. Get going."

XXXXX

Willard slammed his phone in the cradle. He just finished talking to the MTO. The lady that owns the brown sedan was supposed to be long gone.

Out of town. Out of the country, for all he knew.

Is it possible she's back? If so, what's her motive? Why is she going after Luke and Claire anyway?

Picking up his cell, he tried calling Luke. No answer.

Figures. Too busy with the case I sent them to do. Hope they're okay.

Making a decision, he grabbed his keys and stormed out of the office.

XXXXX

After watching the colonel leave, Luke and Claire were in the path next to the third floor. He said to her, "You can stay here for now. But I have to check that room, before we can leave."

"I know," she answered. "But really, I'm fine and coming in with you."

Luke knew there was no arguing with her, so he said, "All right. But stay close to my heels. I don't want to have to worry about you."

"Deal." Claire followed Luke while he kicked the door down again like the other two times. While they were entering the room, Claire was hit by a strange sensation.

Never feeling like this before, she dropped to her knees and put her hands on her head. Not even sure if it was a headache, or maybe a migraine, but she knew whatever was happening to her, it was beyond her control.

Just now realizing she wasn't behind him, Luke turned right around to see Claire on her knees.

"What is it? What's wrong?"

Bending down to help her up, she flung his hand off her and screamed. Standing up to her full height, she was facing him.

Luke couldn't believe what he was looking at. He definitely was not looking at the woman he loved, but someone else who borrowed her body.

The pupils of her eyes were all white, while foaming at the mouth. Then his attention was drawn to her hands.

She held them outward, and the sound that came out of her mouth was a noise Luke has never heard in his life.

Her fingers were spread wide, while bigger fingers were coming out from them. But it didn't stop there. The fingernails started to turn sharp, until eventually they turned to claws.

"Oh my God!" Luke repeated what Claire had said earlier in the other room. "Claire, what's happening to you?"

Claire just stared at him before yelling, "I'M GOING TO KILL YOU! I'M GOING TO KILL YOU NOW!" She rushed toward him. Luke was now paralyzed with fear, and she grabbed his throat with both hands.

Yes, child! Now is the time! Kill him! KILL HIM! KILL HIM! KILL HIM! KILL HIM!

"KILL HIM! KILL HIM! KILL HIM! I'M GOING TO KILL HIM. I HATE HIM! HATE HIM!" Claire yelled. As she was about to strike again, Luke managed to shrug her blow, then force her off him.

She rolled to one side, and for an instant, things became quiet. Luke was hoping she returned to normal so he took a quick glance behind him.

Claire was just getting up, but past her Luke was looking at a rocking chair. It wasn't the chair itself that had Luke's attention, but rather, what was in it.

A skeleton!

But the skeleton was badly burned and had long dark hair. Obviously, a female skeleton, and as though mocking him, the skeleton was staring right at him, grinning. He didn't have time to analyze the situation because his lovely Claire was back on her feet, about to attack.

Luke directed his attention to her and said, "Claire—listen to me. Margo Henderson. Do you understand. Do you remember Margo Henderson!"

Claire rushed him and knocked him off balance; he fell backward, over a table, and on the floor. Luke got up and leaned against the table.

If this was anyone else, he could fight back. Not hold anything back, but this wasn't anyone else. This was Claire.

But Claire or not, he could only take so much. After that, something would have to give. He needed time to think, to get Claire and himself out of this mess.

But not now. Claire was coming at him again to attack.

His neck was sore from her trying to strangle him, and his shoulder, hurt. But even with his injuries, he managed to leap out of harm's way.

For now.

Giovanni Marzolli was in the cabin, looking for anything. Anything to help his men and the two detectives get out of this alive.

Not finding anything useful, he decided to go down the trapdoor. Descending the steps slowly, he gagged and almost vomited.

Wonder what's down here to create such a smell. The north end seemed to be a dead end, but the south part seemed to extend.

He decided to explore south.

Willard was racing his car to get to Luke as quick as possible. Squealing around corners, fishtailing dangerously, he didn't seem to notice. He still had fifteen minutes to make up.

Colonel Fraser had gone outside, to the east corner. There he met up with some of his men, who were gathered around the body of Paul Adams.

"Who found the body?" he asked.

"I did," the kneeling man said. "Exactly like this."

Colonel Fraser lit a cigarette and asked the same man, "Anything else?"

The other man who was standing beside his friend said, "There's another body over there. Near the swamp."

"Another body? Who?"

"Don't know. Not one of ours."

"It's not? Well, who else would be out here?"

The second man just shrugged his shoulders.

The colonel walked toward the second body and looked at the face. "I don't recognize him either."

"Maybe the two detectives know who it is?" the second man suggested.

Colonel Fraser finished his cigarette.

"Claire, please stop this. You can fight her. Please. I love you!"

"NO! YOU HATE ME! YOU WANT TO HURT ME! BUT I WON'T LET YOU!"

Luke was terrified. He didn't know what to do. He couldn't hurt Claire, but he couldn't make her listen to reason.

Claire advanced. She was three feet in front of him. It was then Luke noticed something for the first time.

Along with Claire's new claws, she also had a set of fangs. He must have been so busy trying to stay clear of her, he hadn't noticed until now.

"Claire, fight her! You can win. I love you!"

"Aaaagh—STOP SAYING THAT! YOU DON'T LOVE ME! I HATE YOU! HATE YOU! HATE YOU!

Then when Luke looked defeated, she sprang.

Giovanni stopped dead in his tracks when he heard the screaming. It was definitely a woman screaming, but the only woman here was Claire.

It couldn't be her. She's the nicest person he's ever met. It can't be her. Can it?

It was difficult to tell where the screaming came from.

Probably, one of these three rooms.

But it echoed so much down here, the screams were bouncing off the walls. He had to check the rooms. He was coming up to the first door.

Apparently, somebody already broke the door. The wood around the hinges were all splintered. The door wouldn't stay closed tight anymore.

He just had to push it in. He did so. Very slowly, he took a step in.

Nothing.

Except for a table in the middle of the room and a rocking chair in the corner, it was empty.

Nothing.

He stepped out. He was looking at the second door.

As Claire leaped, Luke managed to grab both her wrists. In doing so, he managed to save his face from the force of her claws.

For now.

But he still had to protect his neck from her fangs. This just wasn't his day.

With the force of her leap, she knocked him down on his back, while she ended on top of him.

That's right child. Kill him. Kill him now. He doesn't love you. He hates you.

"YOU HATE ME! HATE ME! I HATE YOU! HATE YOU! I HAVE TO KILL YOU!"

"No you don't. We love each other. Fight the voice in your head. Fight her. I know you can do it."

For a brief moment, Luke could have sworn he saw his Claire looking at him with those beautiful eyes of hers.

But just for a moment. Then they were gone. Her eyes were all white again.

"Claire. Please listen to me. Fight her. I know you can."

"NO! YOU'RE TRYING TO CONFUSE ME! STOP IT! STOP IT!"

With strength he didn't know she possessed, she ripped her wrists free from his hand. She raised her right hand and slashed down toward his neck. He moved, barely managing to get out of the way, but not without sacrifice. h*AHAHAHAHA!*

Two of her claws struck his left shoulder, causing it to bleed. She was about to strike again, when her migraine got the best of her.

The laughing and yelling in her head was too much for her. As her claws came down on Luke, they did so without any power.

She fainted.

XXXXX

The dark figure had a migraine. The migraines always came when Mother was very upset, or angry.

But mother wasn't upset or angry. Mother wasn't even screaming. What could be happening? There was something else.

Mother was in her room. But she wasn't alone. The sheep found her.

They're trying to take her away. To separate us. NO!

Screaming, the dark figure ran. *Mother's room.*

XXXXX

The door to the second room was almost off its hinges. Giovanni, taking precaution, entered the room. Instantly gagging, he stepped out of the room for a moment.

Taking a deep breath, he reentered the room. Getting used to the dim light, he looked around the room. He saw the wall with the ace of spades, saw the wall with the knives, but nothing compared when he saw two bodies hanging on the far wall.

He thought he saw everything in this job, enough death to last a lifetime.

He was wrong.

Colonel Fraser retraced his steps to the cabin. Finding it empty, he looked at the trapdoor. It was wide open, knowing Giovanni Marzolli went in that direction.

He followed.

"CLAIRE," yelled Luke. "OPEN YOUR EYES! SAY SOMETHING! YOU CAN'T BE GONE! I LOVE YOU!" He put his arm around her and kissed her head.

He was devastated. He couldn't believe he let things get this carried away. He buried his face in her hair and couldn't stop the liquid erupting from his eyes.

XXXXX

Mother was grinning. This turned out better than she hoped. Even though the man wasn't dead, he soon will be.

As for the girl, who cares. She did damage. Even though she didn't kill him, she did damage.

Still wearing that grin, Mother rose from her chair.

XXXXX

Willard finally reached Champ's place. Driving past the sedan that he knew would be there, he noticed that its occupant was gone.

He screamed to a halt, got out of his vehicle, entered Champ's backyard and into the woods.

Hope I'm not too late, he thought. Then he followed the same directions Luke had taken.

XXXXX

Up ahead somewhere in the woods were Luke Myers and Claire Davis. It was pretty easy following their tracks, with all the brush broken and dozens of footprints.

It's only a matter of time before I catch up to them. How shocked they're going to be when they see me face-to-face.

She can hardly wait for the reunion.

XXXXX

The dark figure stopped. Creeping by the edge of the swamp, the two dead sheep were still lying not too far away. It was guarded.

But the entrance to Mother's room is straight ahead.

The dark figure was stumped. To go around would not be wise. Too long. They would take Mother away by then. Only choice would be straight ahead. Through the sheep.

Looking at the hunting knife, the dark figure made a decision.

XXXXX

Luke was oblivious to everything around him. Too upset that Claire was still unconscious, he didn't notice the form of the bony skeleton was slowly advancing toward him.

Arms outstretched, the skeleton moved closer and closer. Her grin was so horrid; to stare for a moment would be like hot acid dripping down your face.

Closer and closer, she was five feet from Luke and Claire, grinning, with arms reaching as far as they could extend.

Giovanni, at the entrance of the third room, couldn't believe what he was seeing. A skeleton, raising from a rocking chair, was walking toward Luke and Claire.

But they were both on the ground, and Claire looked to be hurt. Luke seemed to be unaware of his surroundings.

His gaze returned to that skeleton, who seemed to be alive, but everyone knows that's not true. Is it? But here he was, ten feet away, watching one walk like she's going shopping.

He was mesmerized.

"Colonel Fraser! Colonel Fraser! Come quick!"

The colonel, who was about fifteen feet behind Marzolli, froze. Hearing the distress call, he had to go to them. But if he went back the way he came, it would take too long. There had to be another way out from this end.

Reaching Marzolli, he told him about his call. Giovanni nodded, and the colonel continued down the path. As he got farther, he noticed a door.

Door with no handle.

XXXXX

When the dark figure rushed ahead, they scattered, just like the sheep they were. Waving his knife, slashing wildly, was enough to clear a path.

The door was not far. Wouldn't take long to get to Mother.

Mother.

XXXXX

Luke was still in a trance. Realizing Claire was not actually dead, he slowly got to his feet; every bone in his body seemed to be bruised.

When he straightened up, a shuffling sound seemed to grab his attention. Turning around, he was paralyzed.

He must have died and gone to hell.

That's where all the grinning skeletons go. Isn't it? Wait a minute! Earnest Donnelly's mother! It has to be! Earnest's mother was never found. I bet I just found her.

He may have figured it out, but not in time. In the time it took him to solve it, those bony hands were around his neck.

Choking him with super-raw strength, the skeleton wouldn't let go. Luke was trying to gasp for air. Almost to the point of passing out, he thought he was done.

A shot rang.

Mother! Too late! The sheep are taking her away! It must be stopped! No matter what!

Enraged, the dark figure reached the boulder that served as its door.

Before Luke realized what happened, the skeleton was shot in the head, making it lose its strangle hold on Luke's neck.

It rolled back about ten feet and lay still. Slowly, Luke rose to his feet and knelt beside Claire. Claire, who was stirring, began to moan and opened her eyes.

"L-Lu-Luuke?" she was very weak. "W-wh-what ha . . . happe . . . h appened?" she asked.

"Ssshh, don't worry, nothing happened. Just rest. Get your strength back."

"Ple-please, tell me. I had a dre-dream that I was trying to kill y-you."

Hesitating for a moment, he said, "Don't worry, sweetheart. It's only a dream."

She looked in his eyes and saw how tired he really was. At that moment, she knew he was lying for her sake, and she loved him more if that was possible.

She put her arms around his neck and kissed him deeply.

"Ahem, ahem." Faking a cough, Giovanni Marzolli was in the room standing next to them.

Luke pulled Claire to her feet, but she was still unsteady.

She leaned on Luke for support, while he asked, "Giovanni, what happened?"

Giovanni, still looking at the skeleton, turned to Luke and said, "That thing on the floor had her bony hands around your throat. I know it was a tight shot, but if I waited for separation, I wouldn't have got it. You'd be dead."

Luke didn't know what to say but answered, "Thanks."

Giovanni smiled. "Nothing doing. It comes with the job."

Colonel Fraser was at the handless door but couldn't budge it. He felt the surface but still couldn't find the trigger.

There has to be a way of opening it, there has to be. Otherwise, why is it here? Pretty sure it leads to the east end of the cabin. My men need me. Have to find it quickly, or they may all be dead.

Frantically, he began to search.

The dark figure, was pushing the boulder out of the way. Mother was quiet.

Maybe already too late! Needed to hurry! Not much time left!

The colonel, who was preoccupied with trying to open the door, didn't notice a scraping sound beyond him. As the scraping noise became louder and louder, it was much too late for Colonel Russ Fraser to do anything about it.

The door opened.

The skeleton, lying in a heap on the floor ten feet away, rose. Swiftly and quietly, Mother shuffled towards Giovanni, who was the closest.

They were unaware of her existence, which was perfect. For that mistake, all three will be dead.

Soon. Very soon.

When the door extended itself all the way, the colonel couldn't believe what was standing in front of him.

A nightmarish figure, in the form of the devil, with red welts covered in a hood and a blazing hunting knife raised before him, was rooted to the spot.

He thought he heard some shouting somewhere but couldn't be sure. Never knowing his fate would end this way, he tried to grab his gun.

Big mistake.

While his hand was on his holster, the knife was deep in his chest. With the viciousness of the swipe, the colonel was probably dead by the time he hit the ground.

But that didn't matter, because the blade was pulled out of his chest, and driven again and again in his chest.

Outside, when the men were rushed by, whatever that thing was regrouped and followed at a safe distance. When they saw that thing pushing the boulder all the way, every man instantly recognized the colonel. They all started shouting, but they knew from his reaction he didn't hear them.

They all witnessed his death.

When the dark figure pushed the boulder all the way, a stupid sheep was waiting for him. He acted surprised, but he couldn't fool anyone.

Too dumb for that! In fact, he was dumber than the rest of the sheep. He actually thought he could kill the dark figure. But the dark figure proved smarter.

The dark figure killed the sheep instead. Again and again.

But enough of this game. Mother needs me.

Six feet away. Mother's black eye pockets were boring down the one that shot.

Five feet away. Four feet away.

Suddenly, something entered her mind.

No! Not now! Mother! You're still with me! It's not too late still! Don't worry! Almost there!

Out of the corner of her eye, Claire saw the skeleton advancing toward them. Particularly, Giovanni. He was the closest. The skeleton was targeting him.

With a swift move she hadn't realized she possessed, Claire grabbed Luke's gun out of his holster, rolled to one side, and fired four shots.

The first two were solid heart shots; the next two were head shots.

The head, completely knocked off the shoulders, rolled against the far wall. The torso of the skeleton dropped where it stood.

Suddenly, everything became quiet.

Giovanni, breaking the silence, said, "Um, thanks."

Claire winked at Luke and said, "Nothing doing. It comes with the job." They all laughed.

The men outside were at the entrance, all gathered around the Colonel Russ Fraser. They prayed for his body for the last.

When they finished, they looked the way that monster headed and followed.

No! It is over! Mother is gone! Forever! It is too late! Nothing could bring her back! Ever again!

Continuing to Mother's room, the dark figure would show no mercy!

The men slowed at the sight of the monster ahead. If that thing turned around, they would be spotted. There was no cover until they reached that room up ahead.

That was exactly the room the monster was heading. Something must have gotten that brute's attention.

Luke, Claire, and Giovanni were looking down at the skeleton's head. Luke said to Claire, "I'd like you to meet Margaret Connelly, Earnest's mother."

Claire's eyes were opened wide. "That's Earnest's mother? How do you know that?"

He looked at her and said, "Remember in the library when we discovered that fire burning their house."

"I remember. Go on."

"They never found any bodies. At two in the morning, there were no bodies. If they were alive and nothing to hide, they would have been outside when the fire department showed."

"I'm with you so far."

"Not only did they not stick around, the killings from that one particular class, and Earnest being in that class was unaccounted for."

"It makes sense so far. Go on."

"I wasn't 100 percent sure, until we came across that room with the ace of spades mounted on the wall. Then I was completely sure."

"Everything makes sense, but if you're right, where's Earnest now? Wouldn't he be close to his mother?"

"Yes. He would be."

"Then where is he?"

"Not sure. But I know he's close. Real close."

As if choosing that exact moment, Luke heard a low growling noise and turned to look.

No! Mother is on the floor! Dead! Dead, and the three sheep are just standing in front of her! Just staring at Mother, and making fun. For that, they will all die. The sheep will all die horribly.

The dark figure entered the room, with the hunting knife at his side.

The men advanced toward that room, when they saw that hideous thing enter. "Listen up, men," one of them said. "We need to use extreme precaution. That thing is in the room, but we don't know how far in. So be careful. Let's go."

Luke tried to make eye contact, but the red slits through that hood made it real difficult. It was almost trying to paralyze with that stare. Instead Luke tried something.

"Earnest, listen to me. I know it's you, and that's your mother." He pointed at the skeleton, indicating who he was talking about.

At the mentioning of his name, Claire had to cover her mouth so that she'd stay quiet.

Luke continued. "We're not trying to hurt you. We want to help you, but you need to put the knife down, slowly."

Earnest, at the mention of his name, turned his complete attention toward Luke.

But Earnest doesn't exist anymore. I killed him. Just like I killed his classmates. It was me. Not Earnest.

"Earnest, please. Listen to me. I'm only trying to help you. Put the knife down."

The thing that used to be Earnest shortened the distance slowly toward Luke.

Seeing his words didn't have effect, Luke said to his partners, "Spread out. Make it difficult for him to choose. He's confused."

As they all spread out like Luke asked, Earnest stopped in his tracks. He couldn't decide who to attack. Then he saw his mother.

He let out a low growl.

When the men took position around the door, they all had their guns drawn. Then the man who resumed charge signaled to move ahead slowly.

Hearing the low growl, the men stormed the room. Taking notice of where in the room that thing was, they opened fire.

Upon hearing the men enter the room, Earnest turned to them. Having no chance at anything, the sheep fire and hit him instantly.

He went down hard, but the bullets continued to fly in his person everywhere. When the shooting stopped, his hunting knife fell from his grip.

Then it was quiet.

When Luke went to Earnest Connelly's body, he knelt beside the head and stated, "Those with a weak stomach, look the other way."

When nobody moved, he grabbed the bottom of the hood and pulled it off. His suspicions were correct. Everyone gasped. His face was badly burned, and with the hood off, it gave a smell that came from the grave. Where eyes should have been, maggots were crawling in and out.

Most of the people looked away and held their stomachs. Then Claire asked, "How do you know that's Earnest."

Luke turned the head the opposite way to reveal the scar on the side of his face. "That's how I knew it was Earnest."

When Luke and Claire were left alone, Luke knelt beside Colonel Fraser's body. He never would have thought the colonel would be one of the casualties.

Never in a million years.

He put his hand on the colonel's shoulder and said his last good-byes. When he got up, Claire hugged him. At that instant, he lost it.

He cried on her shoulder, and she held him until he stopped. Getting control of himself, he straightened up and said, "C'mon. We still have two more bodies to account for."

When they reached the edge of the swamp, all the men, including Giovanni, waited for them. Talking to Luke, he said, "This soldier's name was Paul Adams. He was guarding the east end when he got attacked."

Luke looked at the body, giving condolences to the other troopers.

Giovanni pointed to the other body and said, "I don't know who that is."

Luke at the body and said, "I do. That was Bob Gerald. He was known as the Boss. He was the ringleader for all the poaching in the last month or two. We were looking for him."

After he moved away from the bodies, he got their attention and said, "Okay, everyone. This wraps it up. You've all done a marvelous job. Time to go home."

Because of their loss, they weren't in a cheering mood. As they made their way to the front of the cabin and toward the clearing, a shot rang out and dropped Luke.

"LUKE!" cried Claire. She automatically went to his side.

"I'm okay," he said. "Just my shoulder." Without trying to hurt him, Claire and Giovanni helped him to his feet.

"You should have stayed down," the voice screamed. "That's where you're going to wind up, along with your lovely girlfriend."

Luke and Claire turned to the voice.

The woman with the gun, the one that shot Luke, was gloating ahead of them. "I really hope you remember me. It'd be such a bore to shoot both of you and you not knowing why."

"Nancy Trusk. I remember you. You're the girlfriend of one of the victims."

"Yes. One of the victims. You can't even say his name. Do you know his name? TELL ME HIS NAME, YOU BITCH. TELL ME HIS NAME!"

"Tony Reid. His name was Tony Reid," Claire answered.

"Yes. Now wasn't that better? Of course it was."

Claire said louder, "What do you want, Trusk?"

An insane laugh issued from her throat as she screamed, "JUSTICE! I WANT JUSTICE! YOU SHOULD HAVE STOPPED THE KILLINGS LONG BEFORE HE KILLED MY TONY. WE WERE GOING TO GET MARRIED. NOW BECAUSE OF YOU, I'VE LOST EVERYTHING! FOR THAT YOU'RE GOING TO DIE!"

She aimed at Claire and pulled the trigger. But instead of Claire, it was Nancy Trusk who fell on the ground.

A direct hit to the back of the head killed her instantly. Both, Luke and Claire were confused.

Who?

"Am I ever glad to see the two of you alive. I was trying to call you, but you two wouldn't answer your cells. Anyway, I was going to tell you Nancy Trusk was trying to kill you."

"Really?" Luke cried. "You think?"

"Captain." Claire beamed. "Am I ever glad to see you."

Epilogue

Later, at Havenburg Hospital, Claire was given a clean bill of health. She was free to go, while Luke had a few more injuries.

Fighting with Claire when she was under the spell of Margaret Donnelly, along with being shot in the shoulder, was enough evidence for the doctor to keep Luke in the hospital for a couple of days.

After the doctor left the room, Claire sat next to Luke on his bed and said, "Yes."

Luke turned to Claire and asked, "Yes to what?"

"My God! You get beat up, shot at, both by ladies by the way, and you forget everything. You're such a man."

"Okay, okay. I agree with you, but what did I forget."

She laughed before saying, "If you still want me to move in, the answer is yes."

With astonishment in his eyes, he grabbed her and kissed her.

"Oww. That hurt," he said.

Willard entered Luke's room and said, "Hope I'm not interrupting," he joked.

"Hey, Cap. You're still here."

"Of course I am. I wanted to tell you, when I received word that Nancy Trusk owned that car following you, one medical call informed me she was in and out of the institute since the age of seventeen. After that, it wasn't hard to figure out she wanted to kill you."

"Thank you for that, but too bad about the colonel. I was beginning to like him. Oh, I guess that wraps up the Trump Case," boasted Luke.

The captain glared at him. If looks could kill, Willard would be considered dangerous. Finally he said, "Actually, there is something else."

Luke and Claire exchanged glances.

"I did some more checking into Earnest's past. Apparently, he was seven years old when his father left his mother and himself. The mother didn't cope well with that and started abusing him shortly thereafter. There were times when she would lock him in a closet for days on end. The mother was on drugs and maybe didn't know what she was doing."

"That's still no excuse to treat anybody like that," Luke said sadly. "It's no wonder he turned out the way he did."

"I agree totally," Willard said. That's probably why he ended up killing her. He was also diagnosed as a probable psychotic patient. The night of the fire, a neighbor saw someone walking by his house around two in the morning. He was lugging something with him, but the neighbor couldn't make out what it was. He said it was too dark."

Willard looked at his two detectives to see if it sunk.

Claire said, "That poor child. His whole life was a hell. Now he's finally at rest, but I wonder if he's at peace."

No one had an answer. Willard went on to say, "But I'm not finished. I talked to a friend of mine, and he explained how his mother had power, even after death."

"What did he say?" Luke asked.

"Somehow, after death, instead of staying dead, she received some kind of telepathy, of which he has no ideas how that would be. With that telepathy, she was able to control anyone who was a threat, or anyone to take care of a threat. If that's not enough, she was able to control the weather also. That's the toughest skeleton I ever heard of. I hope we never have to go up against such a foe again."

"Amen to that," Claire added.

Five Years Later

Luke and Claire were walking along a sandy beach, hand in hand, while four-year-old Luke Junior, was running ahead of them with their new golden retriever puppy.

"Junior," cried Claire. "Don't run so far ahead of us. Stay in sight."

"Aw, Mom. You're no fun!" Junior showed his displeasure.

Luke and Claire started laughing.

In the distance, junior was chasing the puppy, shouting, "Willy, stop! You're running too fast. I'll get in trouble."

When junior finally caught up, Willy was frantically digging something up from the beach.

"Mommy, Daddy!" yelled junior. "Come quick, see what Willy dug up!"

They named the puppy Willy, short for Willard, in memory of Captain Bruce Willard, who passed away two years prior.

When they reached their son, they saw that Willy dug up a badly burned, scarred skeleton, with long dark hair.

FINITO

Edwards Brothers Malloy
Oxnard, CA USA
October 14, 2013